THE UNINVITED

Barry knew the way by heart and had driven the road in all kinds of weather. By the time she reached the bridge she had met only two other cars.

As the Volvo exited the bridge she had an eerie glimpse of him through the speed of the snow, in the headlight beams. His face – what she saw of it in a split second – showed no emotion: if he hadn't moved she would have thought he was a piece of marble statuary, blurred and crumbling, wells of blankness where the eyes should be. But he was human. and he wasn't wearing any clothes.

Barry turned the wheel sharply, then skidded sideways. She felt the impact of the right rear bumper guard against the man – there was never a chance of avoiding him . . .

*Books by John Farris published
by New English Library:*

CATACOMBS
THE UNINVITED

THE UNINVITED

John Farris

NEW ENGLISH LIBRARY

For Ron Preissman,
friend and partner in shadow shows
and the magic lantern business

First published in Great Britain in 1983 by Hodder and Stoughton

First NEL Paperback Edition June 1984

NEL Books are published by New English Library,
Mill Road, Dunton Green, Sevenoaks, Kent.
Editorial office: 47 Bedford Square, London WC1B 3DP

Made and printed in Great Britain by
Cox & Wyman Ltd, Reading

British Library C.I.P.

Farris, John
   The uninvited.
   I. Title
   813'.54[F]   PS3556.A777

   ISBN 0-450-05715-1

What a piece of work is a man! how noble in reason!
how infinite in faculty! in form and moving, how
express and admirable! in action how like an angel!
in apprehension how like a god! the beauty of the
world! the paragon of animals!

—William Shakespeare,
Hamlet, Act II, Scene ii

What is mind? Doesn't matter. What is matter?
Never mind.

—doggerel attributed by the philosopher
Bertrand Russell to his parents

NOTE:

Tuatha de Dannan is pronounced Tootha-day-danan, and *Daoine Sidh* is pronounced Theena-shee.

THE ACCIDENT

ONE

CLAUDE COPPERWELL owned the antique shop on Main Street in Anatolia, New York. He also did framing for local artists in a back room. When Thomas Brennan finished a panel that was destined for sale – this happened only two or three times a year – either Tom himself or whoever might be driving in from the farm took the new painting to Claude. *Greene House* was completed shortly after Thanksgiving. Tom ignored it for a while – went bird hunting, shot pool, repaired a tractor. Then he hung around the panel, critically, for another day or two, but was reluctant to pick up a brush and so knew he had done all that was in him. On a day in early December, at about three in the afternoon, Tom's daughter Barry put the tempera painting, wrapped in an old quilt, in the back of the Volvo station wagon and drove eleven miles to Anatolia. The sky was dull silver, and there was a tease of snow in the air.

For almost thirty years Thomas Brennan's paintings had come to Copperwell's for framing. This occasion was no different from the others, but there was a minor ritual to be observed. Barry parked by the back door. Snow was coming harder, stinging her cheeks, swirling on the street. She went in for Claude. He carried the painting, thirty by sixty inches on die board, to his workroom and placed it on an old paint-scabbed easel that had belonged to Rockwell Kent.

'That's Greene's, isn't it?' Tom Brennan had painted the eighteenth-century farmhouse, or parts of it, several times.

'Yes.'

'I don't think Tom's ever done one like this. A few things around sundown – that kind of light. This picture's *dark*.'

9

'It's scary,' the girl said.

Claude's wife brought in a tray with wineglasses and a decanter and gave Barry a hug.

'It's been much too long since we've seen you, lovey.'

'I haven't been to town for a while. There's a lot to do at the farm.'

'Here I was thinking you were away at college like the other girls.'

Barry shrugged. 'Maybe next year.'

'Oh, my, it's a big one,' Millicent said, looking at the painting, but quickly and almost shyly, just letting it hit her and not trying to size it up too soon. She poured Dry Sack and they smiled at each other, two gnomes with a tall girl between them. Claude was neckless, without hair except for eyebrows so thick and black they looked tarred; he had a chipped waxen face, large pores in his cheeks like unfinished eyes. She was English, pink and cheery, with an ardor for unpopular causes, the unchampioned: Millicent's friends called her Blighty Mouse.

The three of them sipped their wine and devoted themselves to Tom Brennan's latest work, which Barry already knew by heart. She had viewed *Greene House* in all of its manifestations, from early summer on, first as notations in a sketchbook done in India pink or pencil, then as a series of small watercolors, some in dry brush – twenty or more renderings culminating in this impressive work. She both admired and felt a need to back away from her father's painting.

At a glance, the painting, like all of his work (aside from portraits), was daringly composed, muted in color, and dealt with the ordinary and homely things of a very small area of rural New York State – all that was within walking distance of his home. The distinction of Greene's house, situated in a cleft of a hill and nearly surrounded by a bleak woodlot, was an out-of-proportion, squarely built, twentieth-century addition – a screened front porch. By emphasizing the coldly lighted porch and foreshortening the dark house Tom Brennan had suggested momentum, a voyage; the chalky, brilliant angle of the porch, cutting at a slight diagonal to the left third of the panel, was like the prow of a ship. The moon was down, the hour late, the woodlot raggedly streaked with snow at the turn of a year.

On the porch a woman wearing a cardigan sweater sat erect on the edge of her chair, perhaps caught at the instant of beginning to rise, hands gripping the chair arms. At first she seemed merely tired; her face was turned toward the house, as if she'd made up her mind to go inside. But to Barry the tone of the woman's body, the odd jutting of an elbow, had come to describe fear. What had struck her at this moment? A thought, a sound she'd heard, something physical?

'Why, that's Edie,' Millicent said of the woman in the painting. Then she looked at Barry's face, realizing that Barry hadn't guessed. Millicent saw a flash of confusion and, at the same time, Edie's best features, which had survived in her daughter: the high forehead, pale but ravishing lashes, the tip of the nose elevated a bit importantly. Barry's coloring was all her father's. She was a strawberry blonde, with the high ruddiness of chafing weather, eyes royal blue and so sensitive they turned hazy from any sort of brilliance.

'I dunno,' Barry said, looking again. 'I guess it looks like her.'

Edith Brennan had died in an automobile accident when Barry was nine, so Barry's memories lacked depth and precision. There was a good store of family photographs that she sometimes consulted when, caught out in the lonely drift of being eighteen and motherless, she needed to get her bearings. Also, she had seen countless impressions of a younger Edie in the pages of the artist's notebooks – skinny, unpretentious, dun-colored Irish, but with that native cheekiness, a sly wit, and a good-humored indulgent smile any sensible man would have killed for. And Edie was fey, which came of possessing too much knowledge of the world both here and gone. She was always on edge from intuition, using herself unsparingly for the sake of others, burning to excess the pale marrows of her body.

11

Barry's eyes smarted; like all of her family she was too quickly in the full flood of her emotions. She drank her remaining sherry, accepted more, and quelled the self-pity. But drinking softened her focus and momentarily dizzied her; it left her with an uncertain disposition. She turned her back on her father's painting and drifted toward the door that, half opened, revealed a gleam of old mirrors and dark furniture chockablock in the shop beyond. She heard voices, a man and a woman exclaiming over objets d'art.

'I suppose this one's sold already,' Claude said, his eyes still on the new painting.

'There are a lot of buyers,' Millicent said, 'but not nearly enough Brennans.'

Claude turned, looking at Barry. 'Tell the gallery they can come up and get this one a week from Saturday.'

Barry didn't reply. She had glimpsed a young man in the shop, bending over a Shaker rocking chair. He had sandy long hair and was wearing an orange-and-black plaid wool jacket. Barry's heart lurched and her right arm jumped in reflex; wine spilled from the glass she was holding, but she was oblivious. The young man in the shop was joined by his wife, or girl friend. The woman murmured to him, pointing out something of interest. Still he hadn't turned his head so that Barry could see his face.

'Barry?' Millicent said.

She heard her name through the singing of blood in her ears. She turned and almost stumbled, catching the door frame with her free hand, sloshing a little more of the wine.

Millicent looked from Barry's face to the couple in the shop.

'Ned had a jacket like that one,' Barry explained in a small neutral voice.

'Oh, lovey.'

'Nobody could ever mistake him for a deer. That's what he said.' Her shoulders lifted slightly. She smiled, but sadly; her cheeks burned. She stared at Millicent and bit off a stammer. 'So w-what did they think he *was*, when they shot him?'

Millicent went to her without seeming to move very

quickly, deftly closed the door, and put an arm around her waist. Barry was downcast. The cuff of her parka was stained.

'I spilled my wine. I'm sorry.'

'You've got to put it behind you. Honestly.'

Barry nodded. 'I know. It was just the jacket – and for a couple of seconds he looked like Ned. That's all.'

Millicent and Claude went outside with her to the Volvo. In a half hour's time the village had begun to turn white, except for the draped muzzy tinsel and gilt-edged stars on the lampposts, the Salvation Army's sentry box and red kettle in front of the bus depot. Thoughts of Ned had plunged Barry into the deep backwater of her recent sorrow. She fumbled for her keys, dropped them in the cold carpet of white at her feet.

Claude retrieved the keys for her. 'You be careful driving back; we're supposed to get six or eight inches by midnight.'

'Give Tom our love,' Millicent said. 'You two are going to have to stop acting like recluses and come to *see* us.'

'We will. I promise.'

'Everyone at the hospital's been asking, When is Barry going to put on another show for us?'

Barry forced a smile. 'Oh, I don't know. Soon.'

She drove away, not too cautiously, fleeing the town. The Copperwells waited in the snow until she was out of sight.

'She still has all that grief bottled up inside,' Millicent said. 'That's more of a tragedy than Ned's death. I don't know why Tom can't do something to help her.'

'All artists are alike. Tom's in his own world.'

'Perhaps I shall just drop by one afternoon soon and have a heart-to-heart with Barry.'

'Let's go in. My feet are freezing.'

Barry, aching for the seclusion of the farm, her lamplit room, drove too fast, depending on the snow tires of the wagon to keep her out of trouble.

Trees that an hour ago had been skeletal along the road now were shapely from snow that came thick and wild from

13

the northwest. The snow was piled up in translucent slabs at the edges of the Volvo's windshield by the action of the wipers.

The two-lane country road from Anatolia to the farm seldom ran straight for more than a hundred yards. There were hills and more hills, no settlements of any size along the route. A few miles from town the road bisected a state park with a small pretty lake, a century-old spillway and a covered bridge in the cove below it. Here there was a hairpin turn, down to the bridge and sharply up again, through crags and tall trees.

Barry knew the way by heart and had driven the road in all kinds of weather. By the time she reached the bridge she had met only two other cars. The headlights of the Volvo were on. She had a slight tension headache; she felt famished, dispirited, quarrelsome, with no one to talk to, to object to – how *meaningless* Ned's death was, such point-blank cruelty and absurdity. *Had everyone else forgotten*? She could still blow herself away with just a twist of memory – but her mind was definitely on her driving. She was not, as Mrs Prye frequently – and maliciously – observed, carrying her head around under one arm.

Later Barry was asked what she thought the young man had been doing on the road when it would have been sensible (no, instinctive) to seek the shelter of the bridge and wait, out of the blowing snow, until someone came to his rescue. But of course nothing about the advent of Draven made the least sense, and afterward he was unable to provide an explanation of his actions up to the moment Barry ran into him.

She came out of the full downfall of the storm into the rumbling dark of the one-lane bridge, where the snow was limited to a delicate drift through the chinks and spaces of the sideboards. She slowed, as it was prudent to do, then pressed the accelerator again on the other side, needing momentum to make the upcoming turn and hill.

As the Volvo exited the bridge she had an eerie glimpse of him through the speed of the snow, in the headlight beams, raising his hands by the side of the road. It was either a gesture of pitiful defense, or surprise, but his face – what she saw of it in a split second – showed no emotion: if he hadn't moved she would have thought he was a piece of marble statuary, some misplaced Greek, blurred and crumbling, wells of blankness where the eyes should be. But he was human. And he wasn't wearing any clothes.

Barry turned the wheel sharply, hitting the brake pedal for an instant, then skidded sideways. She felt the impact of the right rear bumper guard against the man – there never was a chance of avoiding him, only a possibility of not killing him – and steered in the direction of the skid to try to bring the Volvo under control. She was too intent on avoiding a bad smashup to be shocked by the accident.

The Volvo came to a slant stop a couple of hundred feet uphill from the bridge with the front bumper nudging the protective cable that separated the road from a precipitous drop to the watercourse below. There was a red warning flasher in the station wagon that plugged into the cigarette lighter. Barry got it out and placed it on the roof of the wagon to alert anyone coming down the hill.

Before she was finished her hands began to shake. The blood drained from her head and her knees wouldn't support her. She had to sit down again, numbly, her head almost on her knees, the door open, snow flying in. The thought of what she had done, even though she was sure it hadn't been all her fault, dismayed her.

But he was down there somewhere in the snow, undoubtedly with broken bones. He wouldn't stand a chance if she didn't help him quickly.

Barry reached for the microphone of the radio that her brother Dal had installed in the wagon at the height of the CB craze. She knew, just barely, how to operate it.

'Breaker breaker – this is, uh, Barry. *Barry*. Does anyone copy? I'm by the covered bridge in Tremont Park and I've – I've had an accident. Uh, there's someone hurt. Need help. Please copy!'

Holding the microphone, she looked down the hill, trying

15

to make him out by the side of the road, but she couldn't see much. The swaths she had carved on the blacktop already were whiting out. Tears scalded her frigid cheeks. It was almost as if the man had never been there – but she knew she hadn't imagined the solid thump of the skidding Volvo against his body.

A voice, indistinct, squawked at her. Barry made some frantic adjustments on the tuner, spoke again into the microphone.

'Would you repeat that? I d-didn't –'

The voice this time was clearer, but still faint.

'Uh, Barry Barry, this's that Tidewater Lefty, westbound on eight-four, about three miles from that Brewster town. Want to give me your ten-twenty and I'll notify the state police.'

Barry guessed that he had asked for her location and repeated it.

'Uh, ten-four, Barry Barry. Just hold on and I'll get some help there right away.'

'*Have them call my father!*' Barry yelled, but there was no reply. She replaced the microphone. Her fingers were tingling inside her driving gloves; she no longer felt as if her head might nod off her shoulders. Adrenaline had reawakened her.

Barry snatched the old quilt from the back of the wagon and went downhill, slipping, falling, sliding on her rump part of the way to where the Volvo had struck the man. How could he have been out in this weather without, apparently, having a stitch on? Some sort of lunatic, she thought, and was alarmed. But after being hit and nearly run over he couldn't be a danger to her.

He was a long way from the edge of the road, the tone of his skin so chalky he nearly blended with the snow halfway down the embankment. He was lying on his face; his tumbling fall had been arrested by a small hawthorne tree, and one arm hung limply in the low tangle of branches. He looked, from her vantage point, washed up, homeless as a fish on a beach.

Barry went down backwards, dragging the rolled-up quilt, grasping at small bushes and ledges of rock for purchase. Just above him she slipped, and her momentum carried her jarringly against his body. She heard a faint groan, but he didn't move of his own volition. *At least he was alive.* She looked at his partly obscured face, at the smooth, well-muscled, youthful body, and realized with a pinch of the heart that he was about her age.

His hair was glossy black, thick over the ears and at the nape. He hadn't appeared to have so much hair, or hair at all, when she'd first sighted him. There was no hair on his forearms or legs. The soles of his feet had a faint purple blush. He couldn't have walked far – there wasn't a trace of grime, although the snow might have rinsed his feet. Barry saw no blood, no obvious deformity resulting from a broken bone. She took off one glove and felt his neck gently, then the small of his back. She was distressed by a lack of heat, an extraordinary quality of bloodlessness. His skin, this close, was turning blue. Barry remembered a little first aid from her high school physical education courses. Was he in shock or suffering from hypothermia? The important thing was to make him warm without delay. Barry realized it would be hopeless, even if it was safe to move him, to try to get him to the Volvo by herself. He was about six feet tall and weighed, judging from his solid build, at least a hundred and seventy-five pounds.

She opened and spread the quilt beside him, hesitated, biting her lip, then put her hands under him and rolled him carefully onto his back. His right hand fell from the tree. His eyes were closed, his lips slightly parted. She took a few moments to press her cold fingers against the carotid artery in his neck. There was a pulse, but his face was so blank it scared her. Barry looked him over quickly. His left thigh above the knee was swollen, turning a mottled purple. That was where the Volvo had struck him, fortunately knocking him aside. She pressed gently on his rib cage and then his abdomen, wondering if something was torn inside, leaking blood into the abdominal cavity. She remembered a

17

childhood friend, kicked by a cow, who had nearly died from a ruptured spleen. But she didn't feel swelling anywhere. His scrotum, gnarled and blue, was tight to the body. His ample penis tapered almost to a point, like that of Michelangelo's *David*.

Barry straightened, unfastened the toggles of her parka, and took it off. She was only three or four inches shorter than he was, and she had long arms. She managed to squeeze him into the fur-lined parka. Then she wrapped him in the quilt, tucking it in around his feet. But even that wasn't going to be enough ...

'Hey! Anybody around here?'

Barry straightened, looking up toward the road. She saw a crimson glow from the flasher atop the station wagon. The day was darkening, and it seemed colder. She wiped freezing snow from her lashes and shivered; she was wearing only a lightweight cotton sweater.

A figure partly materialized out of the storm above her. A man with a flashlight.

'Down here!' Barry screamed. 'I need help!'

The flashlight beam, diffused, highlighted the branches of the hawthorne tree and the young man's unconscious face. The newcomer studied them for several seconds, then abruptly vanished.

Barry slumped bleakly in the snow, teeth chattering, wondering if he was just going to drive off again. But within a minute he was back, picking his way cautiously down the slope in his Vibram-soled boots, a coil of rope over one shoulder, a rolled-up square of pearly plastic on the other. Barry recognized him, jumped up, and almost lost her footing.

'Albert!'

Albert Tweedie raised his head. 'Barry?' He was a hulking young man of twenty; he had been in Barry's classes, off and on, from the first grade, but had fallen steadily behind her. A year ago he had dropped out of the high school to marry a homeless girl with two small children. His family was still upset, but Barry had heard the marriage was going pretty well; Albert was good with the kids.

He kneeled beside the victim, then glanced at her again. 'What happened?'

'Well, I – I don't know where he *came* from. He was just on the road, and I – I couldn't help it, I didn't see him in time –'

Fresh tears threatened; Barry blinked hard. Albert studied her, taking time to think over everything she was trying to tell him. He was excessively prognathic, with acne like blackberry stains on his jaw. His eyes were on the small side, and everyone thought him irredeemably stupid. Barry had decided long ago that Albert had good sense and a willing heart – he was just a little slow and socially inept. With Albert, as with most people, patience and understanding paid off.

'You run over him?'

'I hit him. His leg looks b-bad above the knee – it m-may be broken.'

Albert unfolded the quilt and chewed his lip vigorously upon discovering that the other young man was naked; but he said nothing to Barry. After a while Albert wrapped him again and looked back, pondering the steepness of the slope behind him.

'Can you c-carry him?' Barry asked.

Albert shook his head. 'Better not try. He's big.' He unfurled the plastic, which had metal grommets around the edges, and began threading the Dacron rope he'd brought with him through the grommets. Barry, rocked by shudders, guessed what Albert was up to and looked at him admiringly.

He was aware of her distress. He paused to take off his down-filled vest and handed it to her.

'No, n-no, I'm o-k-kay.'

'Go on – cold don't bother me.' He even seemed to be perspiring lightly as he worked. Barry slipped into the old vest, which needed cleaning.

'What'll we do?'

'This is like a hammock, see? This way we can drag him uphill and he'll be wrapped tight, won't be moving much. In

19

case there's broken bones.'

'I don't know what I'd've done if you hadn't c-c-come along, Albert.'

'Don't worry. You hold his head steady now, and I'll move him.'

Together they laced the young man into the dropcloth until his arms were tight at his sides, hands overlapping his thighs. Albert went first up the slope, moving backwards, grunting with effort, feeling for handholds behind him. The rope was belayed around his waist. Barry followed, trying to act as a brake, holding the wrapped victim steady when Albert paused to be sure of his footing.

They were near the top of the slope when they heard a siren; a police car appeared in the tunnel of the bridge. Albert had left his pickup truck on the other side of the road, engine running. He hurried to flag down the cop with his flashlight.

TWO

THE OFFICER'S name was Mix; he was in his thirties, wore a
khan's mustache, and had popped brown eyes that gave him
a look of constant asperity, as if he found even the routine
matters of life infernally perplexing. He asked for Barry's
driver's license. Then, with Albert standing behind her,
chewing his lip, Barry stammered through a brief explanation of events.

Mix went down on one knee, pulled a pencil flashlight
from his shirt pocket, opened the victim's right eyelid, and
shone the light on the dilated pupil. It contracted, but a little
slowly. Mix unwrapped the young man, looked him over for
a few seconds, then rose and put his hands on his hips.

'You a witness?' he asked Albert.

'He just g-got here a few minutes ago,' Barry told the cop.

'And you don't know who this is you hit?'

'I never saw him before,' Barry said, and knew that Mix
didn't believe anything she'd told him.

'Okay, he's a male Doe. Probably going into shock. Best
thing now's to get him to the hospital. We ought to use your
station wagon, instead of waiting for an ambulance. You
okay to drive?'

'Uh-huh.'

'Bring it on down here.'

With Albert pushing from the front Barry was able to get
the Volvo back on the road. Down by the bridge Mix took
the time to look inside, using his big flashlight. He read the
registration and insurance card, then continued, madden-
ingly, to poke around. He was searching for dope, or
clothing, or both, Barry decided. So he thought ... Barry's

21

cheeks fired up, and she began to stammer again from the cold.

'He wasn't r-r-riding with *me*,' she said in exasperation.

Mix didn't reply. He and Albert lifted the injured man into the station wagon. Albert volunteered to ride along to keep an eye on him. Barry was grateful to have his company. She still felt shaky, but perhaps the worst was over.

Mix led the way to the Anatolia Community Hospital, siren going, blue and red roof lights twinkling in the deepening gloom and snowfall. Albert was crouched behind the front seat, keeping the victim's head from rolling side to side; Mix had stressed the importance of this, in case there was an injury to the cervical spine. Barry had the Volvo's heater on full blast, which intensified her headache. The ordeal had nauseated her, but she was determined not to yield to the urge to pull over and let Albert take the wheel.

'How is he?'

'Not so cold.'

'Good.'

'You know what I think?' Albert said hesitantly. No one ever cared what he thought.

'What's that, Albert?'

'He was out there camping.'

'Without any clothes on?'

'Could've gone swimming.'

'In this weather?'

'My uncle goes swimming at Coney Island every weekend. Even in January. And he's sixty-three. It's like a club he belongs to. He says ice water is good for his circulation. Well, he's in pretty good shape except he's deaf in one ear.'

Barry had another idea. 'It could have been a dumb initiation stunt.'

'One of those college fraternities?'

'It wouldn't be the first time they've left them in the woods around here. Maybe they didn't know it was supposed to snow.'

When they reached the hospital the victim was still unconscious. A doctor and two nurses were waiting for him

22

at the emergency entrance, and they hustled him on a gurney to a treatment room inside. Barry and Albert stood around while Mix advised the charge nurse how to fill out her forms. There wasn't much to tell her about the young man.

To Barry, Mix said, 'There's an investigator on his way over, like to talk to you.'

'I'm not going anywhere. But I want to call my father. And what about Albert? He left his truck at the bridge.'

'He can leave anytime.'

Barry looked at Albert and shrugged apologetically. From the treatment room she heard a nurse call out, 'Blood pressure one-ten.' A heart monitor was beeping at a steady clip. '*Can you hear me?*' the doctor said loudly. '*What's your name? Tell me your name.*' Barry, itching with curiosity, started to drift toward the room. The charge nurse sternly shook her head. Instead Barry and Albert went to the hospital lobby to look for telephones.

The housekeeper at the farm, Mrs Aldrich, told Barry that her father had been notified ten minutes ago by the state police and was on his way to town.

'Should I wait supper?'

'I think so, Mrs Aldrich. Is Dal home?'

'No, but the last I heard he still planned to drive up from the city with his young lady. There's Ethan outside honking for me now – if I stay any longer we'll never get up our hill tonight. Everything's ready for the oven when you get here.'

'Thanks, Mrs Aldrich.'

In the gift shop in the lobby Barry bought presents for Albert's stepchildren: a windup bear that played cymbals, a rag doll with floppy curls and an ear-to-ear sewn grin. She had enough money left for a copy of *Seventeen*, which featured on the cover a model friend of her brother's, and a Snickers bar, a lifelong addiction. Barry wolfed the candy, but her stomach complained. She wrapped the other half and put it in her purse.

'Jessie's coming for me,' Albert said when she caught up to him in the lobby.

'Good. My dad's on the way too. Albert, you probably

saved that guy's life. I couldn't have done anything by myself. This is just something for the kids, okay?'

Barry went back to Emergency. The patient was still in the treatment room. Barry had a quick look at him, lying there, unresponsive. The shadows of a doctor, a nurse, and a man in a topcoat were on the curtain that was partially pulled around the table. There was something else – a bundle of rags or cloth on the floor, black and orange and bloody. Unexpected. Too vivid. Barry felt a touch of darkness, a passing fever. She backed away and gave herself a pinch to partially restore equilibrium. She cornered the charge nurse, who smiled distantly at her questions.

'How bad is he hurt?'

'That's hard to say.'

'Why is he still unconscious?'

'I don't think you should worry.'

'*What do you mean I shouldn't worry?* I'm the one who ...'

The man in the khaki topcoat came out of the treatment room and smiled at her. He wore big round fishbowl eyeglasses. He had the general contours, the pussyfoot amble, and slightly manic air of Garfield the cat.

'Are you Barry? I'm Stewart Ivorson. You used to take piano lessons from my mom.'

'Oh, sure. How is she?'

He wiggled the fingers of one hand. 'Arthritis. Cuts down on her teaching. Why don't we sit over there, I need to ask you a few questions about the accident.'

They walked toward a row of blue and orange molded plastic chairs that reminded Barry of nursery school. Ivorson flipped through the pages of a pocket spiral notebook, musing.

'Do you know who he is?' Barry asked.

'Not yet. Couple of men over at the park trying to find out where he was camping, if he was.'

'What does the doctor say?'

'He's cautiously optimistic. Let's see, we've got a male Doe approximately twenty years of age, in good physical condition. Body temperature when he was brought in was

24

94.2 degrees. No signs of frostbite or prolonged exposure to the elements. The patient's pupils were reactive, all other neurological signs were normal. There's no trauma on the outside of the skull. Pretty good contusion on the left thigh between the hip and the knee, possible fracture of the femur, patient's going' to X ray in a couple of minutes. His respiration was shallow, now it's near normal. Blood pressure is on the low side, but not dropping. That means there's probably no serious bleeding anywhere. But he's out cold, hasn't responded to verbal or physical stimuli. Do you know what time the accident happened?'

Barry told him approximately when she had left Anatolia.

'Given the driving conditions, we can say that the accident occurred about ten minutes after four. Posted speed limit on the bridge is twenty-five miles an hour. Think you might have been going faster?'

'A little,' Barry admitted.

'Let's say thirty miles an hour. I don't suppose you thought to notify your insurance company?'

'God, I forgot! Maybe Dad –'

'One of you take care of that as soon as possible. Okay, Barry, want to go through it again for me?'

Barry closed her eyes for a few moments, anxious again, trying to get rid of the fog in her mind, to clearly relive the accident. She needed to go to the bathroom, but she wanted to have the investigation over with.

She concentrated and saw it all again: the dark shaft of the covered bridge, the hard gusts of snow at the other end, then the figure immediately in front of her on the narrow road, suddenly big as life and too close, head turning, hands raised ... But this time she saw him a little differently – something about the victim was reminiscent of Ned Kramer.

Barry stiffened, stopped talking, stared openmouthed at the opposite wall with an expression of anguish.

'He's going to live. *He has to.*'

'Take it easy, Barry,' Ivorson said, misinterpreting the look on her face. 'Visibility was poor, and you had almost no time to react. I'd say you did a good job of saving his life.'

She turned wearily to him.

'I'm not in trouble, am I?'

'Doesn't look that way to me. I've got everything I need for now. Why don't you go home and get some rest?'

'I better wait for Dad. I don't think I could drive right now.'

The charge nurse brought her parka to her from the treatment room. Barry took it eagerly, feeling cold from shock. But, although the young man had worn it for the better part of an hour, he'd left no clues to himself. Putting on the parka was worse than going blind; it was like stepping into the featureless eternity of a grave. Barry reacted violently, shucking the parka and dropping it on a chair.

Two hospital attendants wheeled the young man out of the treatment room on the other side of the nurses' station. A sheet covered him now, from his ankles to his chin. His eyes were closed. His hands were folded on his chest. He was handsome, but lifeless. He seemed to her bewitched, a fallen prince.

Barry rose as if she intended to follow the gurney. She wanted to see his eyes open, hear him breathe. She staggered a little, feeling a sharp pulse of blood almost like a blow to her left temple.

She felt the grip of a supporting hand and turned. Her father was there. She hadn't seen him come in. He was staring at the young man on the gurney as it was taken away. A muscle near Tom Brennan's left eye twitched as it usually did when he was snatched out of his studio or creative reverie and presented with a crisis. He adjusted slowly, and sometimes with resentment, to the reality of the world. And he'd always hated hospitals.

It was a treat then just to lean against him with her eyes closed for a few moments. Tom Brennan's arms went around her. She knew what he must be thinking. Remembering. Edie had been brought here from the smashup; she was dead minutes before the ambulance reached the emergency room doors. And the stranger who had been in the car with Edie had not survived her by more than half an hour.

'You okay?' Tom asked Barry, squeezing.

'Shaky. It comes and goes.'

'How is he?'

'Nobody's saying yet, but he's alive. I can go home.' She looked at Ivorson for confirmation. He nodded and extended a hand to her father.

'Mr Brennan? I'm Stew Ivorson, state police. It's a pleasure to meet you, sir. I've always been a great admirer of your work.'

'Thank you. Any charges against Barry?'

'Not likely to be.' Ivorson smiled approvingly at her. 'She's quite a girl. Well, I'll be in touch.'

'Let's get out of here,' Barry said thankfully.

THREE

TOM HAD brought the Chevy Blazer, which was equipped
with heavy-duty suspension, tires that could chew through
six inches of fresh snow, and a plow attachment to push the
really heavy stuff aside. A ten-year-old dyspeptic bloodhound with a voice like the thunder of doom made room for
Barry in the cab of the truck, then lay with his head in Tom's
lap. The bloodhound's name was Kipper, but Barry had
renamed him Meanness for the volatility of his bowels, and
that name had stuck.

They left the Volvo in the hospital's parking lot and
headed for home. Meanness broke wind. Barry groaned and
rolled the window on her side down halfway.

'Not sticking to his diet, is he?' Barry said accusingly.

'He must have got hold of something ripe in the woods.'

'Ugh.'

Tom wore his old corduroy coat, a faded pumpkin color,
leather at the elbows. He was a lanky, fair man with a
freckled forehead and a trace of the Irish accent that had
accompanied him to the States forty-odd years ago. He
looked at Barry over the edges of his driving glasses.

'Feel like talking about the accident?'

'Sure. Wait till we get to the bridge, though.'

He nodded. Barry seemed collected to him – a little tired,
but not ready to subside into one of her wordless brooding
studies that both annoyed and worried him.

At the west end of the bridge there was a place to pull off
the road. They got out of the truck, leaving a complaining
Meanness behind, and walked through the long shaft of the
echoing bridge. Tom had a six-battery steel flashlight with

28

him.

Barry explained everything that had happened. They stood looking down the slope of the hill, snow fluttering through the beam of the light.

'It's strange that he was walking away from the bridge, into the snow,' Tom said.

'If I only knew what he was doing out here.'

'I'll go along with Albert's notion. I doubt that he's a local boy.'

'He could've escaped from the reform school,' Barry suggested.

'In Cairnstown? That's twenty miles.'

'You're right. It's too far.' She turned, blinking, as the wind shifted and snow flew at her eyes. 'Something keeps going through my mind.'

'What?'

'Ned's plaid jacket. You remember the one – it was orange and black.'

'Why were you thinking about that?'

'I saw a boy in Copperwell's wearing a jacket like Ned's. And then at the hospital I was looking into the treatment room and I swear I – I saw it again for a second, all bloody, lying on the floor just where they'd thrown it after he was brought in.'

'After *Ned* was brought in?'

'Yes.'

Tom touched her, as he sometimes did for reassurance, not knowing why he needed it. 'What does that have to do with –'

'I'm trying to remember what was going through my mind while I was driving across the bridge this afternoon.'

His ungloved fingers felt her tremor.

'Too cold for you out here. We could be sitting in the truck.'

'No, I think better when I'm cold. Don't rush me, Dad, please. This is important.'

'Take your time.'

Barry closed her eyes for half a minute. Her head turned

29

slowly in the direction of the bridge. Light from Tom's flashlight seeped upward to her face. He felt the power of her concentration as a tingling across his forehead, in the tips of his fingers. It was all he could do to keep from stepping back, as if something awesome and vaguely threatening were contained by the shut lids of her eyes. Here was the differentness that challenged his love for his daughter, Edie's difficult legacy.

'That's it,' Barry said after a freezing interval. She looked around at her father, rather blankly, wiping away snow tears. 'What I thought – what I *saw* – was Ned, holding his stomach, bloody, staggering, falling, trying to get down to the road for help, and then the next thing I saw was this other guy, in my headlights, acting sort of –'

'How?'

'I dunno – dazed. Like he was already hurt and didn't know where he was. Then I braked and, *bam*!'

'What do you make of it?'

Barry sighed and shook her head. 'I don't know. It doesn't explain anything, does it?'

They were driving the last mile home when Tom asked cautiously, 'Do you think Mrs Prye might have something to say about all this?'

Barry was jolted from a reverie of music, a piece she'd been composing in her head for days. Her shoulders came up rigidly.

'I haven't heard from Mrs Prye, and I'm not going to.'

'No?'

'No. She was – definitely getting out of hand.'

'To say the least.'

'You were right when you said we had to banish her. She won't be back.'

Tom sighed, glad to hear she'd been cured from that obsession. 'Well, it's for the best. I wondered how you felt about her. There's no point in bringing her back just to ask a couple of questions. She probably doesn't know the answers anyway.'

He glanced at his daughter for confirmation, but Barry's

face was clean of expression; she had no more to say about Mrs Prye.

Tom signaled for the gates to open and turned off the road to Tuatha de Dannan.

They all hated the black iron gates, which were obtrusive in the natural landscape of old rock walls and tall trees that formed one boundary of the farm. But as Tom's reputation and popularity grew it had become necessary to protect the privacy that was essential to his creative process. As it was, too many admirers and well-wishers still turned up unexpectedly, confident of their welcome, wanting to pass the day or a weekend with their favorite artist; they clambered over walls, tromped through hedges and gardens, and snapped photos of Tom while he was trying to sketch by the gristmill or pond.

Tuatha de Dannan, named for the second race of people to settle in Ireland (according to Celtic mythology, they were descendants of the Roman goddess Diana), had been in Edith Brennan's family for more than a hundred years: the farm was her legacy and her dowry upon her marriage to Tom, who had not yet begun to make a reputation as a painter. There were three hundred and fifty acres, including a spring-fed pond of some sixty-five acres. In places the pond had some unexpected, rugged depths, going down more than twenty-five feet. About half of the remaining property was woodland or orchards; the rest was lease-farmed, producing cash crops.

The centerpiece of Tuatha de Dannan, on a knoll three hundred yards in from the road, was a clapboard saltbox house, remodeled and enlarged during each century of its existence. The northwest wall of the house, the most recent addition, was sheathed from the peak of the roof to the ground in twenty-eight panes of reflective glass, a stunning visual departure from the traditional architecture of the rest of the house. This mirror wall provided light for Tom's studio.

Sharing the knoll was a stone barn that housed riding horses and chickens. Somewhat more distant from the house

31

stood a working gristmill on a stream that fell in steps to the northeast shore of the pond.

In the middle of the house were two columns of stone chimneys. Several of the rooms upstairs and down had fireplaces. Mrs Aldrich had left a kindling fire going on the Texas grate in the kitchen. Barry busied herself putting soda bread and steak-and-mushroom pie in the oven; she tossed a salad. Meanness whined for his supper. Tom gave him a soupbone from the refrigerator, and he retired to a scruffy braided rug by the laundry room door to chew on it. Tom poured a stout for himself and one for Barry and set to work sharpening some knives.

Barry said, musing, 'What if he was locked up somewhere, almost all of his life?'

'Like Rochester's wife in *Jane Eyre*?'

'Chained in the attic, shut away from the light of day?' She loved it. 'Wow!'

Tom grinned at her and went to dig more kindling out of the barrel on the hearth.

'No. No.' Barry's face fell. 'He looked too good for that. I mean, really *put together*. A hunk. If he'd been a closet case, he would've been all skin and bone and runny sores. Twisted out of shape.'

She turned away from the sink, one shoulder canted high, fingers crooked, mouth agape. She made distressing sounds in her throat. Meanness looked up warily from his soupbone.

'Delightful,' Tom said, turning away from the fire to catch her act. 'Hold that thought until after we've had our supper.'

Barry's appetite evaporated, as it often did, after the first bite of food. They went over the latest financial statement from Tom's business manager. He had sold some stock at a profit and added, at auctions, to their store of rare collectibles: a mint-condition Army Colt .45 made in 1881, a Dürer etching. Royalties from two collections of Tom's work had come in; the totals for the coffee-table art books were impressive. Condominiums in Paris and Manhattan, along with the farm and orchard operations, provided essential tax shelters.

'Did you call Les?' Barry asked her father. Les was his agent, who with his brother operated the Mergendoller Galleries in New York and Washington.

'Forgot. I'll do it tomorrow. When will the new one be framed?'

'Week from Saturday, Claude said.'

'What did Claude and Blighty think of it?'

'Knocked them over.'

'How about you?'

Barry drank the rest of her stout, wondering how to accurately express what she felt.

'It's like you were painting the end of the world,' she said.

Tom's eyes were on his plate, but she discerned a gleam of satisfaction. Barry knew she was right on the button.

'But I didn't like it. Houses ought to be *safe*. What other safety is there?' She looked at the cold windows and heard the rising wind. 'Is that how you felt after Mom died?'

'Yes.'

'I did too, but I don't want to be reminded.' She sensed she had hurt him by being too candid. 'Look, what difference does it make how I feel? It's a great painting. People are going to talk about it. You know what I think Les will get?'

'No.'

'Half a million. A new record for a Brennan.'

Tom whistled and got up to pour himself another glass of stout.

'Did I ever tell you what my first show in fifty-three brought in? It was a sellout, remember.'

'I know exactly. After commissions you took home twenty-three hundred bucks.'

'Half a million, huh?' he said softly.

'The Sharmans and the Kameos will go to war to get their hands on it. But I'd rather see it at the Whitney or the Philadelphia, if you want my opinion. It's too good to be in a private collection.'

'Eat, you're thin as a rail.' He always reacted to praise with some minor criticism of her. Barry had learned to ignore him

33

– it was just a personality flaw – but years ago his habit had hurt her a lot and led to woeful misunderstandings. 'And quit looking at the telephone.'

Barry was surprised. 'Was I looking at the phone?'

He nodded. 'All during supper.'

'So what?'

'Don't get huffy.' Tom sat opposite her again. Meanness got up and padded over to his chair. Tom let a hand dangle; the hound licked his fingers. Barry cringed. Then she gazed thoughtfully at the wall telephone.

'Maybe I ought to call the hospital. He might be conscious now.'

'Barry –' Tom rubbed flaking skin off his upper lip with a knuckle. 'Whoever this boy is – whatever the circumstances – I don't want you feeling guilty about what happened.'

'I don't!'

'Then stop brooding.' He took a piece of bread, soaked it in cooled meat gravy, and slipped it under the chair to Meanness.

'No, Dad! He's going to get off his diet and then he'll stink up the whole house.'

Tom smiled contritely.

'Well, you better not let him sleep upstairs tonight.'

Now out of sorts, Barry got up and began scraping plates into the disposal.

'And I'm *not* brooding. You don't understand. Maybe he's going to die and we'll never know anything about him.'

Her tone made Tom edgy. He thought about the unknown young man in the hospital. Probably he wasn't hurt too seriously. In a day or two he'd be released and Barry's concern would lessen, before it became obsessive. There really wasn't anything for him to worry about. Plenty to be thankful for – the accident could have been much worse if she'd lost control and the Volvo had left the road. Time to count his blessings and not think of the coincidence, his own obsession, now deeply buried but capable of stirring, resurrecting with it all the old horrors that for two years had left him a man in a trance, incapable of working.

34

Tom took his pipe, matches, and tobacco pouch out of various shirt pockets. 'Give you a hand with the dishes?'

'No thanks. You better start plowing the drive. Dal's driving up tonight, and he won't be able to get to the house.'

FOUR

STEWART IVORSON returned to the Anatolia hospital at a little after nine o'clock to find out how the accident victim was coming along and to talk to the head of Neurology, Dr James Edwards, a man in his forties with a short haircut and the wiry thinness of the marathon runner. Edwards took the policeman to an intensive care unit on the second floor to see the patient.

'Do you have a name for us?' Edwards asked.

'Not yet, There was no indication he was camping out in the park. No missing persons reports have been filed locally. We checked all schools and colleges in the area, but nobody wandered off or was absent without permission. What do you have?'

'Contradictions,' Edwards said. 'This one has me baffled.'

They stopped by the bedside of the patient. He was wired to both electrocardiograph and electroencephalograph machines, which monitored his heart rate and produced tracings of his brain waves on a continuous strip of paper.

The young man's eyes were closed; he was unconscious. Fluids dripped from bottles on either side of the bed into veins in his arms. A catheter had been inserted. His urine was a flawless yellow. But his heart rate and respiration were noticeably slow. He was on oxygen and an endotracheal tube had been inserted in his airway. To Ivorson the face in repose looked unfinished, smoothly sculpted but without so much as an irregular pore, a vein, a pimple, a tinge of life. The face gave Ivorson the willies. He looked away.

'How long has he been out?'

'He was admitted at four fifty-three this afternoon. Call it five hours.'

'What's wrong with him?'

'Physically, not much. Everything works, but slowly. There's no indication of intoxication with alcohol, barbiturates, or tranquilizers.'

'Diabetic?'

'First thing I thought of. Negative. Also we've ruled out hepatic and hypothyroid comas. His urine is normal. He's not bleeding internally. There are no broken bones. We did a spinal series and an angiogram. All vertebrae are intact, and the flow of blood to the brain is unobstructed. Temperature remains subnormal – it's down to eighty-seven degrees. That and the absence of a maculohemorrhagic rash rules out infection: meningitis, a host of viruses like Rocky Mountain spotted fever. I'd like to do a CAT scan, but we don't have the equipment.'

The doctor took a rubber-tipped reflex hammer from a pocket of his hospital smock.

'Watch this.'

He pressed the metal end of the hammer against the patient's right heel and drew it sharply toward the toes. The foot flexed and the toes curled tightly. He did it to the other foot, with identical results.

'What does that prove?' Ivorson asked him.

'If his corneal, pupillary, pharyngeal, tendon, and plantar reflexes are within normal limits, we should be able to wake him up. But we can't.'

'This guy goes against the books.'

'And how.'

'So he's in a coma?'

'Not really. Coma is a condition produced by disease or encephaloma. The EEG doesn't indicate the presence of scar tissue, intercranial bleeding, or episodic dysfunction of any kind.'

Edwards picked up a handful of EEG tracings and studied them, frowning. He looked up at the policeman. With a pen he pointed out lines on the graph paper. 'The brain is constantly producing electrical energy. By pasting electrodes around the head we can record the amplified neuronal activity as waveforms. These nice steady steep waves indicate alpha activity, which is linked to eye movements; they tend to disappear during wakeful periods. The size of these delta waves indicates deep sleep. I ordered the EEG two and a half hours ago. He's been in delta sleep all that time. All the waves are diminishing rather drastically now because he's cooling off, but still there hasn't been a trace of beta or theta waves.'

'What are those?'

'They're associated with a flow of imagery and thought: with anxiety and dreaming. Even newborns have enough mental activity to produce increased frequencies. But he doesn't.'

'In other words, his mind is a blank.'

'A couple more hours like this, I might be convinced. He's not in any kind of sleep cycle I'm familiar with.'

The doctor studied the blips on the oscilloscope that reported heart activity. The rate was thirty-two beats a minute. A little slower, he thought, than when he'd come in. Edwards put the handful of graph paper back in the collecting tray. 'If we just knew who he was, if we had a medical history ...'

Ivorson shook his head regretfully.

'It's almost as if he's running down to a full stop,' Edwards said, staring at the face of the young man. 'And there's nothing we can do to prevent it.'

FIVE

SNOW WAS still falling heavily when Dal Brennan showed up, his Mercedes coupe like a white mushroom in the lights of the dooryard. Barry had been curled up in a favorite wing chair in the family room listening to an old Beatles album, *Rubber Soul*, searching for an offbeat inspiration for one of her own compositions. She put her guitar aside, went into Tom's den. He was dozing slipperless by the fire, a book in his lap. Barry helped herself to a little of the Jameson's he'd been sipping, then gently shook him awake.

'Dal's here.'

Dal came into the house with two small Gucci cases and a girl in a hooded shearling coat. She was superbly blond, blue of eye and blood, undoubtedly finished to a high gloss at the most exclusive schools in Switzerland and America. She had a wide smile and dimples more valuable than anything they could sell you at Cartier's.

Dal gave his sister a road-weary grin as he took off his glasses. 'Barry, this is Tinker Botsford.'

'Hi! I feel like I know you already. Dal talks about you so much. I think Barry's such a cute name for a girl.'

Barry held her own smile for a count of ten, letting her silence go on almost too long. Dal fidgeted and shot her a look.

'So is Tinker,' Barry said slowly.

'My real name's Eunice. But who needs it?'

'Good point. Where d'you go to school?'

'Columbia.'

'Fabulous.'

'Isn't it? I really like it a lot.' Tinker looked all around, nodding her approval of what she had seen so far. 'This is *cozy*.' Her eyes settled on Barry again. 'Are you a painter too?'

'No. I write music. Sometimes.'

'I'll just put these bags upstairs,' Dal said.

'I think I'd better go too,' Tinker said, showing her dimples again. 'It's been a long time between stops. Oh, has it been snowing! I didn't think we'd get here. I thought we might have to spend the night in *Port Chester*, or some god-awful place like that.'

'I'll put the coffee on,' Barry said, holding back a yawn. 'Great to see you, Dal. Why don't you come home more often?'

Dal and Tinker were nearly twenty minutes in his bedroom, long enough for Tom to start nodding off again as he waited with Barry in the family room. It was almost an hour past his usual bedtime. But he perked up, as Barry knew he would, when he laid eyes on Tinker. She did a poor job of concealing her hero-worship of the artist. Dal sat with his ankles crossed and drank whiskey. He grinned and said little and ran a hand nervously through his hair, already thinning drastically though he was just twenty-five. He was smaller and brawnier than his father, with a much more difficult psyche: he could be as dark and forbidding as a cave in the woods, a bad drunk, prickly with nerve endings. At his best he soared with the poetry of his kind. He came from a long line of schemers and deluders, saints and crackpots. Sometimes after an hour with Dal he'd have you believing he could turn dogshit into stars. He was a natural ladykiller.

'I did my art history thesis on Pieter Brueghel the Elder,' Tinker said to Tom. 'The parallels between your work are amazing. I don't think anyone's ever noticed. The sense of historical mystery in the *mise en scène* just knocks me for a loop. Were you influenced by Brueghel?'

'*Hunters in the Snow* is one of the pictures I keep going back to.'

'I knew it!'

'He may be the best painter of winter scenes who ever

40

lived. I've tried to get that light of his, but I think he must have been divinely inspired.'

'A genius.'

'The rest of us,' Tom said modestly, 'just work at it. More coffee?'

'Oh, no, sir, thank you.' Tinker leaned forward intently in her chair, high color in her cheeks; she moistened her lips and clasped her hands between her knees. She was talking Art with a Major Figure. This was serious business. Barry wondered if Tinker was going to have to run to the bathroom again. Dal sat back, his body relaxed from the heavy drinking, his eyes half-lidded, a courteous smile that no longer seemed to fit his mood still on his lips. Tinker said, 'Brueghel was obsessed with man's essential lack of freedom. There's so much space in many of his landscapes, but it's *forbidden* space. His people are constantly circling back on their lives, going nowhere.'

'It was a brilliant age, the Renaissance,' Tom said. 'And there have been few periods in history so filled with human suffering. The Hundred Years' War. The Peasants' War. Religious persecution. So he painted *The Blind Leading the Blind*.'

'And *The Fall of Icarus*. You've painted your own *Icarus*. Do you know which one I mean?'

Now she was just plain hitting on him, Barry thought. Barry was both amused and infuriated. An hour from now Tinker would be in bed dutifully and no doubt strenuously screwing Dal and wishing it was Tom, and both men already knew it. Another cross for Dal to drag around, but he should have known better than to bring her home with him.

'Umm, well. No,' Tom said, responding to Tinker's question.

'*Edgar Valence*. That wonderful old black man sitting in his chair in the back of that pickup truck. His head tilted, just a little gleam of sun on his forehead as he looks at the sky. His eyes, God! Like he's traveled through time, seen all there is to see of the universe. My father has six of your watercolors, but that is one painting of yours he would

41

literally *kill* for.'

'He'll have to work his way through the entire board of directors of the Met,' Barry advised her.

'I used to go there every Saturday, without fail, just to see *Edgar Valence*. Then I'd leave.'

'Tinker,' Dal said affably, 'I'm pooped and I need to talk to my old man for a few minutes. Why don't you let Barry show you around the rest of the house?'

Thanks a lot, Dal.

'I don't suppose I could see your studio?' Tinker asked Tom.

'Sure.' Tom waved Barry to her feet. Tinker got up too.

'It's really been a revelation, talking to you like this. I feel just like I did the first time I walked into the cathedral at Chartres.'

'We're just plain folks,' Barry assured her. 'Descendants of bog trotters. We want you to make yourself at home, Binky.'

'Tink-er.'

'Tink-er,' Barry said, beaming. 'I forgot.'

Tinker was predictably impressed with the three-story studio pavilion, the northwest wall of which was mirror glass. Fins and shutters on the inside could be adjusted against the summer's glare. For now, despite the snowstorm, the studio was comfortable from stored solar heat. Tom hadn't been in to straighten up for a day or two, and nobody else was allowed to touch anything. The sketches and watercolors that had been the models for *Greene House* still littered the tops of tables, cabinets, and even the floor around his easel.

'I'd give anything to watch Tom work on a painting,' Tinker said wistfully.

Barry shook her head. 'He just finished one – probably won't do another for a while. Anyway, he doesn't like having anyone around. Even me. He draws a magic circle around himself when he's working. Step inside that circle and he turns into a werewolf.'

'Oh. I see.' Tinker tugged at a couple of cabinet drawers, which were locked. There were several such cabinets, at least fifty drawers in all. 'What are these?'

'Where Dad keeps all of his working drawings. From way back.'

'They must be worth a fortune.'

Barry shrugged. 'We have enough money.'

'Does Dal have a studio here?'

'Before he bought the loft, he worked in a room off the barn. Too much snow tonight, or I'd show you.'

Tinker wandered around, examining props and curios: bleached animal bones, a bull-shaped weather vane, a collection of birds' nests, an antique marionette stage and a forties-model pinball machine.

'Does this work?' Tinker asked of the pinball machine.

'Sure. Dad likes to bang around on it when his painting isn't going so well.' Barry plugged in the machine and ran a couple of balls. 'We picked this up along with some other stuff from an amusement park down by the Sound that went bust. We have an old popcorn machine in the kitchen, a nickelodeon – you name it. Most of it's stored away. We drag a few things out for parties, but we haven't had any parties since Dal moved to SoHo.'

While Barry was using body English on the pinball game, Tinker approached another machine, partly concealed behind a dropcloth, in one corner of the studio.

On the front of the machine, a scuffed scarlet box about five and a half feet high, there was printed, in jaded white glitzy script, LET MRS PRYE TELL YOUR FUTURE. The box had an electronic numbered keyboard below a transparent but badly scratched glass dome. Tinker saw what looked like a shadowy human head inside the dome. She cautiously pulled the dropcloth aside. There was a film of dust on the glass. She brushed some of it away.

'What's this?'

Barry looked around and frowned.

'Oh, that's Mrs Prye. She doesn't work.'

Tinker cupped her hands against the dome and peered inside.

Mrs Prye was done up as a Restoration-era medium.

There was a jewel in the middle of her forehead. She wore a luxurious *tête*, had a beauty spot on one rouged cheek, and thick sable eyelashes. The whole of her head was about the size of a marmoset's, or a large man's fist. The head was tilted forward slightly, as if in repose. The eyes were closed.

'God, she's spooky! What does she do?'

Barry, annoyed, abandoned her game and unplugged the pinball machine.

'She's just an illusion. And she doesn't talk anymore. Maybe you'd better get away from there, Tinker.'

Tinker was a little surprised by her tone, but she dutifully walked away from the machine.

'And cover her up,' Barry instructed, adding softly, 'please.'

Tinker studied Barry's face. Her lips had thinned. She appeared to be looking, not at Tinker, but at some place considerably beyond the walls of the studio. Tinker shrugged and turned back, grasped the dropcloth on which paint had run and hardened. She glanced again at the head under glass, gasped, and jumped away, letting the cloth fall across the machine.

'What's the matter?'

'Her eyes were open! She was looking at me!'

Barry shook her head and said scornfully, 'I told you, she's just an illusion.'

'Oh, you mean – it's like a three-dimensional sort of thing, and it depends on where you're standing, right?'

'That's it,' Barry said. She smiled, but she seemed preoccupied. 'Come on.'

'I really love this house,' Tinker said as they left the studio. 'What do you call it?'

'The farm is named Tuatha de Dannan. The Tuatha ruled Ireland a long time ago until they were conquered and became fairy people. They were great magicians and artists. Still are, I guess.'

'Still are?' Tinker dimpled. 'You don't believe in fairies and leprechauns, do you?'

'Yes,' Barry said in a no-nonsense tone.

'Have you seen any?'

'No. They stick close to home. They don't travel well. But I've seen a few ghosts.' Tinker's eyes widened. Barry was bored and tired, and decided to torment her. 'Ours is named Enoch. He was killed in the Revolutionary War, but nobody's been able to convince him of that. If he comes around looking for Abigail, tell him to go out on the road and wait for the stagecoach. That always gets rid of him for a few days.'

Tinker had a surprisingly robust laugh. 'Ba-loney. Barry, you have a wonderful sense of humor.'

Barry leaned against a cabinet, her arms folded.

'I hope you do. Us Brennans can be hard to take sometimes.'

SIX

Tom Brennan's study was the smallest room in the house; the door and single window were enclosed by walnut bookcases with glass doors. The other two walls were painted a warm cream color and contained a few paintings by those artists Tom most admired: Dürer, Homer, Hopper, Andrew Wyeth. There were two framed posters of Tom's first important shows, a pen-and-ink sketch of Edie at twenty-one, and a blowup of a *Time* magazine cover that featured a self-portrait of the artist. Tom's reading chair, near the fireplace, was a Barcalounger. There was a magazine rack beside it that Dal had made for him as a birthday present when Dal was fifteen, a standing lamp, and a refurbished peanut dispenser that had seen a tour of duty in the Times Square BMT station before World War II.

Dal got up from the arcade-style Space Invaders game he'd been playing, helped himself to a handful of peanuts, and swished melting ice around in his glass. He slumped on the small sofa in the room, which was printed with autumnal hunting scenes: pheasants on the wing and barking bird dogs.

'Barry looks like she's taking it all right.'

'Nobody in his right mind could say the accident was her fault. She's worried, though.'

'Check with the hospital? How is he coming along?'

'I called. They aren't giving out information. But he's in Intensive Care. Somebody there was worried about the bills since he's a John Doe. I said I'd take care of it.'

'How's Barry been acting?'

'Okay. She keeps to herself – you know how she is. Tells

46

me she's composing a pop opera. She works at the piano nearly every day.'

'Does she talk about Ned?'

'Once in a while,' Tom said.

'That's good. But not good enough.'

Meanness scratched at the door and whined. Dal reached out to open the door and let the bloodhound in.

'Do you think she would have married Ned?' Dal asked his father.

Tom smiled. 'I don't think there's any way we could have stopped her.'

'He was a good guy. Steady. But she was too young to get married – she doesn't have any idea of her potential yet. It's been – what? – a year? Barry's just not reacting normally, Dad. I mean, first love and all that, and a tragic end to it. But she should have recovered. She ought to be in school with girls her own age, dates.'

'I can't force her, Dal.'

'Well, she has to be damn lonely around here, and you know how off-the-wall she is – anything can happen.'

'I think she has all that under control,' Tom said evenly.

Dal shrugged. 'Look, she could come down to New York and live with me, go to school at NYU. It's the best town in the world to party in, and the intellectual stimulation wouldn't hurt.'

'Did you ask her?'

'Ask her? I've twisted her arm. She comes for a weekend, she loves it, then she zips right back to the farm. Dad, you know it's up to you.'

Tom was silent. He poked at the fire on the small hearth. Sparks flew crackling like a flight of bees to one flanneled arm. He shook them off moodily.

'I don't think I'm one of those possessive fathers. Remember, she's only eighteen. Some girls can be on their own at that age, others need another year in the nest.'

Dal got up a little unsteadily, searched the bookshelves, took down a rare copy of Arthur Conan Doyle's *The Coming of the Fairies*, signed by the author to Edie's father,

47

who had been a devout folklorist. Dal leafed through photographs of small people, some with gossamer wings and pointed ears, taken by two young girls in a glen in Yorkshire, England, with plates Doyle himself had marked and provided to preclude fakery.

'Doing any work, Dal?' Tom asked.

'Yeah. I've been working. Trying to. It's hard.'

'If you're serious about what you do, it never gets any easier.'

'I can't focus,' Dal admitted. 'I – my ideas are bad. I feel washed up. Isn't that a bitch?'

'Critics can do that to you. For years they almost had me convinced I wasn't good for anything but magazine covers.'

'The critics still don't buy you, but the museums do. And everyone who cares anything about art in this country.' Dal looked at his empty glass, struggled with himself for a few moments, then helped himself to whiskey. Tom watched him pour, and pour, and looked away.

'I guess you were right when you said I wasn't ready for a show. I should have listened to you.'

'Expectations were running too high. Yours. Everyone else's. Lousy reviews are a risk you run when you exhibit.'

Dal exploded. '*Sure* I still paint like you! What do they want from me? I learned here, right here. But I'm not a clone – that was about the best thing any one of those sons of bitches had to say.'

Tom tried to appease him. 'I went through a few bad years before I felt that something unique was happening. You absorb from others, you use what you can, and one day there's a breakthrough. It's like putting on corrective lenses when you've been nearsighted all of your life.'

'O happy day,' Dal said mournfully.

'Dal, you're wasting your time in New York. You may think you're working, but you're not. I know the routine: saloons, lofts, openings, hoopla. There's always something diverting around. It's the same old mob down there. Everybody gets into a feeding frenzy when the bait is juicy enough. You get a better class of groupies nowadays, that's

48

all. Put a padlock on your place and come home. You have more talent than anyone I've ever taught. But technical proficiency alone won't get you anywhere.'

'I just can't be as sure as you are that there's anything to reach for.' Dal smiled at his father. But his eyes simmered with frustration and anger.

'You're afraid of the pain,' Tom suggested. 'But believe me when I say you can't succeed without it.'

SEVEN

BARRY. HOW do'st thou, mistress?

The only light in Barry's room was from the television console in one corner. The 'Tonight' show was winding up in fine style, with the acerbic Don Rickles, sweating quarts and grimacing like a frog, breaking Johnny up. Barry had snuggled down under two comforters half an hour ago and drifted off to sleep with the sound low, the voices of the comics indistinct, only the laughter audible.

Let me come back, my angel, Mrs Prye wheedled. *I fancy not this purgatory you have cast me into.*

Barry thought she must be dreaming. But she couldn't be dreaming the Carson show and Mrs Prye simultaneously. She stirred and groaned and pulled a pillow over her head.

'Go away, Mrs Prye.'

Talking back to her was a mistake; it only gave her confidence.

Nay, you're too severe. Let's have no more hasty temper. For my part, I vow I'll not be sly, nor unfit for the company of your friends.

Barry tried burrowing deeper into the bed. 'You talk too much. You tell people things they shouldn't know. Then everyone blames me. You can't come back. I mean it.'

The TV picture disappeared suddenly, hopelessly scrambled. Barry felt the emanations from the screen as a tingling on the back of her neck. She knew she was licked. She sat up. Outside it was still snowing.

Don't despise me, my dove. Is it the young man who has you in such a bitter passion? Sure, he's vastly handsome. Let me tell you more of the matter. I know his name.

50

Barry looked at the TV screen, where Mrs Prye had materialized, simpering, batting her long eyelashes.

'You *don't!*' Barry said hotly.

Well, well, may I serve thee now? Art thou yet in the proper spirits? Back on speaking terms with her mistress, Mrs Prye was well pleased with herself.

'You don't know anything about him. You just think you do.'

Impudent cub! I have the gift of prophecy. You know 'tis so.

'You're not getting me into any more trouble!' Barry said, too loudly. She was afraid she'd wake up the rest of the house. If her father came in he'd be upset. She had assured him that Mrs Prye wasn't going to be a problem ever again. Barry lowered her voice but said threateningly, 'I can make you go away.'

Mrs Prye prudently turned the other cheek.

Ay, you can. But fetch me away now and you may ne'er know more of his soul and bones.

Barry studied the face on the TV screen, her heart beating faster. The young man in the hospital had been on her mind as she dozed off; no denying she was curious now.

'All right. Tell me your big secret. Who is he?'

Mrs Prye unexpectedly let loose a peal of laughter.

Ned Kramer Ned Kramer Ned Kramer Ned Kramer

'That's the dumbest thing I ever heard!' Barry said, and began to sob, her face twisted in indignation.

Immediately the medium's image was replaced by the 'Tonight' show; not so much as a whisper of her delighted laughter remained. Johnny, however, was convulsed, nearly falling out of his chair. The sound was louder on the TV. Rickles displayed a goblin's grin. The drummer in the band was dealing out sardonic rim shots. Ed McMahon, as familiar an artifact of Americana as Uncle Sam, appeared to sell dog food.

Sullen and mad, Barry wiped at her tears. She was shaking, which often was the aftermath of an encounter with Mrs Prye.

When she had herself together, Barry turned on the lamp beside the four-poster bed. She kept Ned's picture on a mahogany rent table there, a last photo of him, bare to the waist and enjoying a big slab of watermelon that idyllic August before his death. Next to the framed photo was a statue of the Brennan family saint, Veronica, an ancient Celtic cross, and a rosary that her mother had left Barry. The cross, handed down through generations, at one time had been the property of family priests, very holy men who, Edith had claimed, gave it special powers.

Barry saw her own face, elongated, in the slant glass of the picture frame. Ned's hair, long as Lancelot's, was wheat-blond, the bridge of his nose broad and hawkish. But of course Mrs Prye hadn't meant that the other young man was literally Ned. Her pronouncements, sometimes to the point, were more frequently obscure.

It was almost twelve thirty on a Friday night. Sleep now was out of the question. She had a chill, a chill of events set in motion about to whirl out of control. She wanted to go to the hospital. She was afraid, but eager. She *had* to go.

Barry dressed in wool pants and an alpinist's sweater, pulled on fur-lined boots, and went down the hall to Dal's room. He hadn't locked the door. She listened for a few moments, heard him snoring, then walked in and left the door ajar so that the light from the hall fell across the bed.

'Dal. Dal.'

He struggled up, bleary-eyed. 'Wha?'

'It's Barry.'

'What are you doing in here?'

Tinker sat up suddenly beside Dal, looking dismayed. She was wearing a flimsy peach-colored nightgown. Barry glanced at her boobs. Dal sure could pick 'em, she thought.

'Who's that?' Tinker said, wide-eyed but apparently not in focus.

'Oh, hi, Tinker. I didn't mean to disturb you. I'm sorry. Listen, Dal, I need a big favor. I want you to drive me to the hospital.'

'What's matter, you sick?'

'Don't ask me a lot of questions now – it's really important. Just help me out.'

'Do I have to go too?' Tinker said. 'I'm really not a night person.'

'Barry, for God's sake –'

'Come on – we don't have much time. Night-night, Tink.'

Tinker, her eyes closing, fell back into her pillow with a soft little groan.

'Barry, it's freezing and snowing – listen to that wind.'

'Dal,' Barry said severely, 'we once took a blood oath. Neither of us would ever deny the other anything within his power to grant.'

Dal sat tenderly massaging his head.

'Jesus. There ought to be a statute of limitations on blood oaths.'

EIGHT

THEY TOOK Dal's Mercedes. Dal, in spite of a headache, insisted on driving. It was still snowing, but the county plows had made one pass already, and the worst of the slippery spots on the hills had been sanded. Barry tried to find something on the radio they could both listen to, but gave up after Dal snapped at her three times about the garbage she was into. His preference was for gloomy cellos. She sat with her hands folded in her lap, gazing straight ahead, wondering if Dal was going to pick on her anymore.

'Listen, you could give Tinker a break.'

Barry sighed.

'She's just somebody I brought up for the weekend. I don't know why you have to dump all over her.'

'Me? What did I do? I promised we'd never have another argument about your taste in women, and I meant it.'

After a few seconds Dal shot her an accusing look.

'You're laughing.'

'I am not. I have perfect control over my lips. See? A straight line.' She glanced at him and stifled a giggle, looking as startled as if she'd farted in church.

'There you go!'

'Honestly, Dal. I could see why you're attracted to her.'

'Yeah?'

'She was really cute in her little fly-by-nightie.'

Dal hit the brakes; Barry's hands flew up placatingly.

'Don't make me walk! I'll be good!'

Only the Emergency entrance to the hospital was open. An ambulance had pulled up. Inside the building the ER nurses and intern on night duty were busy; someone had taken a serious fall on a flight of icy steps. Barry led Dal past the vacant nurses' station and down a hallway.

'Where're we going?'

'Dad said he was in Intensive Care. That's on the second floor, isn't it?'

'I think so. Now tell me what we're doing here.'

'I have to see him again. I don't think I'll have another chance.'

'He's *that* critical? I thought you didn't do any real damage.'

'I wish I could explain, Dal. I've just got this terrible feeling.'

They went up a stairwell, down a hall with laboratory and conference room doors closed on either side, past a porter who was swabbing the floor. He had a transistor radio hooked to his belt, a cord running to an ear button: he didn't look at them as they went by.

'Barry, do you know more about this guy than you've been saying?'

'No, Dal,' Barry said, hurrying on ahead of him.

At the second-floor nurses' station a woman wearing a pink sweater over her uniform turned around and glanced up at Barry from a chart she'd been reading. She had grim gray curly hair and bulging jaw muscles. She looked like a tough cookie. E. MAYO was printed on her name tag.

'Yes?'

Barry started to explain. Mayo's mouth opened and closed like the snap of a scissors before she got very far.

'I can't give out information about the patient. Neither of you has any business bein' up here at this hour of the night.'

'But I only want to see him for a couple of minutes!'

'If you're not a relative, you don't belong here.'

'That's just the point,' Barry said in exasperation. 'He doesn't have anybody else right now!'

Mayo's eyes narrowed; her formidable chin bulged down against her chest. Dal smiled languidly and moved in between the two of them, turning his head so that Mayo wouldn't see the wink he gave his sister.

'Barry, would you excuse me for a few minutes, please? Wait over there.'

Barry withdrew, fretting, to a water cooler and had a drink. Dal turned back to the nurse. His cranky look had vanished, his eyes were brighter, his cheeks flushed handsomely. He leaned on the counter. Mayo watched him stolidly.

'Eileen, is it?' Dal asked, his phrasing subtly more Irish, his voice richening to a brogue.

'Elizabeth.'

'Our mother, God rest, her middle name was Elizabeth. I'm Dal.'

He put out his hand. Mayo was startled. She almost took it.

'I'm sorry, but you have to leave.'

Dal sighed, shaking his head. He sneaked a look at Barry. Then he turned his eyes on Mayo again, beseechingly.

'Elizabeth, my poor sister is beside herself with guilt.'

'Guilt?'

'It was her in the car ran the unfortunate fellow down this afternoon.'

'Oh.' The nurse stared at Barry, who hung her head in a dreary way.

'Never mind the accident wasn't her fault. She'll be scarred the rest of her life if he doesn't pull through. Tonight she was *six hours* on her knees at Saint Boniface.'

'Tch!'

'Father Tim himself couldn't console her. "Dal," he said to me, "take the poor child home." But I just had a feeling that somehow a glimpse of his face could ease her suffering. Do you understand my thinking, Elizabeth?'

Barry sniveled, almost inaudibly, then bravely got hold of herself, clenching her fists at her sides.

Mayo pursed her lips, stole another look at Barry, then glanced over a shoulder at the wall clock.

'Well –'

'Two minutes. That's all I'm askin.' Her mother's been dead these nine years. Dad and me, we do our best, but –'

56

'Say no more.' Mayo put her clipboard down, opened the gate, and beckoned to an incredulous Barry. 'Follow me, girl. But quiet, please.'

In the intensive care unit a slender Jamaican nurse was taking some readings that detailed the young man's steady, slow regression into oblivion. Barry took one look at him from the doorway and had to swallow hard to keep her heart out of her throat. She advanced cautiously to the side of the bed, stood looking numbly down at him. His chest scarcely rose and fell with each well-spaced breath.

'Eight beats a minute,' the Jamaican nurse whispered to Mayo. 'I didn't know it was possible.'

Dal was shocked. 'What the hell is going on?'

Mayo shook her head. 'I've seen 'em come, and I've seen 'em go. Most have been hurt a lot worse than this boy, and they've survived. But it's like he doesn't have one iota of the will to live.'

Barry couldn't breathe for a few seconds; she could not have imagined a more dreadful scene than this neat small space with its machines and low lights, the profusion of wires and tubes – oxygen, fluids – that snaked to his body. Her vision blurred from tears. She sobbed, catching her breath at last as the electrocardiograph pens scribbled like beastly fingers and the oscilloscope yielded up yet another isolated heartbeat.

She groped for the hand of the young man. He was so cold her fingers jerked away involuntarily. It was a toss-up then, whether she turned and fled or tried to find the courage to touch him again. She jerked a look at Dal, who was frowning. Dal started to shake his head. Barry winced and turned back and made contact again with the nearly lifeless hand of the patient. She held on, bowed her head, and said a silent prayer. It was brief. She let go of his hand slowly; there was no perception in the trailing fingers, no change in the motionless twilight body. He was dwindling imperceptibly, like an ice floe in a warming sea. She wanted alarms, flashing lights, doctors swarming in and out of the room, drastic action.

Barry turned on Mayo.

'But he can't be like this! Why wouldn't he want to live? Somebody has to do something!'

Dal put an arm around her shoulders and led her out. Mayo said, 'Doctor tried stimulants, directly into the heart muscle. Nothing happened.'

'But – he's –'

'Won't last the night, I'm afraid. Now, girl. Why blame yourself?'

'I don't. That's not it at all.'

'Okay, Barry,' Dal said. 'I guess there's nothing more we can do.' He put discreet pressure on her with his arm. Barry balked and looked at him, red-eyed, pleading, her voice a squeak.

'I can't go home, Dal. Can't leave him. There's *nobody*. It's terrible to be as alone as he is. Don't you see?'

'I know how you feel, but –'

'I'll be okay. I'll just sit here the rest of the night, until –' She glanced at Mayo, whose lips were pursed in disapproval. 'That'd be all right, wouldn't it? I won't get in the way.'

'You need to get yourself a good night's sleep, darlin'.'

Dal attempted to put more pressure on his sister, but she broke away from him. 'I'll sleep. I can always sleep.' She appealed to both of them. 'Don't make me go home.'

Mayo looked at Dal. He fidgeted, glanced at his sister, and shrugged. The decision was up to the nurse.

Mayo hemmed and hawed and came up with an idea. Barry could stay in the nurses' lounge, on the sofa. A blanket and a couple of pillows would turn it into an adequate bed, and nobody used the lounge during the wee hours. Barry jumped at the idea.

They had coffee in the lounge. The Jamaican girl brought in bedding. 'No change,' she said to Mayo, and went out again.

'You're sure this won't be any trouble, Mrs Mayo?' Barry asked.

'Not if they don't find out about it up top. Well, I don't care if they do. Twenty-three years, I run my floor the way I

58

see fit – like to see them manage without me. Get yourself some shut-eye.'

Dal finished the last of his coffee. 'I need to get home to my own bed.'

'Oh, I don't *blame* you,' said Barry.

He chuckled, smacked her with a pillow, kissed her cheek.

'Thanks, Dal,' Barry said, hugging him.

'You've got a good heart, kid. Call me if you need me.'

NINE

THE CLOSER he got to home, the more misgivings Dal had
about leaving his sister at the hospital. Self-doubt made him
surly and in need of a drink. He was surprised to find Tom up
– it was now a little after two – and apparently waiting for
him.

'Where did you go with Barry?'

Dal just looked at his father, took his coat off, and hung it
up in the foyer closet under the stairs.

'She's at the hospital.'

'Christ, Dal, what are you using for brains?'

On the defensive, Dal said, 'You know how she is. She'll be
safe there. What's the use of arguing with her?' He went into
the family room and opened the bar cabinet, took out an
unopened bottle of Jameson's. Tom had followed him in. He
stood with his hands in the pockets of his robe.

'I think we'd better go get her.'

'Why?'

'Because I don't like the way she's acting.'

'Barry's okay. She feels sorry for – Dad, the guy's dying.
He can't last the night, that's the shape he's in.'

'Are you sure?'

'Yes. I saw him.'

'I thought he wasn't seriously injured.'

'Well, something happened to him. His vital signs are all
going straight down. You want a drink?'

'No.' Tom sat down, still looking worried. Dal leaned on
the bar.

'I hope you're right,' Tom said.

'That he's going to die? Sure. What a thing to say! What
the hell is eating you?'

'Barry, I guess.'

'What about her?'

'Dal, I don't know. Something strange about the way all this happened. Where did he come from?'

'Who cares? Somebody will claim him eventually. It was just a freak accident. Why are you dwelling –' Dal drank, put his glass down, grimaced. Tom turned his head and looked at him.

'I had a dream about Edie.'

'Oh.' Neither man said anything for a minute or so. Dal chewed on a thumbnail, knocked back more of the Jameson's.

'Dad, it's just a lousy coincidence.'

'I wish I was that sure.'

'I know what you're thinking, and it isn't healthy.'

'We never found out who *he* was, either. Where he came from; what he was doing in Edie's car. Or what he had to do with the accident that killed her.'

Dal's breath was audible, a sharp burst of exasperation.

'Dad, come on. *Don't.* Mom had lovers, that's all. You have to face that fact. The one in the car, the others she was seen with sometimes. Nobody knew who *they* were, either. Just pickups. Guys off the road. She was lonely – what the hell. It's the way you are, the kind of life you have. Jesus, Dad, I loved Mom too, but – that was the reality of the situation.'

Tom got up deliberately, without a change of expression, walked over to the bar, and stood within a foot of his son, looking him in the eye.

'Your mother was faithful to me until the day she died.'

'Dad, what are we talking about? Everybody knows –'

'Oh yes. She was seen with strangers. *That's* what everybody knows. She was seen talking to men. But not – Just talking to them, Dal. And nobody has ever known who they were because – they were from another world. Some place that Edie knew well but a world we'll never know anything about.'

Dal's mouth dried up; he felt a clutch of anger in his

61

stomach and turned away to have another drink.

'I don't want to talk about that! You know what I think, you know how I feel about all that spiritualist crap Barry and I were raised on. I've spent my life trying to get away from it! Faces at the windows, noises at night, Mom wandering around here for days with that woebegone look in her eyes and her mind hanging by a thread – Let me *alone*, Dad.'

'I can't. Because Barry might be in trouble.'

'Why? All right, she's not your average kid – she's a sensitive and maybe a little like Mom. But not anywhere as bad. You're acting like Barry's doomed in some way.'

'Do you remember what happened when we got Mrs Prye?'

'Yes. Some people just can't mess around with stuff like that – it's worse than a Ouija board. She's not hanging around Mrs Prye, is she?'

'No. I put the machine in my studio.'

'Good. Go one better and have it hauled to the dump.'

'I will. I'm not saying Barry's doomed, but we have to be careful.' Tom's hand was on Dal's shoulder. 'Do you understand?'

'Yes. Yes.' Dal laughed unhappily. 'Barry really laid it on Tinker tonight. Gave her the whole occult history of Tuatha de Dannan. Tinker had me looking under the bed before we –' He shook his head, looked up, looked all around while avoiding Tom's level gaze. 'God! I don't know why I can't get away from this house, why I keep coming back.'

'Because you can work here.'

'I can also drink myself to death here. Maybe if I'm lucky I'll paint a couple of masterpieces before my liver turns to a cinder block.'

'Better get to bed.'

'You too.'

'I think I'll go to the studio for a while. Then, maybe I'll drive over to the hospital.'

'Barry's *okay*, Dad. I wouldn't have left her if –'

'I trust your word, Dal. I guess I just have to see him for myself. I didn't have a very good look this afternoon.'

TEN

WITH THE door to the nurses' lounge closed and a single lamp burning, Barry stared at a small-screen TV for a while but couldn't make sense of a movie she was watching, a spy story in which the characters took endless walks through picturesque streets in the smart spots of Europe. She took her boots off, turned out the light, lay down, and squirmed to get comfortable. When her eyes closed she saw the oscilloscope vividly and suspended her breathing until her mind's eye saw it blip. To get her thoughts off what was happening she pulled the blanket over her head, turned her back on the TV – now there was an interminable car chase going on, ineptly filmed in long shots – and relived deliberately every mile of the afternoon's drive from town to bridge in the snow.

She had believed, since she was a child, that if she concentrated hard enough after the fact she could change the course of unwelcome events. Her bicycle, carelessly left in the drive, would not be backed over by the delivery truck, her mother would not smile her benumbed good-bye smile, the stranger would appear by the side of the road, safely out of her way, thumbing a ride. She would fall asleep absorbed in this mental effort, certain of awakening refreshed with the bad things erased from time's scheme – her bicycle now standing where it belonged, unscratched beside the porch, Edie as always in the morning kitchen, smoking too much, churning pancake batter in a greased bowl with a big wooden spoon.

Blip.

In Barry's dream he appeared first like an apparition, then as a man made of snow with a lump of coal for a heart, and was struck by the skidding station wagon. Her feet, when she went to his rescue, were torturously mired in snow that mounted alarmingly, to her ankles, her knees; she struggled to get through it. She heard his loud heartbeat. The snow was speckled with blood. She somersaulted downhill, but slowly, and was about to plunge by him into an abyss. In panic she seized an outthrust naked foot and twisted it to stop herself. The foot turned clockwise, winding like the propeller on a toy airplane. She thought she heard him scream, but when she looked at his face it was frozen – all the handsome features lay an inch below a slick coating of ice. The sun came out, blazing hot, and he was melting, pockmarks in the ice, water running everywhere. She licked frantically at the melting face. His tongue, surprisingly human, warmly receptive, protruded stiffly from his mouth. She touched it with the tip of her own tongue and, shockingly, had an orgasm.

Barry came awake in a tangle of blankets, sweating, a hand clenched between her thighs. She rolled to her right and fell off the couch, hurting her knee. The TV screen flickered to her right. Then it was blocked from view as something stepped noiselessly in the way of it; moments later she heard a labored breath.

She looked up with a jolt of terror vivid as lightning ripping through her and saw him huge, looming over her, trailing red dripping tubes from the adhesive strips across one forearm, a catheter from the applelike glans of his semierect penis, the thin wires of those electrodes that were still sticking to his forehead and chest. He was only a few feet away from the sofa, trembling violently, his eyes wide open. They stared blackly at her. He had a look of stark incomprehension.

Barry tried to get up, but her body felt as if it had been clumsily reordered in sleep by a drunken maniac. When she moved, he raised a hand slowly toward her. Later they told her she'd screamed loud enough to bring the roof down, but she wasn't aware then of making a sound.

Her scream did something to him. His head came up as if

she'd jolted him with a punch. His lips trembled momentarily, and then his lights went out. He swayed and came down hard, but the couch cushions absorbed most of the shock of his fall. Then he just keeled over slowly sideways, into her arms. And that was how Nurse Mayo found them both, huddled mock-amorously on the floor of the nurses' lounge, when she came running in a few seconds later.

ELEVEN

THE TELEPHONE got Dr Edwards out of bed at ten past two and he made it to the hospital from his home on Wendover Street in just under eight minutes. The patient, again unconscious, had been lugged back to bed by the two ICU nurses and an overexcited Barry. The Jamaican nurse was mopping up the mess from a shattered IV bottle and a spilled urine pouch. When Edwards walked in with snow droplets sparkling in his hair Mayo had already made note of the young man's vital signs, including a heartening pulse that had climbed to seventy-two beats a minute. He was breathing more quickly, the shallow breaths of an uneasy sleep, and he had tremors. Edwards gave Barry a puzzled, disgruntled look, took the clipboard from Mayo and glanced at it, then looked at the disconnected EEG and EKG machines. He bent over the patient and checked his pupils. The young man was in a light sweat, spread-eagled on top of the bed, one IV tube half filled with backed-up blood like a vivid lash mark across his flat stomach. Edwards listened to his heart. He straightened up, looking distantly exasperated.

'What happened?' he asked the head nurse.

'He got up and *walked*,' Barry answered.

'Who the hell are you?' the doctor snarled. Barry retreated to a corner of the small room. Edwards raised an eyebrow at Mayo, who despite a stiff upper lip was unhappy. She'd never anticipated this turn of events.

'She's Barry Brennan.'

'Oh.' Edwards didn't waste another look at Barry. 'He walked? When I left the hospital tonight this patient was close to death. I tried everything I could think of to revive him. Doesn't make *sense*.'

'Well, doctor.'

'He came to me,' Barry said in a small but insistent voice.

Edwards turned around, winding the rubber tubing of his stethoscope around one fist. 'And where were you?'

'In the nurses' lounge. Sleeping.'

Mrs Mayo winced. Edwards addressed her but kept his eyes on Barry. 'Mayo, what were you doing when he snapped out of it and decided to take a stroll around the second floor, dragging an IV stand along with him?'

'Something went wrong with the respirator in Mrs Schaefer's room, two thirteen, down the hall. Tillie and me had our hands full.'

'You didn't hear anything?'

'Not until the girl screamed. I ran to the nurses' lounge. When I got there he was passed out on the floor, much as you see him now.'

'Get rid of those electrodes and IV's and clean him up.'

Edwards walked from the room, beckoning to Barry. She followed him, at a safe distance, to the nurses' lounge. There was a trail of dime-sized drops of blood and urine that hadn't been cleaned up yet. The lounge was in another hallway of the oblong building, out of sight of the intensive care units across from the nurses' station. The doctor opened the door and looked at the crumpled blanket on the couch, the pillows, the television screen. He looked back at Barry.

'Door was closed?'

'If you're just going to give me a hard time, I don't want to answer any more questions. I'd like to call my father.'

Edwards softened his tone. 'I'm the one who's having a hard time, Barry. Let's start over. I'm not even going to ask you why you thought you had any business being here this time of night. Were you watching television?'

'No, I was ... asleep. I had sort of a funny dream.' Her cheeks flushed; she rubbed her forehead with the palm of one hand as if she feared the last rhapsodic image of her dream was pornographically tattooed there. 'When I woke up he was in the room with me.'

'How did he know you were in here? Why did he get up out of bed and – with several ways to go – walk straight to this door?'

'I don't know. That's weird, isn't it?'

'It is if you're telling –'

'*Doctor!*'

Edwards whirled and ran past Barry, back to the IC unit. This time Barry was right on his heels.

The young man's eyes were open. He was awake and trying to sit up in bed, making sounds of effort. Mayo and Tillie tried to restrain him. He was too strong for them. Edwards rushed in and took hold of the patient, a viselike grip at the right elbow, before he could lunge off the bed and possibly hurt himself. Cords stood out in the young man's neck. He made incoherent noises. His head came around and he stared at Barry with black eyes that might have seemed tragic if there had been a corresponding cast of emotion, of human trial and suffering, in his face.

The sight of her seemed to calm him. He breathed with his lips parted, eyes steady on Barry.

Edwards ordered a tranquilizer from the Jamaican nurse. To his patient he said, 'Okay, okay, nobody's going to hurt you. Try to relax. You're in a hospital. You had an accident this afternoon, but you're not seriously hurt. Want to tell me your name?'

There wasn't a flicker of reaction. The young man went on staring at Barry, who moved a couple of steps closer to the foot of the bed. She tried a smile.

'What's your name?'

He didn't seem to understand English, or else he was stone deaf. Edwards snapped his fingers next to the young man's ear; the black eyes swung to him and then jumped back to Barry.

'His hearing is at least adequate. That isn't it.'

'Do you know any other languages?'

Edwards, picking the only foreign language he knew, tried German. The young man watched him closely while he was speaking but didn't reply. Barry had studied Spanish in high school. She put together a couple of sentences. It got them nowhere.

'What'll we do now?'

'One thing is for sure. He likes having you around. I can feel his heart thumping through his rib cage. See if you can get him to lie down.'

Tillie reappeared with the syringe and an ampule of Thorazine. Barry moved around to the other side of the bed. The young man shifted his full attention to her again. She touched him gently. She could feel his tension flickering in waves beneath his skin. He was warm now, perspiring, blood racing. He didn't seem to mind being touched.

Sometimes she was able to receive impressions from those she touched, odd bits of revelation, secrets; but she was too keyed up now; she had to be in a tranquil, almost thoughtless, mood to be receptive. Nothing came to her. His history was a blank.

'You'd better lie down,' Barry advised him. He didn't move. He seemed content to sit there looking at her. She felt very strange: heartsore and light-headed, prickling all over. She hoped it was just a language problem with him; otherwise he might be some kind of retardate. But she'd worked with the weak-minded, the brain-damaged, performed shadow shows at their schools. He wasn't like them at all. His eyes were clear and attentive. Intelligent. He was trying to understand her. The rest of his face had a sort of frozen immobility. But when she smiled there was a definite softening around his mouth, a muscular twitch, as if he yearned to smile back but couldn't. Paralysis? She raised her hand and placed her fingers to his lips. Absorbed, she traced the outlines of his mouth, his chin. He sighed, almost inaudibly. His eyes closed partway, then opened wide again.

While Barry had his attention, Tillie swabbed a spot and Mayo deftly pricked him in the hip with the needle of the syringe. Either he was too tense to feel the injection, or it didn't matter to him.

Edwards picked up the EEG tracings to see what had happened to the young man's brain waves before he

69

awakened.

'Good God Almighty,' he said, amazed and distressed.

'*What?*'

He glanced at Barry without focusing on her. 'He was flatline EEG just an hour before he got up from that bed and walked.'

'What does that mean?'

'It means brain death: he was necrotic. No electrical discharges to record. Then all of a sudden they started up again. His brain came alive.' Edwards winced.

'Is that impossible?'

'It should be. I've *heard* of a couple of cases where there was no EEG, then later they woke up.'

Barry shuddered; it sounded like something from Edgar Allan Poe. The two nurses had tied the patient into a hospital johnny. The tranquilizer was taking effect. His head nodded, his eyelids drooped. Barry helped him lie back. Soon he was dozing again, fitfully.

Edwards gave instructions to the nurses. They were to take his pulse and respiration every fifteen minutes, his temperature on the half hour. He wanted the fluids resumed. Someone was to be in the room with the patient at all times.

'I'll stay,' Barry said.

The doctor hesitated, instinct in conflict with his professional judgment.

'I think he trusts me,' Barry pointed out. 'I don't know why. When he wakes up again, I'll just talk to him, try to keep him calm.'

'He'll be calm enough from the Thorazine, but ... I guess it won't hurt. He may not understand what happened to him or know where he is, but he knows a good-looking girl when he sees one.' He smiled at Barry, then stifled a yawn.

'Do you think anything's seriously wrong with him?' she asked.

'Barry, I have no idea. I've never seen a case like this one. Tomorrow he might be sitting up in that bed eating a good breakfast or he might be comatose again.'

After Edwards had gone home, Barry helped Mrs Mayo

carry in the most comfortable chair they could find, and she padded it with pillows. She borrowed a radio from Tillie, dialed it low to an easy-listening FM station. She settled down near the bed for her vigil, fully awake, watching him breathe, observing the movements of his eyes beneath the lids. Dreaming at last, she thought. Occasionally he moved, always a jump or a sharp twitch, and moaned. She got up whenever he made a sound, leaned over him, hoping he would say something in his sleep.

Once during the night he turned his head on the pillow and looked at her for a few moments. Barry smiled and murmured to him. She wasn't sure he was actually awake, but she thought he recognized her. Either her presence or the music gradually soothed him. His body relaxed visibly. Despite the restricting IV tubes, taped with his arm to a splint so he couldn't rip them loose again, he was able to turn on his right side and draw his knees up beneath the sheet and thin blanket. His left hand groped for something, closed, relaxed, curled against his body.

Toward dawn Barry dozed for an hour, satisfied in her own mind that he was going to be just fine.

TWELVE

THE PRESS conference was scheduled for eleven o'clock on the morning of December 22, eighteen days after the accident. The Anatolia hospital administrator, whose name was Jacobs, realized too late that there was much more interest in their John Doe patient than anyone had anticipated. A half hour before the scheduled conference the boardroom was overflowing with representatives of the media, including a dozen or more from the foreign press services and TV networks. Journalists with no place to sit and camera crews without space to set up their equipment were in an uproar. The cafeteria was then closed, despite the inconvenience, and they moved everyone there. The noise and confusion disrupted the choir, composed of hospital volunteers, who had gathered in Dickensian costume in the lobby to sing carols for patients and their families. The lead soprano, wife of a prominent patron of Anatolia Community Hospital, flew into a tizzy and went home. Dr Edwards was unavoidably detained and the journalists gathered in the cafeteria became vocal again, particularly when a rumor went around that they weren't going to see John Doe in person.

ABC complained to CBS. 'What a hell of a way to run a press conference.'

'Amateurs,' the *Daily News* groused.

There was a further delay when no one could seem to find the folder of photographs of the young man that were to be handed out. Finally, at eleven forty-two, Edwards walked in with Jacobs and sat down in front of eleven microphones, sitting back a little too far so that he had to lean toward them when his first words were hard to hear. The television lights emphasized his leanness, the deep sockets of his eyes.

'Good morning. I'm Dr James Edwards, chief of neurological services at the hospital. I'd like to read a brief statement on which Mr Jacobs and I have collaborated, and then I'll be glad to answer as many of your questions as I can.'

'*Where's the mystery man? Don't we get to see him?*'

Edwards ignored the demands from various parts of the cafeteria, staring at the sheet of paper in his hands.

'On Friday, December four, an accident victim was brought to Anatolia Community Hospital by police. He had been struck by a vehicle in the vicinity of the covered bridge in Tremont Park. His condition upon being admitted was stable. He did not appear to have serious injuries, but he was unconscious and remained so for nearly eleven hours. We were not able to establish his identity when he was admitted, and as of this morning we still do not know who he is.'

Barry had slipped into the cafeteria while the attention of the journalists was focused on the doctor and on the photos of John Doe that were being distributed as he spoke. When Edwards paused, he was asked three questions at once.

'Let's proceed one at a time, otherwise there's bound to be confusion.' He paused to hear a question from the reporter for the Gannett chain. 'John Doe is five feet eleven and a half inches tall and now weighs one hundred and seventy-seven pounds. His hair is black, his eyes black. He is approximately twenty-one years of age. Yes?'

The young woman from the *National Enquirer* was on her feet. She was a red-haired aggressive snip who had been hanging around the hospital for several days. She'd easily established the connection between Barry and the young man and had been pestering Barry for an interview.

'Won't his dental charts help in establishing his identity?'

'He's never had any dental work done. His teeth are in perfect condition. His fingerprints are not on file with any law enforcement agency. He also lacks scars or marks that might aid in identification. Including, I might add, a vaccination scar.'

This statement caused a lot of comment; Edwards waited for the assembly to quiet down, then chose another questioner.

'I'm told there's no such medical condition as total amnesia.'

'Global amnesia may be a more appropriate term, but whatever we choose to call it, the condition is extremely rare; and I've never heard of a case like this one. We have good reasons to doubt that he should be categorized as amnesiac.'

'Is it true he has to be toilet-trained?' a seedy-looking man in a tartan vest loudly inquired.

Edwards ignored him and continued, 'At this point, after tests, observation, and consultations with experts in the field, we have determined that John Doe's condition is not due to structural or metabolic changes in the brain.'

'You mean he's not brain-damaged?' the *Times* asked.

'He is not.'

'But he's suffering from aphasia,' the *Times* persisted.

'In John Doe's case the proper term is mutism. The effect is the same. He has a nearly total inability to understand spoken and written language. But we have noticed some modification in this condition during the last two or three days.'

'Is it possible that he understands only an obscure language?' Metromedia asked.

'We did consider that,' Edwards replied. 'One of my daughter's projects for her high school course in international relations was to assemble a tape with as many different examples of modern language as she could come up with. My understanding is that in New York City it's possible to hear more than sixty-five root languages or dialects spoken on any given day. I borrowed the tape that she and her classmates made at the UN and played it for John Doe on three occasions. He was not responsive.'

Near Barry the man who had asked the question about toilet training studied John Doe's photo and said to a colleague, 'Kid looks good enough to be an actor. Maybe he'll suddenly get his memory back when his new picture's about to come out.' Barry could have strangled him.

'What are the chances he's suffering from a mental disorder?'

Barry pricked her ears at this question; she had often asked herself, and Edwards, the same thing, and she knew what he would reply.

'It's one explanation, but it seems more unlikely with each passing day.'

'Why?' asked *The Christian Science Monitor*.

'In treating John Doe we've been guided by some of the research conducted with severe amnesiacs. We've given him vasopressin and amphetamines without eliciting helpful results. In the future sodium amytal might prove beneficial, but for now he exhibits none of the syndrome of abnormal mentation, mood, or behavior. Our problem is almost entirely communication on an elementary level. The patient has adjusted well to his environment; he's alert and well motivated. He quickly learns and retains complex physical skills, which is an indication of above-average intelligence. We believe he has no past memories; this is typical of global amnesia. But other important indicators are asymptomatic.'

A reporter who was trying to get all this down in writing groaned. Edwards smiled thinly and apologized for the involved explanation.

'Again I'd like to stress that this is a most complicated case. There are no easy answers.'

'Could you give us an example of a complex physical skill?' *Paris-Match* asked.

'Well ... juggling. He watches television avidly, and he must have seen it done. There were some oranges in a bowl in his room, and one morning about a week ago a nurse walked in and found him juggling four oranges, as if he'd been doing it all of his life.'

'Maybe he was with a circus,' *Newsday* suggested.

Edwards smiled. 'We're looking into it.'

Barry gathered up the bags from a morning's belated Christmas shopping and left the cafeteria as unobtrusively as she'd come. It was almost noon and the young man would be returning after a lengthy EEG to his room for lunch.

Alexandra Chatellaine was standing near the nurses' station on the second floor. She was in conversation with a gout patient named Simmons but nodded pleasantly to Barry over the elderly man's shoulder. Alexandra had come to the hospital ten days ago for treatment of complications arising from a foot injury suffered in a moped accident. She had been confined to bed until a blood clot could be dissolved, but now she was ambulatory with the aid of a strong and intriguingly crooked black cane. There was nothing remarkable about her accident, except for the fact that she had been on a moped in the first place: Alexandra was nearly eighty years old.

Barry had never met anyone like Alexandra. She could have passed for fifty-five. She was a rigorously erect woman with a level to her shoulders that was both bones and breeding, a good square upthrust chin, skin like fine old porcelain wearing down to a tracery of veins thinner than thread, and more good bones, cheeky and broad, above which her eyes shone as if the pupils were lacquered. She had her own teeth. Her hair was abundant, gathered and pinned in a hard hay-looking tussock on the back of her head. In her room she did complicated yoga exercises that did not involve the injured leg, would not touch hospital food, and had accepted only the medication that was required to dissolve the clot.

Alexandra had shown a great deal of interest in both Barry and the young man, although she and Barry hadn't spoken much to this point: Alexandra was neither obtrusive nor talkative. Her manner was unpretentious, yet something about her could be unnerving: she had a quality of stillness that went beyond ordinary calm and self-possession. Her curiosity, her searching intelligence, was like a big weightless hovering thing: a fog bank, an Olympic cloud.

Barry acknowledged her with a quick smile and went on to John Doe's room. His lunch had been delivered and was waiting beneath a plastic tray cover. She tore into a shopping bag, came up with a conical artificial Christmas tree already decorated and wired with Lilliputian lights. She placed the tree on the deep window ledge and plugged it in. On one melon-orange wall she taped a cutout Santa Claus, Three Wise Men, and Norman Rockwell's *Christmas Trio*, reproduced from a long-ago *Saturday Evening Post* cover.

Two unwrapped presents came from another shopping bag: a poplin storm coat with diagonal zippered pockets on the sleeves and a big metal zipper toggle, and a pair of Wellington boots with cleats.

Nurse Mayo arrived at the door, pushing the wheelchair that hospital regulations made him ride in, although he could easily have walked wherever they wanted him to go.

'Oh, look! Surprise! Merry Christmas! And there's a *tree* too.'

As soon as they were in the room John Doe got up out of the wheelchair, which he hated. He was wearing the clothes Barry had brought him, the staff having decided it best for him to be out of his hospital garb: Top-Siders and vanilla corduroys and a rust-colored knit shirt with long sleeves. He looked first at everything Barry had added to the room, then, inquisitively, at her. He smiled slowly. He had a disconcertingly beautiful smile, at odds with his normally placid lack of expression. She had slaved for that smile – clowned, babbled – but still she saw it rarely.

'Where've you been all morning?' Barry asked him.

For several seconds he was motionless, watching her. The smile, having dazzled, now faded like fireworks into the spacey black of his eyes. Then he raised a hand to his forehead, where white electrode paste slicked the dark hair at his temples. He extended the hand to Barry.

'They put the wires on your head again?'

Mayo said, 'It's amazing how he responds to you, Barry. He's beginning to understand you.'

Barry soared; the press conference, with its squabbling journalists and stink of cynicism as sharp as overboiled coffee, had turned her stomach, but the day was looking better already. She turned to the bed and held up the new storm coat for his approval.

'I talked to Dr Edwards. He thinks you should start going out every day. How about it? Would you like to go for a walk after lunch?'

As always she had his rapt attention, but there was no response. Barry pointed to the window. She said slowly and distinctly, '*Out*side. We'll go together.'

Without hesitation he walked to the window, glanced at the tree on the sill, the tiny winking lights. He touched one with a fingertip, then lifted his eyes to the smoggy radiance of noon, the hospital grounds, a walking flock of pink and gray pigeons. He looked back at Barry with what she interpreted as interest.

First, he needed to eat. Lunch was a sandwich, soup, crackers, fruit cup, chocolate milk. Like all hospital meals this one was superficially attractive but as flavorless as week-old chewing gum. John Doe ate every bite, still a little awkward with a spoon in his hand. He used the left and the right hand indiscriminately. He had had to relearn eating, dressing, brushing his teeth, going to the bathroom: it was as if the part of the brain responsible for retaining these basic patterns of childhood achievements had gone out of business. But once he was shown how to do something, he repeated the action with little difficulty. His imitations were unerring, to the smallest detail. If Mayo pursed her lips while tying his shoes, he also pursed his lips.

Barry wished she had stopped at Wachter's for brownies; she just hadn't had time lately to bake for him herself. The first two weeks she'd overdone the treats, milkshakes and popovers, and he'd taken on a tummy. Dr Edwards had asked her to use better judgment about what she stuffed him with.

John Doe watched TV while he ate. He wanted it on constantly when he was in the room. Now *Days of Our Lives* played out a segment of its slow-moving Byzantine drama. There was nothing he could understand of the characters but their emotions: heartbreak, despair, malice. He seemed so frequently on the brink of the unfathomable – silent, sometimes apprehensive, at other times with a flicker of aspiration.

The press conference was long over by the time they rode downstairs in the elevator and went outside, but a hospital guard accompanied them in case a reporter or two might be hanging around waiting for a break. Their walk was confined to a broad quadrangle with a parking lot on one side. The sun was a heatless flare, the spoiled snow like mildew.

'Dr Edwards gave out pictures of you at the press conference,' Barry said. Sometimes it was hard to know what to say to him, to keep on talking when the words obviously slid off his mind like rain on a piece of slate. But he was so clever and observant and willing; already he was understanding her a little, as Mrs Mayo had pointed out. None of her effort was wasted effort, and the day would come when he would not only smile but speak to her. She felt a childish ache, as if she were anticipating a birthday that seemed suspended, shimmering, in time, unreachable. 'You'll be on the network news shows tonight, and in the papers tomorrow. It's been almost three weeks. That's a long time to be missing. You're bound to be recognized – you didn't just pop up out of nowhere.'

Then what? she thought drearily. Someone would turn up to claim him – parents, girl friend, perhaps even a wife. Her fingers curled, clawlike, as if she were afraid of sliding precipitously into the background of his unknown life.

'More than anything else, I just want to know your name. Because I'm positive that eventually you'll be a hundred percent okay. I feel it in my bones.'

Barry also felt that he was missing from her side, and she looked around quickly. He had stopped walking ten paces behind her. He was watching a group of boys having a snowball fight in the parking lot. It was one of the few times she'd ever lost his attention. She sensed he was intrigued by the aggression they displayed. On impulse she packed a handful of the sparse mushy snow, took aim, and drilled him high on the right arm with it.

John Doe studied her, surprised. Barry put her hands on her hips.

'The least you can do is hang around me when I'm talking to myself.'

He brushed at the snow clinging to his coat, looked at the boys again, then bent and dug a double handful of snow out of a pile of scrapings. He packed it as he had seen Barry do and fired the snowball at her. She laughed and ducked, barely in time. He could throw hard and accurately. He was pokerfaced, but she was certain she'd seen a gleam of mischief in his eyes.

'You want to play, huh?'

Barry started making another snowball, but he was faster. She darted behind the rim of a dormant fountain, took aim, hit him in the center of his forehead. John Doe looked startled.

'Oh, lucky shot!' Barry called out, but she held her breath, wondering how he was going to take it.

There was something in his lack of expression more threatening than anger. He bent down for more ammunition. But instead of a handful of snow he came up with a rock big enough to crush her skull, uncovering, magically, a flattened but pretty little blue flower.

Barry backed up instinctively, unable to speak. He took a step toward her, holding the rock higher.

'Hey – no –'

Barry tripped and fell backward, sprawled with her nose pink and the snow cold beneath her legs, her heart trying to tear free of its moorings. His indistinct shadow blotted her. Her stomach gathered in a tuck. She raised her hands, flinching, but there was a smile on his face, the rock held high, dripping in his hands.

She got up slowly. He didn't move. She smiled too, uneasily, put out her hands, took the rock away.

'No fair.'

She pitched the rock a dozen feet away. It sank into the snow. His hands had been cold and wet, but when she touched them again they were suffused with blood and heat;

80

they dried almost instantly. She looked at his face in astonishment and at once felt, for the first time, the hard impress of his mind, communication without words – a question that only confounded her.

I am I; you are you. Who are we?

THIRTEEN

Alexandra Chatellaine turned away from the window at which she had been observing Barry and the young man with bare-faced enthusiasm. She had fastened herself to the periphery of their lives like a great green-eyed moth, invisibly palpitating. The fact of age, the accretion of wisdom had done nothing to still her curiosity, which had, seemingly forever, leapt over mountains, forded torrents, charmed moguls, viziers, and aloof mystics, the scoundrel and the ascetic, the wild and the tame. She was an old beauty and no longer, as in her youth, daft with wanderlust, half crazed by the limitations of mind and body. But Alexandra could never resist the suggestion of a mystery.

Bored with the enforced waiting to see if a blood clot below one knee might tear away before it could be dissolved, drift undetected through channels to the brain or heart, and put an abrupt stoppered end to her life, Alexandra had turned her attention to Barry – the girl had been spending hours a day, and many nights, on the second floor, which was, as a rule, only for very sick or imminently threatened patients. Alexandra saw herself in this vivid girl; Barry, unaware of the attention, was absorbed in her self-appointed duties as mentor to the young man so stripped of human apperceptions he had needed help buttoning his shirt and, according to one of the nurses on the floor, had seemed to be unacquainted with the usage of toilet tissue.

What most attracted Alexandra to the two of them was the possibility that something even rarer than amnesia was responsible for the young man's condition.

Musing on the evidence, or lack of it, Alexandra poured

herself tea made from rose hips and herbs and flavored with a little butter and salt. She ate half of a barley and oat cake. Someone much less her age would have cracked a tooth – it was like a hockey puck – but she chewed effortlessly She had turned the hospital room, which was already austere – one wall an unfortunate avocado shade, the others white – into a chamber suitable for her lengthy meditations, her spare, structured, rhythmic life. She had had brought to her by her late husband's niece a simple mat for the floor and a little folding table about sixteen inches high, carved all over with a floral and vine pattern so painstaking the artistry could be fully revealed only with the use of a powerful magnifying glass. The table was made equally of ebony, ivory, and rosewood. On it she had placed a small delicate bowl of Chinese porcelain for her tea, a silver saucer with a cover shaped like a pagoda roof, studded with polished rose coral and turquoise. There was an incense burner, the fumes from which obscured the institutional odors she detested.

Beside the table was her prayer wheel and some of her Tibetan books, made of detached oblong sheets of rice paper and wrapped in silk cloths. She never turned on the television. A cassette recorder not much larger than her hand played religious music, lamentations of Tibetan trumpets, hautboys, kettledrums. She wore, in her room, the ecclesiastical robe of a lama; she was one of a handful of women in history entitled to the honor.

Alexandra's father had been a British Colonial officer posted to India. She had been always less than he required in a daughter and quite unmanageable when he asserted himself on behalf of the traditional role for a woman in society. She was, from an early age, obsessed with geography and fascinated with the machineries of life – the ordinary, the superhuman. A summer's holiday in Sikkim when she was fifteen fueled her fascination with the mysteries of thought and perception. Two years later, with only the jewels left by her mother to provide for the necessities of arduous travel, Alexandra bravely set out for the top of the world.

For the next thirty-one years, with excursions to Nepal,

Burma, and China, she devoted herself to the study of Lamaism in Lhasa and at such monasteries as Tashilunpo. She had lived, for two years, as a hermit in a cave in order to be near, and study with, a renowned thaumaturge. Alexandra had decided, once she knew the extent of her ambitions and what was required to achieve them, to resist the dangerous beehive of man's sexual nature and remain a virgin. She was attractive despite the rigorous life she led and thus had her fair share of narrow escapes from assaults on her virtue – from libidinous monks, merchant traders, and princes; during the siege of Shensi; and again after a bandit's attack on a caravan crossing into Nepal by the Jongsong Pass.

Ultimately she married, late in life, a French scholar and devotee of Buddhism who had some very rich cousins across the Atlantic. And so she came to be in America.

Her physician, a young harried man named Bovard, came to see her at two o'clock. The clot was a thing of the past, she could get around with the aid of her cane, it was time to be discharged; but he had been concerned by a persistent anemia and had urged her to reorder her diet.

'Can you eat meat?' he asked her.

'Yes.' Alexandra smiled. 'But only after reflection on the nature of the animal from which it comes and after I understand how the psychic elements of what I am eating will be of benefit to me.'

'Lean beef and calves' liver,' he prescribed. 'Don't overcook it.'

The nurse had taken Alexandra's temperature. It had been normal for days; now it was 101. Bovard couldn't believe his eyes. He touched her forehead. She was hot.

'Now where did that come from?'

'Does this mean I can't be discharged?'

'Not with that fever. Sorry, Alexandra.' He looked at her, puzzled. 'You've been champing at the bit for days to get out of here. Aren't you going to give me a fight?'

'I'm disappointed, of course,' Alexandra said serenely. She had decided, moments before her doctor's visit, that a mysterious fever was the best means of prolonging her hospital stay. She had produced the rise in temperature with ease, by means of a discipline that enables adepts to sleep outdoors in freezing weather and even snow without clothing.

'We'd better take some more blood and put her on Tylenol every four hours,' Bovard advised the nurse. To Alexandra he said sternly, 'No more prowling around. Into bed.'

'Yes, doctor.' The stratagem would be good for three or four more days, and she knew she was not taking up a bed needed by a genuinely ill patient: with the holidays on hand several rooms on the floor already were vacant. Her extended stay would give her ample time to become acquainted with the young people who had caught her fancy.

Bovard grabbed his handkerchief and sneezed; the incense bothered him.

'I know you've been here almost two weeks, but at your age we can't take chances. Try to be patient, Alexandra.'

She almost smiled again. He was young, earnest, impressed with himself. He knew so much, and so little. A living being was an assemblage, not a unity. One of the first things the masters had taught her. She could live within herself for weeks, perfectly content, her senses detached, scarcely in touch with the world. She had an enigma to think about. There were many known laws of nature and as many yet unknown. She had lived a long time, traveled in and out of the body. Answers would come. Perhaps they would be surprising. Alexandra doubted it. She had already sensed, in passing, the true nature of the young man, his sought-after identity.

Only one thing had to be decided, and as soon as possible. Could anything be done about him?

FOURTEEN

ON THE night of the twenty-second Tom and Barry decorated the family Christmas tree, a few days late this year because of Barry's preoccupation with John Doe. Dal had promised to be there and wasn't. Barry simmered with resentment but didn't express it; her father would only defend Dal.

By eight thirty the work was almost done. Decorating had taken almost four hours. The tree by the front windows in the family room was huge – nearly eight feet to the star on top – and their ornaments were antiques – handcrafted beauties, exceptionally fragile.

Earlier they had taken time off to watch both the CBS and NBC newscasts. The networks had run stories about the young man, with film clips from the press conference.

'I don't want you to get your hopes up,' Tom said when they discussed the impact that the publicity might have. 'I remember the big circus fire in forty-four, over in Hartford. There were seven thousand people in that tent when the fire started. A hundred sixty-eight people died. One of them was a little girl. She might have died of smoke inhalation or been trampled in the panic. Anyway, the body wasn't claimed. There were pictures of her in all the papers, even the newsreels. But not one person in the entire country came forward to identify her. To this day she's still unknown.'

Barry scowled. 'That's a *terrible* story. And it's Christmas, Dad.'

They turned out the lights in the family room and admired the tree by firelight. A little after nine Barry heard a car in the drive; she went to the windows.

'Dal has somebody with him.'

Dal came in reeking of wassail, eyes stewed to a pulp. He was singing 'God Rest Ye Merry Gentlemen.' His companion was leggy, with Oriental eyes heavily made up and bold front teeth when she smiled. She wore coral-colored cowboy boots with silver and gold butterflies on them.

'Oh, your tree looks terrific!' the girl said.

'Dad, Barry, this is, uh, JoJo.'

'Hi!'

Dal wrapped an arm around his sister. 'Barry, let's go to a party. There's this party we're all going to.'

Barry sidestepped him. 'No, thanks. Wish I could.'

Dal helped himself to Bushmill's from the drink cabinet. His hands shook. His eyes swarmed. JoJo stood with hands clasped at her waist gazing up at some of the ornaments on the tree.

'These are *precious*.'

Dal squinted at his father through amber and crystal. 'Having one, Dad?'

'Just finished mine – you go ahead.' Tom took his pipe out and glanced at Barry, who had her chin up and was staring at a blank space on one wall, perhaps wondering if Dal's head, suitably mounted, would fit there. Dal swung around to her exuberantly.

'Come on, Barry – you need a little fun in your life. You're so uptight these days I don't recognize you.'

'Is that a fact?'

'I can get you a real cute date,' JoJo said.

Barry shrugged; her smile was closer to a wince.

'I need to wash my hair. Then I thought I'd go back to the hospital for a little while.'

Dal tried to embrace her again. 'Barry, I am here to save you from yourself. We're all going out and have a good time, and that's the last word on the subject.'

'You're fine the way you are,' JoJo assured Barry.

'Dal, I'm just not in the mood.' Dal stood back appraisingly and raised his glass to his lips. Barry said softly, 'I don't think I could catch up to you anyway.'

Dal belched unbecomingly. JoJo looked concerned rather

than offended. Dal's complexion was blotchy, and he hadn't shaved well that morning. Barry wondered how long it would be before he fell on his face and stayed that way for the next forty-eight hours. Merry merry Christmas.

'You'd rather go sit and talk to John Doe? That's the next worst thing to talking to pigeons in the park. Turning yourself into a little old bag lady.'

'Dal –'

He ignored the warning tone, giving her a big savage grin. 'Heard you, uh, had to grab hold of his peepee and point it in the right direction to teach him to –'

Barry turned and nailed him with a straight jab, knocking his glasses askew. The drink in his hand went flying. JoJo gasped. Dal staggered but didn't fall. Tom caught him. Blood and snot dripped from Dal's left nostril.

'Of all the stupid, cruel, vicious things to say!' Barry raged.

'Oh, he's bleeding!'

Barry rounded on JoJo. 'Listen, you. When Brennans fight it's Brennan business. Why don't you go outside and slip on the ice?'

'That'll be just about enough out of you, Barry!' Tom wasn't particularly upset by the shot she had taken at Dal, feeling that it was well deserved, but he hadn't brought her up to be rude to guests. Barry turned instantly to JoJo.

'I'm sorry,' she muttered, her lips white.

Dal took his bent glasses off and daubed his nose with a handkerchief. He glared at his sister.

'You're obsessed with that guy. Come on, JoJo, let's get out of here.'

Holding the handkerchief to his nose, he sullenly escorted his date from the house. Barry twisted away from her father.

'Okay, okay, I know! I made an ass of myself.'

'Don't tell *me*.'

She nodded, close to tears. She ran to the foyer and opened the door Dal had slammed, calling him.

'Dal!'

He turned from helping JoJo into the Mercedes. Barry ran outside and sprawled into his arms, sobbing.

'I don't know what's wrong ... I'm jumping on everybody ... I'm sorry ...'

'Barry, I just don't like what's happening to you. Why're you so on edge – what's this guy doing to you?'

'Nothing! It's just – Christmas, and he doesn't know who he is. Dal, I apologized. Give me a break.'

She touched his nose cautiously. It was swollen and blue. He smiled wryly.

'Oh, God, I really hurt you!'

'I'll live.'

'Still invited?' Barry asked meekly, and gave JoJo a shy glance.

'Sure you are,' Dal said. 'Grab your coat.'

Barry flew back into the house, looked at her face in the powder room mirror, made emergency repairs, and took a ski vest from the foyer closet.

'Barry?' Tom said from the doorway. 'You drive.'

With his glasses needing repair Dal couldn't see anyway. He crouched in the back of the coupe, giving directions to the party. Barry made a determined effort to be chatty with JoJo, who had been born in Manila and worked as a bilingual secretary for an import-export firm in Manhattan. By the time they reached Pound Ridge Barry had convinced herself she was out to have a hell of a good time.

The house on Butternut Lane was a country estate, an old Colonial with a broad flagged terrace in back that overlooked a covered swimming pool and several miles of forested valley. The party room was crowded, stifling, weed-infested. She had a couple of Scotches right away, then met a boy named Egon who was a foreign student at Yale, from Hungary or someplace, very good-looking and with a wonderful opinion of himself. He wasn't that hard to take, and he wanted to jump her bones ten minutes after they met. It was fun to relax a little and let the flattery roll over her, but casual sex wasn't on her agenda. As soon as she had him convinced of that, Egon excused himself politely and went beaver shooting elsewhere. Barry had a fourth Scotch, then took a hit on Dal's reefer when she located him propped up in a corner with a death grip on JoJo. His eyes were crossing and his knees were all but gone – it was just a matter of time for Dal. His nose was still swollen and looked like it hurt – she felt lousy about it. The heavy-metal music was antiholiday and ultimately depressing. Eventually Barry went outside on the terrace.

She'd been drinking since she was fourteen and had a curious capacity. There were times when a glass of mild white wine was enough to knock her over. At other times, in a more complex mood, she could absorb up to half a bottle of Scotch, if she took it wisely and didn't bolt it down, and never feel a thing. Right now she was sharply, perhaps disappointingly sober, but with a stuffed-up head.

A full moon over frozen hills was echoed by the white round globes of a lighting fixture attached to one corner of the house. Barry stayed in the lee of the house, out of a knifing wind, exhaling plumes of vapor.

How do I find thee tonight, my charmer? Hash Old Bedlam broke loosh about our headsh?

Mrs Prye's voice startled her. It was raucous, the words slurred, as if she had failed to put her teeth in before making a hasty appearance. Barry looked up, at one of the round globes. The medium's head was lolling, her wig ridiculously askew. Barry was struck by another notion – one that made her smile incredulously.

'Don't I get any time off for good behavior?' she asked in mock despair.

But thou hash not been good! That ish something we both know – and only I understand.

'Mrs Prye, you're drunk,' Barry remonstrated.

The medium giggled, delighted with her debauchery.

'Don't you think you should go sober up?'

Firstly, I would tell newsh of your departed mother – mosht gratifying newsh to be sure. She is a princesesh now, of the Daoine Sidh, the Magic People.

Barry's lips felt numb from the cold; she shuddered.

'I know that. From the day she left us, I knew where mother must have gone.'

90

She ish more beautiful than the tearsh of God. But her own eyes are brazen from weeping, lamenting the foolish-ness of her daughter.

'What do you mean? I haven't done anything!'

I'll warrant you've already done more than the mind of man can comprehend. But before foolish becomesh wicked, you have the power to stop. Do not trifle too long.

'I don't know what you're talking about,' Barry said hostilely.

I have a prophecy for you, my poor sulky. You enjoy my prophecies, don't you?

'You're geting to be a bore, Mrs Prye.'

This time the medium's voice was clearer; her eyes regarded Barry unwinkingly despite the fact that her image had begun to evanesce at the edges.

The eye must lie
The heart deceive
Until in the month of Midsummer's Eve
The truth pours out
In a rain of blood:
What thought has engender'd
Need never surrender.

It was some time before Barry was aware that a sliding glass door had opened behind her. She had a crick in her neck from looking up. She saw JoJo standing a few feet away. The wind tore through the arborvitae at the edge of the veranda, and the tall trees made slashing shadows on the expanse of blank wall between the girls.

'Somebody said you came out here,' JoJo explained, clasping her hands bowllike at the belt line as if she were begging alms. 'Dal passed out and I don't know what to do with him.'

'Time he went home,' Barry said, her voice hoarse.

JoJo looked around, big-eyed. 'Who were you talking to? I don't see anybody.'

'Well, there *was* somebody,' Barry said furiously. 'I don't talk to myself.'

FIFTEEN

INQUIRIES REGARDING John Doe began the evening of the twenty-second after the newsbreak on television; by the day after Christmas the hospital's telephone lines were over-burdened. In five days they logged more than six hundred calls, many of them collect.

A young woman who spoke in a hushed voice said that she was phoning from Balmer's Gap, North Carolina, and identified herself as the recording secretary for the Fellowship of the Supernal Ark. John Doe, she said, was really Ra-Mel, a member of their commune. It was very important that he be returned to Balmer's Gap at once. Main Sequence had been initiated, and Ra-Mel's group was due to depart New Year's Eve for a planetary system deep in a remote asterism of the Milky Way.

A wealthy woman who did not discuss kinship offered to pay his medical bills, but she wanted him removed without delay to a wing of her mansion in Palm Beach, no questions asked.

An elderly irate gentleman claimed to have been mugged by John Doe in the vicinity of the Museum of Science and Industry in Chicago three months ago, and he said he was notifying the FBI.

A paraplegic teenager in Bemidji, Minnesota, wanted to start a John Doe fan club.

Maisie de Hart, a professional mud wrestler in Manhattan Beach, California, admitted that she couldn't vouch for his present identity, but maintained that in a past life in Marblehead, Massachusetts, she and John Doe had been pilloried by the community for adultery.

Several parties informed hospital authorities that they

were organizing prayer vigils to facilitate the speedy return of his memory. John Doe received a kind message from a member of the Belgian royal family who had also been briefly amnesiac in her youth. Representatives of three talk show hosts inquired about his availability.

Journalistic freebooters of all kinds were thick as thieves around the hospital; Barry took to arriving in borrowed cars, wearing disguises. Security guards were permanently assigned to the second floor.

What looked like a real break occurred on the morning after Christmas, when Mr and Mrs Wallace Umber arrived, dead tired after driving straight through from their farm in western Iowa.

Wallace was wearing a tight, wrinkled, out-of-style suit that fitted him like a pair of long johns, and a florid tie with a knot the size of his fist. His wife, Cis, clutched a summer straw purse filled with photos of Wally junior, who had disappeared from their home a little over two years ago at the age of seventeen.

The boy in the photos was uncannily like John Doe. Jacobs, the hospital administrator, spent almost an hour talking to them, gradually delving into young Wally's medical and dental history. He had had measles and mumps, was vaccinated like every other preschool child in the state of Iowa, and had suffered a badly broken ankle when he was eleven. His teeth were far from perfect. Jacobs regretfully had to deny them the opportunity to see John Doe, who owned flawless teeth and had no vaccination mark on his left arm. The Umbers were brokenhearted and bitter.

'We'll take him!' Cis cried. 'We'll take him anyway if nobody wants him!'

On the second floor Alexandra Chatellaine manipulated her body temperature according to whim, distressing her physician. She used the time she gained before discharge to strike up a friendship with Barry, observed John Doe closely, and meditated. Barry was fascinated by Alexandra's colorful pilgrim's life and her knowledge of the mysticism of Tibet. She confessed to the lama a lifelong interest in faerie, the lore of the supernatural and inexplicable that her mother had passed on to her.

Faeries, Alexandra told her, also played an important role in Lamaism. They were called, in Sanskrit, dâkinî, had a motherly air about them, and functioned as teachers of secret, ancient doctrines. They often appeared in the shape of aged women, but with a signal distinction: they had bright red or green eyes.

'Like mine,' Alexandra said with a conspiratorial wink and a smile.

At the hospital Barry had run into Blighty Mouse, who functioned on several good-works committees. Blighty urged the girl to find the time to put on a shadow show for those unfortunate kids stuck in the pediatrics wing over the holidays. They'd had Santa Claus and carolers and now they were bored silly, with nothing to look forward to.

Barry brought from home her slide projector, a cassette recorder, and a bag of props, and invited Alexandra to sneak away to pediatrics to see the show.

She hung a makeshift curtain in the lounge of the children's wing, focused her projector to throw a beam of light on a blank wall, and darkened the room as much as she could. The beam shone through a gap in the blankets she was using for the curtain. A dozen kids from four to twelve years of age walked or were wheeled in. Barry sat behind the curtain and just to the left of her projector, where she could place her hands in front of the light. Alexandra took a seat by the door. The nurses who had seen one of Barry's shows before also took time to be on hand; some came from other floors of the hospital.

Barry turned on the recorder. It played wistful Irish airs as she narrated her story, at first making shadow images adroitly with her fingers and hands and such props as paper cutouts, feathers, and twigs.

'This is a legend my mother told me, when I was eight or nine. I've never forgotten. Do any of you know where faeries live?'

A boy wearing a hip cast mumbled an answer.

'Could you repeat that? I don't think we all heard.'

'In the woods.'

'That's right, most of them do, although some live on islands in the sea or even under the sea. But the faerie troop I'm going to tell you about lived deep in the woods inside an enchanted hill on top of which thorn trees grew. Now, in Ireland, most country people know that a hill crowned with thorns is a sure sign of faerie kingdom. And if they're wise they avoid such places, especially at night when the faeries are having their revels ...'

'What's that?' a girl asked, and giggled. They were all intently watching the hill and high thorn tree Barry had made for them on the wall.

'Oh, it's like a party, or a picnic, where there's lots of music and dancing. Faeries love to have a good time. Leprechauns too.'

The hill vanished and, almost instantly, a slouch-bellied, big-eared leprechaun, wearing a pointed cap with a feather in it, appeared on the wall.

'And sometimes they invite ordinary people like you and me to their revels. But that can be dangerous. Do you know why?' Barry paused; no one had an opinion. 'Because the faeries will cast a spell on a human, if he's not careful. And then he must dance with them until he falls down dead, or turns into a very old man.'

The leprechaun was replaced by a gangling man with a long nose who stood peering at the hill of the faeries. Alexandra, glancing at Barry through a slit in the curtains, admired her dexterity as she manipulated props and, seemingly, all ten fingers at once.

'Now there was a man named Jemmy Rilehan who thought he could outsmart the faeries and take away all the gold he knew was stored in their enchanted hill.' On the wall Jemmy Rilehan sidled closer to the realm of faerie. 'He discovered the entrance by walking nine times around the hill in the light of the full moon. A door was opened to him, and the brilliant lights of the kingdom shone forth.' Barry approximated this mystical effect by allowing glimmers of the light beam through her cupped hands. 'He heard the voices of the faeries bidding him enter.'

A boy who remembered the dimensions of Jemmy Rilehan and the enchanted hill, as Barry had projected them, said, 'Wasn't he too big?'

'That's right.' She reproduced Jemmy Rilehan, this time on all fours. 'He had to crawl along on his hands and knees through a passageway, like this. But once he was inside, he found a wonderful palace, with the king and the queen of the faeries at one end of a long table around which hundreds of other faeries were eating and drinking.' She created Jemmy Rilehan in profile, his head turning this way and that. 'They were all so beautiful his eyes were dazzled. He'd never even dreamt of such beautiful jewels and fabulous dresses. They offered him food and drink – but Jemmy knew that to touch anything he was offered meant he would be enslaved. Yet there was one thing he couldn't resist for long: their music. And so they lured him to the dance. And once he began to dance in a faerie ring, the faeries showed their true selves to him –'

A remarkable thing was happening, as Barry launched into the climax of her tale. Alexandra looked alertly at her. Barry's hands gradually fell still in her lap. As she spoke she gazed at the source of light, the blinding pip of the projector bulb. The crude images she had heretofore projected with her hands, of the leprechaun and Jemmy Rilehan, gave way to elaborate full figures dancing in a ring that took in all of the wall. Then the shapes began to change – into horned goatmen and hunchback goblins, banshees and werewolves, all prancing around poor cowering Jemmy Rilehan. The piping, fiddling music reached a crescendo. The children were enthralled, as was Alexandra, who had been a few places and seen some sights in her time, but nothing quite like this.

people and their feelings.' She got up, knocking her chair over. 'The least you could do is try it for a week. A week! Is that too much to ask? Can't you stand having him here for one week? He *hates* the hospital. What good does it do having him locked up with sick people all of the time?'

'Barry, climb off your high horse,' Tom advised.

'Am I a member of this family or not? Don't treat me like I'm ten years old! I'm inviting a friend home for a few days, that's all.'

'I think,' Tom said softly, 'you just may be asking for trouble.'

'Don't give in to her,' Dal said to his father.

'Dal, damn you, shut up!' Barry yelled.

'How would you like a swift kick in the ass, kiddo?'

'Both of you shut up,' Tom said furiously. While Dal and Barry glared at each other, he sat thinking, still not liking it. He turned his eyes on Barry.

'What do you mean, trouble?' she asked him. 'He is *not* mentally deficient, if that's what you're thinking. Dr Edwards can tell you that. He's been tested and tested. He has a wonderful mind! He never stops learning. Are you saying he might murder us in our beds or something?'

'Jesus, there she goes,' Dal said despairingly.

'Well, are you? Are you scared he's dangerous? Of all the ridiculous –'

'Barry, I'm not scared of anything,' Tom said. He hesitated. 'Maybe you're right. We get a little bit too much to ourselves out here, too self-absorbed. So – sit down, will you.'

Barry picked up her chair and sat in it. She wiped a last tear and began to smile expectantly. Tom smiled back. Dal laced his hands behind his head and bit his tongue.

'I don't want to be that way, Dad. Not anymore. I know what I've been like since Ned died – dreary as hell. It got to where I couldn't even stand my own company. This is something positive I can do. I can help someone else instead of brooding my life away.'

'I guess we could take a shot at it,' Tom said after a while, and Barry lunged across the table to give his cheek a peck.

'Dr Edwards wants you to call him right away,' she said. Then she glanced soberly at Dal, not wanting to lord it over him, though she was bursting inside. He stared back, shrugged slightly.

'Beat you at Pac-Man,' Barry said.

'That'll be the day.'

'Thanks for trying, Dal. You'll like him when you get to know him, I promise.'

'We'll see,' he said.

NINETEEN

ON AN afternoon of the first week in January John Doe was discharged from the hospital. Barry drove him to the farm in the station wagon. On impulse she stopped at the covered bridge. There had been a fresh snowfall for New Year's. This day was cold and clear, a dry cold that hurt the sinuses and burned the throat. The snow squelched beneath their boots as they walked beside the cleared road.

'This is where it happened,' she told him.

He looked back at the bridge, the ruled oblique shadow on the snowbanks. His eyes were inquisitive. They stopped at Barry's face.

'This is where it happened,' he repeated, but clearly the words had no meaning for him. He waited patiently to hear what else she might have to say.

Barry smiled sadly. 'You just don't remember a thing, do you?'

He also smiled. 'I don't remember.' Then something stirred in him, the smile disappeared. She sensed that he might be trying to express something, an original thought, not just mimic her. This was hard.

'I want to remember.'

She nodded encouragingly.

'You will. It's all going to come back to you – who you are, where you're from.'

Words came so fast they took his breath away. 'Who I am. Who I am. Who am I? I don't have a name. I should have a name. Everyone has a name.'

She linked an arm with his, pressed close to him, the full weight of her assurance against his body.

'So do you. It's coming. Just a little more time.'

The spare bedroom in the house was next to Barry's. They would share the bath. While she put his things away in an armoire, he looked carefully around the second floor. Tom and Dal were at work. Mrs Aldrich was in the kitchen baking. He walked from one end of the upstairs hall to the other, looked at the tall pendulum clock, the framed sketches and photos of the family, a painting from Picasso's blue period. He went into Barry's room.

She found him there by her bed, absorbed in the photograph of Ned Kramer.

'I laid out your shaving gear in the bathroom. Your room gets a little cold at night – I'll have Mrs Aldrich put an extra comforter on the bed.'

He looked at her, a question clear in his eyes.

'Oh, that's – that was – a boy I – He was killed, in a hunting accident.' Barry turned to the hall door, straightened a Mary Cassatt on the wall there, then took a deep breath for buoyancy, aware of an ordeal in the making. 'Come on down – let's meet everybody.'

'Barry.' He was looking at Ned's photo again.

'Yes?'

'He was killed. In a hunting accident.' The young man's eyes were drawn tight in concentration. 'Killed is –'

'He's not with us anymore.' The shock of it somehow failed to grip her as urgently as she'd come to anticipate. 'He will never be with us again.'

'What happened to his name?'

'I don't – oh, you mean – now that's a strange question.' Barry was tempted to laugh it off, to take him by the hand and lead him from her room, where he was unnerving her. But if she was going to do him any good, if she hoped for a truly significant recovery, she couldn't let any question go unanswered, no matter how difficult the explanation might be.

'His name – didn't die with him, you see. Names are immortal. They always belong to a person, even if that person's dead – not here.'

She'd tried her best, but in line with his present analytical ability she had offered little more than a shadowy abstraction. He was tense, thinking, realizing that there was a contradiction; but he couldn't deal with it. He looked helplessly at Barry, with an expression of sorrow, a severe disappointment.

'Why don't we see what's on television?' she suggested, and took him downstairs.

She'd hoped to find her father returned from an afternoon's tramp, building up the fire in the family room while Meanness scratched and drooped by the hearth, but it was Dal she found in the dusky room, popping ice cubes deliberately into a glass, tension evident in his stance, in the way he held his head.

Barry switched on a lamp and said to his back, 'Hi, Dal – how was your day?'

'So-so.' He filled his glass nearly half full of whiskey and gave it a spritz. Barry opened the woodbox.

'Let's get a *fire* going in here! Want to go to the movies tonight? DeNiro.'

'Got a date. She's picking me up in a little while.'

He turned then and stared at John Doe.

'Look who's here,' Dal said in a nasal voice that cut across the grain of the mood Barry was trying desperately to construct.

She raised her head, smiling, and said to the young man, 'This is my brother, Dal.'

'Hello,' Dal said, drinking, staring rudely.

'Hello.'

The young man held out his hand tentatively; after a moment's indecision Dal chose to ignore it. He turned back to the bar, oblivious of Barry's quick frown, and said, 'Glass of wine, Barry?'

'No, thanks.'

'Well, what about him?'

Barry straightened, a chunk of kindling in one hand. She raised it deliberately, pitched it onto the grate.

'I wouldn't know. He's our guest. So why don't you ask

him if he'd like a drink?'

The young man looked curiously from Barry to her brother, aware of disharmony. Dal glanced at him over one shoulder.

'Care for a drink? By the way, what do we call you?'

Barry's breath hissed in exasperation through her teeth. The young man looked slightly troubled.

'I don't have a name.'

Dal snapped his fingers. 'That's right, I forgot. Little memory problem. Suppose we just call you Mr X.'

'Mr X,' the young man repeated agreeably.

'Dal, would you stop being such an asshole?'

'Asshole,' the young man said, so quickly and smoothly that Barry had to laugh. Dal went red from the neck up.

'Better watch your mouth, pal.'

Barry got a grip on Dal's elbow and marched him away to the windows at the rear of the family room. There were two bright spots of color on her cheeks. Dal separated from her and leaned sullenly against a wainscoted wall, with Barry almost on top of him.

She said as calmly as she could, 'I am not going to lose my temper and I won't fight with you, but *goddamn it*, I'm warning you, Dal, you'd better shape up and make an effort to be nice!'

'Did you hear what he called me?' Dal said, his mouth twisting stubbornly.

'Oh, Dal! He repeats everything he *hears*! That's how he's learning – and he's really amazing. In just a week his vocabulary has gone from almost zero to maybe a few hundred words. He's really very bright and it's not his fault he's this way – his feelings can be hurt, Dal!'

They both glanced at him; the young man wasn't paying attention to them. He had turned on the console television and settled into a chair to watch 'Sesame Street.'

'Like having a five-year-old kid around,' Dal muttered. 'Listen, do we need this?'

'Is he going to bother you so much you have to sulk this way? What is your *problem*, Dal?'

108

'Okay. Okay, I'm sorry, I – there's something about him that – I can't explain why, I just don't like the idea of him being here.'

'Dal, you have to admit that I've done a lot more for him than anybody else! The hospital is just no place for him anymore, not to mention the expense. I want to start teaching him to read again. Dr. Edwards thinks it could be a very important step toward getting his memory back. Please try to be a little more understanding.'

She kissed his cheek and stole a sip of his drink. She grinned to make him grin. Dal's return smile was somewhat fierce, not happy, as he reappraised the young man. He sighed.

'Tell you what. While you're improving his mind, I'll work on his love life. I guess there are some things you don't forget. I know a couple of girls who –'

Barry, only half kidding, gave him a sharp poke in the ribs.

'Over my dead body,' she said.

TWENTY

THERE WAS nothing about the farm and the daily routine of the Brennans that didn't interest John Doe. A mouse in the snow, a kite on the wind, the art of splitting kindling, the warmth of a newly laid egg in a henhouse nest, the textures of oil paint and fine brushes – he was fully absorbed from the moment he awoke with the sun until, exhausted, he fell into a rigorous slumber at night. But he no longer needed the amounts of rest he had required in the hospital. Daily he gained in strength and endurance. There was plenty of snow that winter, and Barry introduced him to cross-country skiing. His coordination was excellent. He learned to ice-skate in a day. When Dal was fourteen and wanting to play high school football he and his father had installed a gym in a corner of the barn. The iron weights were rusting but usable. John Doe spent at least an hour a day in the gym, working up a sweat in the frigid air. Dal occasionally took a minute to teach him some of the fine points of the clean-and-jerk and bench press. Dal was wiry but strong, and he could still, although he was out of shape, bench press nearly two hundred pounds. At the conclusion of a week of workouts the young man beat him by fifteen, then twenty pounds. After that Dal stayed away from the gym.

In his studio Tom took out some dog-eared sketchbooks filled with scenes of villages and the people of Ireland and showed them to John Doe.

'I was eleven or twelve years old when I did these drawings.'

The young man sat on a stool and leafed through the sketchbooks slowly. There was a fire in an iron stove; outside the window wall blunt daggers of ice blazed in the sun. Meanness the hound dozed with blood in his eye. Tom puttered and dreamed in front of a panel on his easel; nothing definite had taken shape. There was a roofline, the head of a man in profile, the body beneath skeletal, hazy, footless, blending with raw earth. He painted in, he painted out.

After an hour of this sort of effort, he took a break with pipe and pinball machine, which featured palm trees and red-lipped bathing beauties from the Hollywood of the forties. The young man quietly returned the sketchbooks.

'How do you do this?'

'Nothing fancy,' Tom replied. 'Just a pencil.'

He took a fresh sketchbook and a pencil from his worktable and with a few deft strokes created a likeness of John Doe, which he showed to him.

The young man was stunned. He sought a mirror, studied his image, stared at the drawing. He looked at Tom in admiration and longing.

'Teach me to do this.'

'It isn't anything that can be taught.'

'I want to draw,' he insisted.

Tom nodded, handed over the pencil and sketchbook, and, after a few moments' thought, went to a cupboard and rummaged in the shelves.

'Usually I start beginners with something simpler than portraits,' he explained. 'Let's see –'

He took out an antique handbell and a big wooden spoon, arranged them against a gray background on the worktable, adjusted lights to give depth and shading to the composition. John Doe watched, holding the sketchbook under one arm. He clutched the pencil awkwardly in his left hand. Tom placed him on the stool, changed the angle of the pencil in his fingers, worked patiently with him until he held it lightly and could draw with long fluid strokes. His student was delighted. Tom guided him through the bare outline of the bell, then turned to a clean page.

'You try. Draw what you see.'

When Barry came to call them for supper the light was gone except for the hot focus of the lamps aimed at the still life on the table. John Doe was hunched over his sketchbook and didn't respond.

Barry penetrated his aura of concentration and touched his shoulder.

He swung around with a look she hadn't seen before, that momentarily chilled her. 'No!' he shouted, and went immediately back to work, turning his back on her. Hurt and confused, she backed away and retreated from the studio.

Tom had gone with Meanness to the kitchen. When Barry came in, he glanced at her and raised an eyebrow.

'What's wrong?'

Barry let out her breath. 'Oh – nothing. I've seen him preoccupied before, but this is something else. You have a disciple.'

Tom broke bread and smiled. 'Could be.'

'But does he have talent?'

'I'm afraid not.'

'Oh,' Barry said, disappointed.

'I thought it was worth a try – he was so eager, and he might have had formal training somewhere that would still be evident despite his loss of memory. But – I'd say he's pretty hopeless. He draws even worse than you do.'

Barry had to laugh. 'He's hopeless, all right.' She slumped a little and glanced at the place set for Dal, who had been missing for the better part of two days.

'Your guess is as good as mine,' Tom said, helping himself to stew.

'Well – he's been working hard and not getting anywhere. He needed a break. What's this one's name?'

'Helga? Heidi?'

'What's she like?'

Tom gazed off, drawing a bead as he visualized the target. He had a knack for succinct word portraits that complemented his brushwork.

'Decorative and crisply sweet, like a good Viennese pastry.'

'Bravo,' Barry said. She poured herself a glass of Harp beer and drank some of it, ate a little of her salad. Her mind was on John Doe again. 'He tries, doesn't he? He tries damned hard to please us.'

'Did you have that session with Edwards today?'

'Yes. He's acting a little miffed because I don't bring John in every other day, but, hell, Dad, he doesn't like the hospital – how can I force him to go? I just think Edwards is jealous – he's always talking about *my* patient, and how unique he is. All he thinks about is making medical history and having a syndrome named after him.'

Barry began to gnaw a fingernail instead of eating her dinner; Tom tapped her gently on the wrist.

'The therapist from Cornell was there,' Barry told him. 'She thought I was doing a terrific job.' Barry fidgeted. 'I hope John gets bored with that sketchbook before he wears himself out. I want to get him off pictures and onto words tonight.'

Barry patiently kept the stew hot for forty-five minutes after she and her father had finished eating. Then she went back to the studio and looked in cautiously.

He was no longer sitting in front of the still life and had put his sketchbook and pencil down. He was off in one shadowy corner, standing curiously before the fortune-telling machine, which he had uncovered.

Barry glanced at his drawings and saw at once that a talented six-year-old could do better.

'Don't you want to eat something?' she asked him.

'Barry. What's this?'

'Oh, that thing – it came from an amusement park. Doesn't work anymore.'

'What is it for?'

Barry joined him and put her fingers lightly on the keyboard. Inside the glass dome Mrs Prye's head was lifelessly, eternally bowed. There wasn't much point in trying to tell him about the mysteries of Mrs Prye, but she always attempted to answer his questions fully, whether or not she thought he would understand.

'It's an electronic fortune-teller. You're supposed to punch in your birth date and what you get back is a recorded fortune – your health, your wealth, stuff like that. There are about fifty stock answers on a cassette inside. Mrs Prye lights up and her mouth moves and it's – it was kind of a weird effect in a dark room, just a fun thing to do at parties. Until –'.

Barry didn't know why she was going on like this – John Doe was gazing at her with a total lack of comprehension as it was – but she continued, 'until one night she stopped giving stock answers and started reading minds – telling people things they thought nobody knew. One of our guests was a vice-president of one of the savings banks in town, and he'd been trying to cover up some serious shortages. You should have seen his face when Mrs Prye opened up. She knew *everything*. There wasn't a secret in the room when she finished. Everybody thought I had something to do with it, of course – that I was being malicious – but I'm not a snoop and I *don't* read minds. I can't explain how it happened. I was as scared of her as everybody else. I guess I still am.'

A shudder made her jump against him. Her heart started to pound. Barry drew the dropcloth over the machine.

'Come on. I don't like being this close to Mrs Prye. I wish Dad would get rid of the machine, but he never throws anything out.'

In the kitchen John Doe put away a heaping plate of stew. After she did the dishes, Barry went to the family room and firmly shut off the television he had settled down to watch. They had the house to themselves. Tom had driven to town to shoot pool at the Black Fox tavern and grill, his regular Tuesday night diversion. The young man looked unhappy at having 'Mork and Mindy' interrupted, but Barry was seething with excitement. She took him by the hand and sat him down at the game table, took the Scrabble box from a cabinet.

She also placed a book in front of him – an Agatha Christie mystery. He was fascinated with books and had spent considerable time turning pages, staring at lines of type

114

without comprehension. She had read to him. Now he was going to relearn the process of making words and understand their meanings.

Barry dumped the alphabet tiles from the Scrabble set on the baize and mixed the letters. Then she extracted the letters that spelled her name and lined them up.

'This is who I am,' she said. 'B-A-R-R-Y.'

He looked at the tiles for a few seconds and smiled slightly. He touched each of them and looked up at her. Barry scrambled the letters with which she had spelled her name, mixed them in with the others.

'Now you spell *Barry*. Just like I did.'

He hesitated, looking at all the letters, then drew the correct tiles out of sequence. He pondered their order for a few moments, and rearranged them. Barry was elated.

'Great! You really catch on fast. Okay, here's Dal –'

She repeated the process with the letters of her brother's name. The word was easier; after she had scrambled it, he reproduced D-A-L almost immediately.

'At this rate I'll have you reading *Romeo and Juliet* by the end of next week. Now for *Dad* –'

They spent an engrossing half hour making words; his touch with the appropriate tiles became quick and sure. His recall – at least within that span of time – was nearly perfect. Barry was almost trembling with a sense of pride and accomplishment while she decided which word to spell next. He had begun to seem a little bored, but she wasn't prepared when he suddenly caught her wrist in his hand.

'Ned Kramer,' he said.

'Why?' she said, startled.

'Spell Ned Kramer,' he insisted. Barry began to feel the strength of his fingers on her wrist. For no good reason she was a little frightened. The silence, the house empty like that – he'd never been aggressive with her before. She made herself smile, but he had sensed her alarm; he let go and sat back in his chair.

'Please,' he said softly.

'All right.' A chill had cut through Barry, saw-edged; her

wrist ached. He didn't know his own strength. She bent to the table, choosing tiles. He was motionless, eyes fixed on the table.

The name took shape.

NED KRAMER

She swept the tiles away suddenly, getting up as she did so. He looked at her, surprised and frustrated.

'I don't think I want to do this anymore,' Barry said woodenly. 'You can watch TV if you want to. I'm going up to bed.'

'Barry. What's the matter?'

'I just don't want to talk anymore. Good night.' She gave him a quick peck on the cheek – it had become a ritual and even a necessity – but tonight her eyes were glazed, unseeing.

He started to follow her from the room, stopped halfway. Barry didn't look back at him as she jogged up the stairs.

John Doe didn't move for almost three minutes, as if she had taken the impulse of his life with her. Upstairs the cabinet clock in the hall struck the hour. It seemed to release him. He turned back to the game table and picked up two of the tiles, examined them in his steady cupped hand.

'What did I do?'

The house creaked in the wind. He heard the click of Meanness's claws on the tiles of the kitchen floor eighty feet away on the other side of the house. The remains of the fire baked redly in layers of ash on the hearth. He took a turn around the family room, uneasy, unsure of himself, then went to the foyer and opened the closet door. With his parka on but unzipped he stepped outside where the black trees showed sides of ice, the rutted drive was deeply frozen, the wind was sharp but nearly silent. Snow was piled against a rock wall like surf overwhelming a breakwater. He looked up at a horned moon and nebulae, the dustbowls of infinity.

He looked into depthless space and felt a corresponding hollowness, a sense of isolation that gave him pain. He shook and whimpered; his eyes burned but no tears came.

116

He turned and hammered a fist against the door jamb and went unheeded; his pain became torment.

Still shaking, he let himself into the house again. Meanness barked perfunctorily behind the kitchen door, subsided grumbling. The young man returned to the family room and stood staring down at the sprawl of tiles on the green baize. The room was dark except for the lamp by the table. He moved it closer, adjusting the cone shade, focusing the light more brightly on the grooved letters. He reached for tiles and spelled NED KRAMER.

'Belongs to him,' he said to himself. 'His name didn't die.'

He scattered the tiles, selected a random four, shook them in his cupped hand, laid them one by one on the table.

RKAM

Looking at what he had made, he felt a stirring of interest. He tried, unsuccessfully, to sound it out.

Slowly, with great patience, he resumed playing with the tiles, absorbed once again, arranging, rearranging, pausing at length to pore over the results with desolate, unwavering eyes.

TWENTY-ONE

PRAY, MISTRESS, wake up! What do you desire?

Barry sat up with a start, her face in a sweat. The room was dark, the pendulum clock ticked in the hall. She was in a daze of black dreams, disoriented.

'I never called you!'

Ay, you did, and in a frenzy. There is a deadly deal wrong. More's the pity, you call but refuse my counsel, spurn my prophecies – you use me extremely ill.

Barry's head reeled; she felt nauseated and paid little attention to the whining of Mrs Prye. She threw the covers back.

O lud! O death! The tale is in the tail of the salamander, snipp'd by the hand of the old dame –

'Mrs Prye,' Barry said, as she stumbled to the bathroom, 'you're making even less sense than usual.' In the bathroom she retched bitterly, cramping, growing faint; her skin was cold, prickling, and moist. Mrs Prye, wherever she was, had the decency to remain silent while Barry was sick in the toilet.

Afterward she slumped to the floor and sat holding her head, smelling of puke and hating it. Her period was late – that had to be it, she thought dully. But in the back of her mind the nightmare refused to be put to rest. It had been about a game she and Dal played as children. They would rake the autumn leaves into big mounds, a dozen or more of them around the spacious yard. Then each would take a turn burrowing into one of the mounds to hide. The finder had only three chances to guess the hiding place. But in Barry's dream it was she and her father who played the game. His turn to hide. She felt a suffocating dread as night began to fall and she searched futilely for him, tearing apart one pile after another of the crisp brown-smelling leaves. To find him sprawled and luminous in the last dense pile, a rotting corpse . . .

When she had the strength, she stripped off her flannel nightshirt and crept into the tub, pulled the shower curtain all around. Shivering, she subjected herself to a tepid needle shower.

The tale is in the tail of the salamander –

'Oh, God!' Barry said through gritted teeth. 'I'm fine, nothing's wrong, give me some peace!'

She was drying herself when the other door to the bathroom opened and the young man came at her with his shapely black eyes and flare of mouth, scaring her witless.

'Barry! Barry!'

'What is it? Why are you coming in here – I'm taking a bath!'

He seized her high on one arm with a keening, pleasurable sound; she lost her grip on the towel and flashed naked before him for several moments before groping, retrieving the damp towel, and muffling herself, now livid with the shock of his presence.

'Come and see!' he cried, only glancing at the upstart pinkness of a breast. 'It's my name!'

'*What?*'

'My name,' he said joyously, trying to drag her from the bathroom; Barry's heels skidded on the mat by the tub. She unlocked her knees and stumbled after him, heart thudding, in a wild disorder of sagging towel and half-wet hair.

'Oh, God! You *remembered?*'

'Yes! Yes! Let me show you!'

'Show me?' Barry put on the brakes again. 'Yes – okay – wait – I don't – I need a – just wait here while I go to my room for a second. I'm coming!'

He let her go and she turned, flung the towel, darted through the doorway into her own bedroom, and came back moments later wearing her bathrobe.

He led the way downstairs to the family room, fairly running, while Meanness rose in the kitchen with a croupy belling at all the commotion. When Barry caught up to the young man, he was hovering over the game table, breathless with passion.

'There it is! My name!'

She moved closer, almost reluctantly, eyes going from his face to the lineup of black-and-white tiles, the trump of identity he had played.

'Mark ... Draven,' she said softly, pronouncing it with the *a* long.

'Yes.' He was at her shoulder, his breath on her cheek. 'That is. Me. Barry. I have. *A name*.'

She turned to him covetously, all but weeping, crooking an arm around his neck.

'I can't believe it.'

'I am. I know. Mark.' He spoke stiltedly, as if he were losing the power of speech even as his vision, the possibilities of his life expanded.

'Hello, Mark.' A tear got away, then another. 'I'm so happy to know you.' She blinked and squinched and was aroused by the sensual liquid, the heated salty flow on her cheeks, lubricity, closeness. He was tense as well but from actuality, a newfound sense of permanence. Overcome with happiness, he could only nod ecstatically.

They had hot chocolate and sugar doughnuts and sat knee to knee talking for two hours in the family room, until the fire she had built up dwindled to a few pale flames. The clock struck three. He nodded off shortly after, and Barry covered him with a blanket, left him sleeping in the wing chair.

Her father showed up at three thirty; he was bleary-eyed and slow afoot, but he responded to her enthusiasm. He was both delighted and relieved by this breakthrough of identity. She made coffee for him in the kitchen. He added hair of the dog.

'Nothing else surfaced?' Tom asked her. 'Where he's from, what he was doing there in the park?'

'No.'

He scratched a stubbly chin. 'Well, now that we know his name, it shouldn't take the police long to find out more about him.'

'They won't,' Barry said.

'How can you be so sure?'

'Dad. They've been working on it for *six weeks*. Mark's picture has been everywhere. And they haven't come up with a thing.'

'His parents might have been abroad. There are a thousand other possibilities.'

'Nobody's missed him – nobody cares,' Barry said. She drew a finger evenly across the tabletop, as if she were signing a disenfranchisement.

Tom poured a little more whiskey into his pitch-black coffee. He felt cross with her for reasons difficult to define. But his strict artist's eye, blurred by memory, was fond and forgiving: she looked very young at this hour, in this light. The tip of her nose had taken on a shine from her habit of rubbing it with a sleeve of the nappy robe. The legend of her growing life was readable by him in almost forgotten nicks and scars, the spot where a bee had stung her when she was six; the stubborn swelling gradually had hardened into a wen. It was a strong face, spade shaped. She was long from the base of her throat to the outcurve of chin, long again in a line from the outer corner of each eye across the bridge of the nose; this line imparted a wonderful balance to a chin that was a shade small, indecisive. Some things in her face worked perfectly – the tip of her nose, standing aloof from the pretty yoke of her upper lip. Other details were awry. She had batty ears – they seemed too large and at odds with the rest of her head. It was a face he loved too severely to dwell on for long without retreating to the perspective of his art. Tonight her eyes shocked him. In the mists of those blue eyes he sensed an obsession soulless in its intensity.

'There are times,' he said, looking away, 'when I think you want him to be an orphan.'

She raised one shoulder, defensively. 'He's *not* an orphan. He has us.'

'He also has a history. Obscure, maybe. But it'll come together, piece by piece. Barry, I just don't want –'

He heard Meanness at the kitchen door, whining; they had let him out earlier to do his business. Tom got up to bring his hound in and turned to find Barry's eyes on him.

'What is it, Dad?' she asked quietly.

'I think you know. I couldn't stand to see you head over heels again and then get torn apart.' Barry shook her head silently, warming to a smile: his concern she took as an absurdity. She was like a born-again believer, drenched with the blood of suffering Jesus, cloaked in the innocent faith and courage of the newly converted. Tom wondered why he couldn't be thankful.

'One thing is inevitable. Either Mark will be found or he'll find himself. And he'll leave.'

'No he won't! He's mine. And he's never going to leave me.'

'Oh, Barry.'

'I don't care if you don't believe that. I can't help how I feel.'

'You make it sound as if I'm condemning you, but –'

She stood. She smiled forgivingly.

'Of course you're not.'

She came to him and kissed him; for a few moments her hand stayed on his arm. Her serene smile lingered long after she'd murmured a good night and left the kitchen.

Tom went into his studio for a few minutes, for nothing much except to indulge an idea that had been kicking around. He laid it out with brush and India ink on paper, no thought of accuracy, of trying to refine the emotion behind the idea; then, calmed, drowsy, he closed his book and shut the lights.

On his way to bed he looked into the family room. Mark slept there in the light of the sizzling fire with his face to one side in a hard, handsome profile, breath sighing between his lips. And Barry was at his feet, in sharper relief, her head back against his knee but with a certain prowess, not relaxed; she gazed profoundly, guardedly, at Tom, an

122

impulse in the depths of her eyes like the sprinting of quicksilver.

He nodded but couldn't speak. The clock struck – it was four, the last hour of full dark. The primal hour of reconciliation and leave-taking. As he climbed slowly to his room the old staircase's slight off-plumb seemed magnified into an unsteadiness of shadow and light and then of vital angles above and below: walls, floors, and eaves. He felt threatened, as if the house might suddenly fold up on him, like a carpenter's hinged rule. A trivial hallucination, although it left a long-lasting resonance of terror. He was half drunk still and heart-sore for his child, the love-galled virgin, vanished now so hugely from the center of his own life.

DRAVEN

TWENTY-TWO

ON THE second Tuesday in May Dr James Edwards got away
from the office early and drove out to Tuatha de Dannan in
his Porsche. The forsythia had peaked, but dogwood and
azalea were taking over, forming estuaries of pink and white
and vibrant red in the country along the road. Above the
covered bridge, which had received a new coat of paint, the
long waterfall brimmed silver. Glimpsed in passing, it
seemed motionless but thrilling, like a long-held inexhaust-
ible note of music.

The gates to Tuatha de Dannan were open when he
arrived; he drove up to the house and parked behind a Chevy
Blazer. Persistent ringing brought Mrs Aldrich to the front
door. The housekeeper was a woman of beak and sinew; she
wore an apron. There was about her – although she didn't
unlatch the screen door and spoke to him from a few feet
back in the foyer – an aroma of cooking fat. She had a high,
hoarse voice.

'Barry's not here – she's at the Shopwell in town. Tom is
upstairs resting. What did you say your name was?'

'Dr James Edwards. I took care of Mark. I just wanted to
see him for a few minutes.'

'I guess it must be all right then. Last time I saw him he was
around in back, working in the garden. You go that way.'
Mrs Aldrich made a sweeping motion with one arm,
pointed, then faded out of view toward the kitchen, where
the theme music of a soap opera was playing loudly.

Edwards walked around the house, paused to admire the
severely sectioned, mirrored north wall in which the serenity
of landscape, blue sky, and becalmed cloud was duplicated

surrealistically. Edwards, an art lover, thought of Magritte.

The knoll on which the house and barn were built fell away to rough fields and willows, a pond. Near the house there was an open expanse, a gentle hillside, part of which lay tilled beneath a benign cloud mass; it was fenced squarely with new chicken wire that glittered in the sun. A cassette player dangled from a fence post, trumpeting Vivaldi.

Meanness rose galumphing at Edwards's approach. Mark, wearing tattered denim shorts, was bending to the task of setting out several flats of tomato plants; he looked around more slowly. His back was a sweaty red, his hair long at the nape.

'Mark? Jim Edwards.'

The young man got lithely to his feet, and Edwards, who had not seen him since the last week in February, experienced a jumpiness, a tilt of perspective, a sense of being out of focus in the sharp daylight. He was amazed by Mark's physique. Mark had been well built before, like a high school athlete. Now he had acquired both bulk and definition in the major muscle groups while trimming his waist to a band of iron. Obviously he'd been working out with weights. He seemed taller, although he wasn't wearing shoes – perhaps three or four inches taller.

When Mark was closer, Edwards realized he hadn't been wrong – the boy *was* taller. He felt confused again, as if he'd been confined too long to four walls, the sight of the unwell. The spacious day, the advent of spring, the turned odorous earth – all had a drowsing effect. The doctor shook his head slightly, as if something sticky had enveloped it. Mark no longer looked like a boy to him. His face was fully ten years older, wearing a little in a good, masculine way, acquiring character lines. He might have been his own, older brother – infinitely more seasoned, the steady black eyes emblematic of the deepest mines of experience and perception a man can explore.

'Dr Edwards? Something wrong?'

The smile, as always, was a dazzler. Edwards recovered his equilibrium.

'No. You look – very well.'

'I feel great.' Mark held up his loamy hands. 'Can't shake – I've been grubbing in the garden all day. Could you hand me the hose?'

Edwards picked up the garden hose strung from a spigot in the barnyard and Mark turned the spray on himself, washing hands, legs, and feet. He stepped into a pair of Top-Siders and peeled back a section of the fence wire through which he and Meanness passed.

'How are you?' he asked the doctor, with a side glance and an easy familiarity; he had still, on their last meeting, occasionally picked over his words, phrased carefully as someone mastering a new language. But there was still a hint of reserve on Mark's part – wariness, perhaps. It had been his wish to discontinue visits to the hospital, not to participate in medical tests that might have facilitated recall of the past. Edwards had acceded grudgingly, hoping his patient would soon change his mind.

'Couldn't be better. Well, I was out this way and I wanted to stay in touch. How's your reading program coming along?'

Mark took the cassette player from the iron fence post and shut it off. ' "A weather in the flesh and bone / Is damp and dry; the quick and dead / Move like two ghosts before the eye.' "

'Sounds like Dylan Thomas.'

'Yes.'

'There's not much wrong with your memory right now. Up to a point, that is.'

'Up to a point,' Mark agreed, sounding unconcerned. 'Come on to the house – we'll have a cold beer. Barry ought to be back soon. I know she'd love to see you.'

Mark left Edwards and the hound in the family room, called to Mrs Aldrich, then went whistling up the steps and reappeared a few minutes later with his hair brushed. He had pulled on a striped knit shirt. He immediately challenged the doctor to a darts match. He seemed barely in control of his store of vitality. With fluid, unstudied moves he threw four

129

bull's-eyes and fell back, gratified, into a chair beside a
reading table that overflowed with books. The windows
were open to a breeze, the lushness of the May afternoon.
Meanness padded over to slump at Mark's feet. Mark
rubbed the tawny dog behind his great fraying ears.
Meanness contentedly cut the cheese.

'Oh, that dog,' Mark said good-naturedly.

'Anything you want to tell your doctor about?' Edwards
asked him. 'How's your appetite? Are you sleeping okay?'

'Sure. I get a couple of hours a night.'

'Two hours' sleep?'

'That's all I need anymore. The last time I saw you I was
sleeping half my life away. And there's so much I want to do.
I don't have enough time.'

Mrs Aldrich brought in a tray with frosted mugs and two
of the big bottles of Grolsch beer, the ones with the hinged
tops.

Edwards was surprised to see her crack a smile. 'Mark, I'll
batter some mushrooms and fry them if you're hungry.'

'That'd be great.' He rolled his eyes and then his head
toward her, a thoroughbred's playful mannerism, but there
was something else too – a wily kind of offhand sexiness she
clearly doted on. 'Thanks, Mrs Aldrich.'

'If you need anything else,' she said, opening a bottle and
pouring for them both, 'you just let me know.'

Edwards stood up against the mantel and raised his glass
to Mark, who acknowledged him and then drank deeply.

'Shows how wrong I can be,' the doctor said. 'I was afraid I
might find you a little depressed.'

'How do you mean?'

'Amnesiacs frequently undergo a secondary trauma called
depersonalization.' Mark frowned. 'That's a sense of
unreality, a feeling of not belonging to the world.'

'Oh.' Mark got up and stepped over the dog, restlessly
picked up the darts, and began sinking them on target again.
'It never bothers me,' he said after a short silence. 'I mean,
not knowing who I was, or where I'm from. I know where I
am now.'

Having rid himself of the darts, he leaned over the reading table and pawed through books liberally stuffed with torn strips of paper to mark pages or passages. He found the volume he wanted, opened it, skipped to the lines he liked, and read one of them aloud.

' "I live not in myself, but I become/A portion of that around me." ' He put the book down and smiled at Edwards. 'Barry and I were reading Byron a couple of nights ago. Great stuff. Do you like the Romantic poets?'

'Sure. Haven't had much time for them lately. Well, there's a new procedure I've heard about involving brain protein synthesis that might be applicable in your case – '

Mark shook his head. 'That's over with. I don't want to do any more tests. I'm not sick – why should I?'

'We know almost nothing about your kind of amnesia, where there's no discernible brain damage. We really don't know much about the human brain, either. I hate to miss an opportunity to add to that small store of knowledge. You might be able to provide medical science with a clue to a rather engrossing question.'

'What is that?'

'Is mind a function of the brain, or is it something quite different, like the soul? Your recovery has been phenomenal. You speak well, you read, you have some understanding of the philosophical complexities of life. Yet at one point five months ago your brain was not functioning at all; it was necrotic.'

Mark said ironically, 'I came from nowhere. I was nothing.'

'That isn't true. Some physiological mechanism of which we're ignorant has suppressed your entire past life. I'd like to know what it was. And you – you're curious about everything else. Why don't you want to know?'

Mark drank deeply from his mug of beer, followed swallows with a sigh, a hint of perplexity in his brows.

'You have a name,' the doctor persisted, 'but where did it come from? How can you be certain that "Mark Draven" isn't just something you accidentally hit on while you were playing with the Scrabble tiles?'

'It suits me. I like it.' He stared at Edwards. 'What difference does it make if I just want to enjoy life? Barry understands.'

'Thought I heard voices,' Tom Brennan said from the doorway.

Edwards turned. He had talked to Tom on the telephone, but they had never met. The painter looked ill, older than he'd imagined. His hair was unkempt, he wore a sagging cable-knit cardigan, house slippers, unpressed chinos.

'Have a good nap, Tom?' Mark asked him.

'Slept too long,' Tom complained, rubbing the back of his head. 'What time is it?'

'About three. Tom, this is Dr Edwards.'

Tom nodded. Edwards shook his hand, which was dry and cold and clawlike. The painter's cheeks were sunken, there was a golf-ball-size notch in his throat below the Adam's apple.

'Pleased to meet you,' Tom said, and subsided into a rasping cough.

'Little under the weather?' the doctor asked him.

'I caught the – the damn flu at the end of winter,' Tom explained. 'And I haven't been able to lick it.' He glanced at his dog. 'There you are, Meanness. Where've you been all day? Come here.'

He snapped his fingers; the bloodhound had lifted his head, but he didn't budge from his place at Mark's feet. Tom looked bewildered.

'That something? Usually can't turn around without stepping on him.'

It seemed to exhaust him to talk; his words trailed off to a husky whisper. Mark bent over and patted the hound on the rump.

'Go on, Mean. Go to Tom.'

The dog got to his feet and slouched toward his master.

'Can I get you a whiskey, Tom?'

'I could use one,' Tom admitted, 'How about you, doctor?'

'I'm happy,' Edwards said, and took a sip of his beer.

Without appearing to pay much attention to Tom, he examined him closely. There was no sign of fever and his hand, while not firm, had been steady. Tom Brennan looked wasted, curiously used up, and Edwards pondered possibilities other than the flu.

'Who's your family doctor?'

'Kesselring, in Pound Ridge.'

'I know him. He's a good man. What does he say?'

'He told me I had one of those rare flu bugs that you can't do much about. He says I'll gradually get my strength back. But it's been over a month, and, damn it, I don't feel any better! Worse. I sleep and sleep.'

'Keeping your food down?'

'When I feel like eating.' Tom looked directly into the doctor's eyes, as if he'd been afraid to before. 'Do you have any ideas?'

Edwards smiled noncommittally. 'What about symptoms you haven't mentioned? Back or chest pains? Is there blood when you cough?'

'No.'

'Do you have problems urinating?'

'No.'

'I can give you the name of a good internist, if you want a second opinion.'

'Maybe I should go see somebody else – I think Kesselring's been taking me for granted. But I hadn't had a sick day in twenty years before this hit me. Like a load of bricks, I'm telling you.'

'How long since you've taken a vacation?' Mark said, bringing Tom a whiskey.

'I don't need vacations,' Tom scoffed, sitting down slowly; rather, he lowered himself into a chair, like a much older, brittle man. Somewhat ashamed of his mysterious infirmity, he gazed at the whiskey in his glass.

'That could be an answer,' Edwards said. 'A complete change of scene.'

Tom had a bracing sip of whiskey. 'I don't know. Getting back to work would be a big help – it's really all I've ever

133

needed.'

Mark produced a sketchbook from under one arm. 'Would you mind looking at these, Tom?'

Tom rolled another swallow of whiskey around on his tongue and opened the sketchbook. Edwards peeped over his shoulder. The pages of portraits were mostly of Barry. The book obviously represented several weeks of work. In the beginning the drawings were barely competent – uninspired, executed tritely, perspectives awry. Ultimately they showed a command of form, a burgeoning passion, and style: in the most recent work the girl leapt at you in all her varied beauty. A profile of Barry with kohl-streaked eyes and streaming hair had been worked into the Mithraic form of a bull: it had the power to raise the pulse. At the bottom of each of the later drawings there was a big, slashing, exuberant *M*.

'Did you do these, Mark?' the doctor asked him.

'Yes.'

'You're getting somewhere,' Tom muttered, fingering his lips as if to still a slight trembling; there was a signal of apprehension in the mannerism. He glanced up at Edwards. 'I was all wrong about Mark. The first time he drew for me, I said to myself, Nope, he doesn't have it.'

'How long ago was that?'

'January,' Mark replied, lounging, his arms folded, smiling vividly.

'That's what I call progres..,' Edwards said, marveling at the talent in evidence on the sketchbook pages.

'I just kept working. I love to draw.'

Tom laid the open sketchbook in his lap and rested his eyes.

'You're ready to try your hand at something new, water-color, oil maybe.'

'I've started work on a tempera landscape,' Mark said confidently.

Tom shook his head. 'No, no. That's a very difficult medium for a beginner. Took me years to really get the feel of it.'

'Barry showed me how to mix the egg yolk and the colors. I've been working a lot at night. In your studio, Tom. You said you didn't mind.'

It was clear that the idea shocked Tom; he seemed to be trying to remember the conversation, his assent. But after a few moments he gave up with a shrug.

'No, I don't mind. Not at all. Need to think about getting back to work myself, but I –'

He opened Mark's sketchbook to a blank page and reached for a pencil in a vase. Mrs Aldrich brought in a basket of crisply fried mushrooms. Mark and the doctor helped themselves; Tom waved the basket away and sat hunched, mendicant, eyes contemplating the white paper. He made an attempt to draw, then stopped, grimacing, feeling the poverty of it. Nothing recognizable had emerged. He looked up, and for a moment his eyes were transparently fearful.

'Can't remember a day when I haven't had a pencil or brush in my hand, drawing something. Now I – feels damned awkward.'

With his left hand he touched his head, then moved the joined fingers lightly to the top of the pencil.

'Nothing happening between here and here. That's strange, isn't it?'

'All artists find themselves blocked from time to time, don't they?'

'I suppose so.' Tom replaced the pencil, handed the sketchbook back to Mark and reached for the whiskey, which Mark thoughtfully had replenished.

'Tom,' Mark said, 'I have most of the tomato plants in. I'll start the beans tomorrow.'

'Squash. Don't forget acorn squash. Tomorrow I – hell, I just might be up to giving you a hand.'

'Hey, terrific!'

Tom drank; his body tensed as if to ward off a chill, or a pain that might have been spiritual rather than physical.

'Cold in here. Maybe I'll go outside and catch some sun.'

'Wait. I'll walk with you.' Tom had already started to rise, but he sank back obediently. Mark flickered a look at Edwards.

'Time for me to be on my way,' the doctor said, taking the hint.

'I'll go out with you. Tom, back in a minute.'

'No, no, take your time,' the artist said vaguely.

On their way to the front door Mark asked in a low voice, 'Do you think there's anything to worry about?'

'Difficult to say. Some strains of flu just have to work out of the system.'

'That's what I told Barry.' He stepped outside with Edwards, gazed at a bumblebee cruising across heaps of starred impatiens flowering by the stoop. He suddenly jumped straight up to touch the wingtip of a bronze eagle atop the lighting fixture over the door; it was more than ten feet from the surface of the stoop. He dropped back easily, with a grunt of pleasure, looked over the red-and-black car parked behind the Chevy.

'Is that your car? What kind is it?'

'Porsche.'

'They're fast, aren't they? Barry's teaching me to drive. What I like – I like to go fast.' One hand shot out straight, palm down. '*Vvvoom.*'

Edwards was amused. Mark could be intimidating – in bulk, the breadth of his mind, his talent. In other respects, including the occasional banal choice of expression ('Hey, terrific!'), he was almost adolescent.

'Thanks for the drink, Mark. If you should change your mind –'

'I won't.' Mark extended his hand, they came to grips, he hurt without seeming to try. He said blandly, 'Barry and I both wish you wouldn't come here again.'

Once more Edwards felt the heady sense of dissociation from reality, as if he were talking to a vaguely sinister stranger who had popped up there in the garden to replace John Doe. He unobtrusively flexed his right hand, which pained him.

'All right. But I'd like for you to know that I'm always

136

available, if you need me.'

Mark said nothing more – just leaned back against the door jamb and regarded him with eyes gone a little dusty from uninterest. He ran a hand through his healthy mane of hair. Meanness appeared behind him, nose thrust against the screen, whining. Mark smiled then and went in; the hound rose and Mark grabbed his forepaws playfully, danced him around.

Edwards paused before getting into his Porsche, took out a professional card, wrote on the back, BARRY, SORRY TO HAVE MISSED YOU, circled the new telephone number on the card, and went back up to the front door. He slipped the card between the doorbell backing and the siding of the house. He was about to leave again, but he heard Tom Brennan weeping.

And Mark said, his tone sharp, 'Tom, don't do that!'

Tom's response, muffled by tears, was unintelligible.

'It worries Barry to see you crying. You don't want to make her unhappy, do you?'

'Nooo.'

'Barry's *very* happy. We both want her to stay happy.'

'I'm sick. I'm sick. I don't know what's wrong. Why do I feel like this?'

'It'll be over soon, Tom.'

'You think so?'

'Yes. I'm sure of it.'

Edwards felt a wormy writhing at the nape of his neck. He had heard physicians whom he hadn't much admired use that exact tone of voice when speaking to patients they knew were terminal.

'I wish I – I wish I could spend just one good day painting. *Why isn't it there anymore?* Oh, God, I wish you'd either let me paint or let me die!'

'*Wishes breed not,*' Mark replied, and to Edwards it sounded like a quote, a snippet recalled from long days of omnivorous reading. 'Come on, Tom. Get on your feet. Let's take a walk. You need the air. You'll sleep better if you have a little fresh air.'

'I don't want to sleep!' the artist cried. 'It's too hard to wake up!'

Mark's voice was soothing now, patient. 'Barry'll be home in a little while. Come and look at the garden. It's going to be the best garden we've ever had.'

Edwards felt he'd overstayed. He backed away from the screen, although because of the angle he was not detectable from the doorway of the family room. Then he turned and crunched across the gravel to the low-slung car that gave him so much pleasure. But at the moment he was at odds with tranquility, simple pleasures, the fullness of the day. Thoughts of John Doe had iced his mood. The homeless John Doe, now more than at home, with a new name and the satisfied, settled-in posture of one to the manner born, an attitude of proprietorship that transcended mere effrontery.

Perhaps Mark Draven knew more about himself than he was telling. And he had decided, as a convenience, or for more urgent reasons, to ignore all that he remembered.

Edwards opened the door of the Porsche and caught a swinging glimpse of his face in the side mirror, a mean-spirited smirk, then the handsome old house in the background, unpainted clapboard and layered stone, strong chimneys and foot-square beams. Some parts of the house, he had heard, were nearly three centuries old. Oak trees on the property had the girth of a similar great age. It was a house that had endured with grace and character. There was a serenity in view that couldn't be denied: streaked sun, flowering crab, and cheery, piping birds.

The doctor felt depressed, dissatisfied with himself and the distorted vision of things he was trying to impress on the household. Perhaps it was just a case of thwarted ego: he knew he could take no credit for the astonishing gains that the former John Doe had made in the last four months. If he believed that something was wrong here, it was due to a cranky misinterpretation on his part. Tom Brennan was weak from a tenacious case of flu, that was all – Mark worked in the garden and read the Romantic poets, Mrs Aldrich suffered with the population of daytime TV dramas and cooked wonderfully in the kitchen.

And Barry – Mark had said it – was happy. She was very happy.

TWENTY-THREE

'Is THAT you, Barry? We meet again.'

Barry had been pondering a shopping list in the dairy section of the supermarket, trying to decipher Mrs Aldrich's loopy handwriting, in which one letter looked much like another. How to tell the *o*'s and *e*'s from the *d*'s and *l*'s? She turned, confused, saw no one paying attention to her, turned in the opposite direction, and spied Alexandra Chatellaine, a market basket on one bare tanned arm, coming down the produce aisle, her sagacious eyes as green as the husks of fresh corn piled in a bin behind her.

'Alexandra – hi.'

She sailed along without the familiar black cane, her head held high as always. She attracted glances through some mysterious, extra dimension of well-being that seemed hers alone by divine sanction.

'You look well. What a lot of colour for this season!'

'I've been outdoors every day for a month. I hope we don't lose this great weather. How have you been?'

'Still working for passing marks in the school of life.' Barry smiled politely. 'Shall we shop together? I need very little, but it's so boring alone, and everyone looks the same, stunned by the prices and that pacifying music that never stops playing.' She reached past Barry for a half-pound of unsalted butter and popped it into her reed basket. 'How is your young man? Come out of the wilderness yet?'

'Oh, he's doing so well! You should see him now. By the way, his name's Mark. Mark Draven.'

'Progress indeed. What does he recall of himself?'

'Nothing.'

140

'Isn't that remarkable? A *tabula rasa,* on which an entirely new personality has – I assume – been impressed.'

'He's one of the most intelligent men I've ever met. And he's *very* talented. He'll make a painter. That's what he wants, more than anything.'

'And of course he still has the good looks that made him such a favorite at the hospital.'

'Ummm,' Barry mused, not so subtly aglow. She put milk and brown eggs into her shopping cart and they went on to Meats, where Alexandra picked out a half-pound of calves" liver and Barry chose a dozen center-cut lamb chops and a couple of big roasting chickens.

'I hope your father is well.'

'No, he hasn't been.'

'That is a shame.'

'It isn't anything, really – he's run down from the flu. And – he's been sort of in the doldrums lately, doesn't know what to do with himself when he isn't working. I'm having friends over Saturday night for dinner – that'll cheer him up.' Barry added, with a belatedness Alexandra pretended not to notice, 'You'll have to come, if you're free.'

'I'd be delighted.'

A bag of brown rice, a large bottle of Perrier, some fresh vegetables and toiletries – Alexandra soon finished her shopping. But she continued to tag along with Barry through the checkout, chatting away in a kind of ecstasy, as if she'd gone weeks without having a soul to talk to. Barry listened with half an ear and nodded tolerantly and became aware that Alexandra had more in mind than merely passing the time of day. Her none-too-casual questions about Mark and their relationship verged on interrogation. Barry became uncomfortable; she began to answer stiffly or not at all.

'He sounds quite ideal for you,' Alexandra said in summary, and they parted outside.

Alexandra transferred her groceries to the racks on the sporty Puch she had ridden nine miles from her home, and Barry loaded up the Volvo in the parking lot. It was nearly four o'clock. She'd been in town since shortly after noon, first at the dentist's, then at Copperwell's; she was anxious to get home and be with Mark.

But as she pulled out of the parking space and headed for the exit she saw Alexandra standing in consternation beside her unchained but motionless moped; she backed up and asked if anything was wrong.

'It won't start,' Alexandra said, exquisitely baffled.

Barry left the motor of the station wagon running and got out. She'd owned a moped when she was fourteen but had ditched it in a rather scary accident; thereafter she swore off everything that ran on two wheels. She tried all she knew, but the little two-stroke engine wouldn't kick over.

'Could be out of gas.'

'Do you think? It quite runs forever on a single gallon. I'm always forgetting to add any.' The gas gauge wasn't working; with a stalk of celery Alexandra plumbed the small tank. It was half full.

'Oh, my. Something very drastic seems to have happened.'

It was obvious to Barry that Alexandra couldn't pedal the Puch home, and though she was running late it would be cruel to leave the elderly woman stranded.

'I think we can load it into the Volvo. I'll drive you home. But how will you get it fixed?'

'Don't worry about that. The gardener's son is a wizard with mechanical things. In exchange for fixing my toaster I taught him to breathe properly, which did wonders for his acne.'

One of Shopwell's bag boys gave Barry an assist with the moped, which wasn't so much heavy as it was awkward, and they made room for it in the wagon.

The Kinbote estate was some thirty acres of botanical elegance surrounding a sixty-five-room mansion of a speckled gray granite that reminded Barry of tombstones. There were several cottages on the grounds, in one of which, a stone's throw from the same brook that ran through their own property, Alexandra lived. Barry wrestled the Puch out of the Volvo and wheeled it into the foyer of the gabled cottage, where Alexandra liked to keep it. The cottage had a

142

small bedroom and a living room with a high ceiling, a kitchen you could barely turn around in without barking your elbows.

Alexandra insisted on brewing tea and Barry didn't have to be coaxed to stay a few extra minutes: there was a great deal to look at within the small space – a wealth of Asian and Oriental art. Brocade drapes closed against the sun produced a churchly interior light, cranberry red, in which swam motes of gold. Alexandra kept dabs of little birds in ornate cages, large cats in gray fur loose as cassocks. Incense in braziers made Barry's nose twinge and ache.

But the tea was good, reddish in color, slightly sour and penetrating – it seemed to flow beneficently through every cell of her body. From a lacquered trunk with as many secret drawers and compartments as a magician's stage prop Alexandra produced mementos of her long career in places Barry scarcely had heard of: Bhutan, Sikkim, Kham. There was a leather face mask, on which the features of a provocative woman with slanted eyes had been painted. The mask was designed to protect the complexion during long rides across steppes scoured by gritty winds. Barry fell hard for a pair of tall snow-white boots made of Tibetan felt with thick red soles and artful piping. She also loved the leather bolero jacket and a silk blouse of a blazing purple shade; she had a strict eye for color and had never seen anything to match this blouse. It was, Alexandra told her, the color of the sky in the highest places of the world.

She lured Barry's attention from this finery by dropping into her hand a small amulet bag that was inordinately heavy; a gift from the Dalai Lama, it was made of pure gold mesh.

'Woven of precisely one hundred and eight strands of gold – a sacred number. I believe I have a photograph, taken in twenty-one or twenty-two. Yes, here it is – my audience with the Dalai Lama, who encouraged me to seriously pursue my ambition to study Lamaism. His astrologers so advised him of my worthiness. You will notice he has placed a *khata* – a silk scarf – around my neck and has shown to me the palms

143

of his hands, a most singular honor. Tibetans believe that all of one's life may be viewed in the palm, if one has sufficient knowledge to read what is engraved there. To show one's palms is an act of openness, of intimate friendship.'

Alexandra produced more photos – of celebrations, processions, dignitaries, beggars. Landscapes of a sun-struck, threatening beauty.

'Tibet is one of the harshest lands on earth,' Alexandra said. 'Only the physically strong and the strong-minded are allowed to survive. They must learn to endure the altitude and the extremes of temperature: great heat at noon in the summers, zero cold by moonrise. Perhaps because of the immutable natural laws, women have always enjoyed equality with men, an equality still beyond the grasp of Western women. Tibetan women, often alone or in small groups, are frequent travelers in the loneliest reaches of the country, such as the northern Changtang. I have seen nuns living as hermits in caves in forbidding wilds.'

A cat jumped to the top of a gong frame and scolded her for some obscure slight. Alexandra took him down and scolded him back. Barry said, 'How long has it been since you were in Tibet?'

'Perhaps twenty-four hours,' Alexandra said, and Barry had to look at her twice to see that she was being mischievous.

'How do you mean?'

'Physically I left my adopted land more than twenty years ago, when the Communist Chinese invaded. But Tibet is still perfectly realized in my mind. By visualization, for which I have had fully half a century of training, I can by stepping outside this cottage door find myself in Lhasa – in the warrens of the Potala, the shops and stalls by the cathedral of Jo-Kang. Perhaps I shall decide to meditate for a day among the rhododendrons and dwarf apple trees of Norbu Linga.' She looked at Barry over the cunningly shaped head of the cat she was holding. 'I think, with a little more effort, I could persuade you to see what I see, share in my experience.' Her eyes were startling in the wine-colored

144

light of the fading day, so that the eyes of the Siamese, doubled below hers, of equal intensity but nebulous color more ashen than blue, seemed reflections swimming on a level of the air.

'You have a *fantastic* imagination.'

'So do we all. Our gods, our evil spirits, the cosmos itself are merely visions that exist in the mind, are created by and erased by mind.'

'You said something like that before.'

'It is the truth of Lamaism from which all truths spring. Each of us has the power to alter experience, to evoke magic. The evocation most often is the result of arduous training and discipline, though there are instances of spontaneous transformation by the naive but exceptionally gifted. It is all a matter of energy rightly directed – our word is *angkur*. Self-empowerment. The most adept at the generation of palpable phantoms and worlds for them to inhabit are near to godlike – *bodhisattva*, supremely spiritual beings. Tibetans are fond of the legend of King Gesar of Ling, who created of himself a multitude, supplied with horses, tents, servants. To do battle he imagined phantom soldiers, which dispatched his enemies with no less deadly effect than if they had been real.'

'That's just a story.'

'Congenial to the nature of a people who have persevered in a wonderland that no single god could conceive, a land of mirage and storm and the silences of the eternal. Aside from legends, I have had many experiences with phantoms, or *tulpas,* as we call them – the creatures of master magicians. I once made one myself.'

'How?'

'By concentration of thought and the repetition of certain prescribed rituals I was able, after a period of some months in seclusion, to visualize a phantom monk. A pleasant and rotund little man who became, after much effort on my part, quite realistic and active around my apartment. My friends became very fond of him.'

'They saw him too? Well, I guess that's not unusual. We

145

have a ghost at home.'

'Ah, yes.'

'Enoch. He's been hanging around the farmhouse since the Revolutionary War. The problem is, he doesn't believe he's dead.'

Alexandra nodded. 'The manor house is rather well populated with similar unfortunate souls. But they do no harm.'

'Neither does Enoch. My father's seen him. So has my brother. Mrs Aldrich *refuses* to see him. Just as well. I don't know how we'd get along without her.' Barry laughed and checked the time. 'Speaking of Mrs Aldrich – she's waiting for the lamb chops. I'd better go.'

Barry arranged to pick up Alexandra on Saturday evening. She felt, in parting, more at ease with the elderly woman. Alexandra was undeniably eccentric, but it was hard to dismiss her as a humbug, and she certainly was lively company. She knew that her father, who had been raised by a septuagenarian aunt of sly wit and fierce independence, would take to Alexandra and her yarns in a big way.

She drove home in a little more than four minutes, paused to pick up the mail. With the remote control unit she closed the gates of Tuatha de Dannan behind her, glanced at an oversized postcard from Greece filled with Dal's microscopic lettering, and continued up the curving leafy road toward the house.

Halfway there, as she was crossing a log-and-plank bridge in a glade of wild rhododendron and white birch trees, she saw Alexandra again, moving a little way off through the woods with the lowering sun behind her.

Barry hit the brake so hard she almost slid over into the rock wall beside the unpaved road.

Alexandra was perhaps thirty yards away, and she was walking roughly parallel to the road in the direction of the house. At least, Barry assumed it was Alexandra she saw, but her practical mind denied the possibility. She had driven away from Kinbote estate with Alexandra standing in the doorway of her cottage, holding an armload of cat, smiling good-bye. There was no way she could have walked from the cottage to this patch of Brennan woods in so short a time. Barry had driven the country road at nearly fifty miles an hour, covering a distance of about two and a half miles. To make the matter more perplexing, Alexandra, or whoever it was, now was completely dressed in the costume that Barry had admired, piece by piece, as it emerged from Alexandra's trunk: the voluptuous, strangely erotic leather face mask, the smashing heliotropic blouse and red bolero vest, a full calf-length black skirt, and immaculate white boots. She was carrying, under one arm, a leather casket with lockwork and hinges of flashing gold; the casket was about the size of a loaf of bread.

Barry got out of the Volvo fast, adrenaline surging.

'Alexandra!'

The woman, as if surprised to hear her name called, turned full face with the rictus of a helmed smile glancing into sunlight. Despite the distance between them, Barry thought she could make out the movement of eyes behind the diagonal slits cut for them in the leather.

She scrambled through the bog near the bridge and uphill toward the torchy treeline where the figure of the woman had fallen two-thirds into shadow, with only the brilliance of one sleeve, the curve of a hand around the end of the casket showing full fleshed in the remaining light. Barry was breathless, aghast, but impelled toward her.

'But you – how could you –'

The eyes were Alexandra's: pungent as mint, appraising. They stopped Barry in her tracks. Alexandra spoke not a word but slowly extended the casket to Barry. It looked very old. There were markings on it in a language she had never seen.

Barry reached numbly for the casket. Her hand brushed Alexandra's.

She felt something that was not flesh and bone; her fingers sank into it. Recoiling, crying out in fright, she saw the figure of the woman go loose as smoke, which streamed through the low branches of the trees. The sharp colors, the fixed

147

smile vanished in the gilded twilight.

From the fingers of Barry's hand ectoplasm writhed
stickily. She knelt and thrust the hand into soft earth –
humus – scrubbed it frantically on a stone as she felt her
gorge rise. She was afraid she would faint; only the more
persuasive fear that she would awaken in full darkness in this
haunted wood kept her sensible.

The ectoplasm dissolved as if it had never been. Her hand
shook, the nails were rimmed in black, Barry's cheeks
burned with humiliated tears.

Why? she thought. *Why did you do this to me?* She
trudged back to the station wagon and locked herself inside,
shivering. With the windows raised she was free to scream,
but couldn't; her throat was too tight. She turned on the
radio, to rock music. Rod Stewart's voice rasped against her
soul like a scrub brush. After a few minutes she found the
strength to drive the remaining few hundred yards to the
house, all pleasure blasted from her day, bound helplessly in
a rage that hurt like a vest of nails.

TWENTY-FOUR

DAL HAD left Tuatha de Dannan the last week in February to spend a few days in Paris and attend the wedding of an artist friend. In Paris other friends and acquaintances had lured him south to Marbella on the Costa del Sol. Then, island hopping, Dal made his way across the Mediterranean aboard Freddy somebody or other's yacht to Greece, and Corfu, where the telephone service was a quaint antique, despite the latest in communications satellites criss-crossing the heavens.

It was nearly eleven thirty at night when Tom Brennan succeeded in getting a call through to his son. He lay slackly on his bed in robe and pajamas, his back propped against big pillows, the telephone beside him, finding it almost too much effort to hold the receiver to his ear. On the Betamax opposite the bed *Casablanca* played out its familiar intrigue, Bogie's harrowed handsomeness, Bergman's face in close-up soft as a cloud, verging on tears. Star-crossed love.

'Hello? Hello – Dal? It's Tom! Can you hear me?'

'*Hi, Dad!*'

The sound of his son's voice, filtered through a wall of metallic noise, brought a jet of tears; Tom trembled and lost his own voice momentarily.

'*Dad, you there?*'

'Yes, I'm – what time is it there?'

'*… Called me to find out time it is?*'

'No, no. Haven't had a letter from you – in a month. I was wondering how you were.'

'*Kay. Getting little work done. They had earthquake here couple weeks go.*'

149

'Earthquake?'

'Wall fell on me.'

'My God, Dal!'

'Masonry wall. I'm little skinned up and sore, that's all. Dad, you don't sound so good.'

'No, I'm not – feeling well. I had the flu.'

'Flu? That was two months ago! Is something else wrong?'

'I don't know. I feel weak. Just can't get out of bed anymore. And I'm afraid –'

There was silence on Dal's end. Tom listened to the susurus of long distance, tuned into another voice sounding as far away as limbo, shouting in an exotic alien language.

'Afraid of what, Dad?'

Tom couldn't suppress a sob. He was trembling. His skin was coppery in the light from the hall, like spoiled fish, the freckles like bloodspots everywhere.

'Barry – she's so infatuated with him – nothing else matters –'

'Do you mean Mark?'

'Yes! He – he has me worried. He's – not like anybody I've ever known.'

'Why that guy still hanging around? Don't you get rid of him?'

'I can't. He's – in my studio, all the time.'

'Doing there?'

'Painting. I wish – wish you'd come home, Dal. We need you.'

The line went dead.

Tom looked up, stiffened from shock. Mark was in the middle of the bedroom, bending over, retrieving the loose phone cord. He had a tray with a glass of milk on it in his other hand. He had come in very quietly. Tom had no idea of how long he'd been there.

'Tom,' Mark said, 'I'm sorry. I didn't see the phone cord. I pulled it right out of the wall with my foot.'

Tom, holding the useless receiver, began to sob again. Mark looked at him, perplexed.

'I said I was sorry. Who were you talking to, Dal?'

On the television screen actors dressed as French soldiers were singing the 'Marseillaise' in Rick's place. Mark didn't bother to plug the phone in again. He sat down on the bed beside Tom, the tray on his knees. He reached out and took the receiver from Tom's hand. Then he held out the glass of milk.

'Barry wants you to drink this,' he said.

Tom's robe was open, revealing all the bones of his sunken chest. He breathed through his mouth, a dry rustling noise. When he made no move to take the glass Mark held it to his lips and put his other hand behind Tom's head to steady him. Tom choked after two swallows and sprayed milk on them.

Mark put the glass on the night table and took Tom in his arms. It was a dispassionate embrace, expressing no tenderness or concern for the artist. Rather he seemed to be taking possession of what was left.

After a long time he relaxed his grip. Tom's eyes had closed. Mark spoke quietly to him, laying him back on the pillows.

'I have to go to work now. I'll work all night, every night, until I'm as good as you. And I will be. Soon.'

TWENTY-FIVE

'How's Dad?' Barry asked when Mark walked into the studio.

He smiled at her. 'Sleeping.'

'Did he drink his milk?'

'Some of it. I left the glass by the bed in case he wants to finish it later.' He went immediately to one of the easels and set to work. He had several things going at once in the studio, in tempera, in oil, in chalk; he was insatiable, learning his craft at a phenomenal pace. Barry watched him work on the landscape that he'd nearly finished, a familiar hill of the farm made exceptional by his placement of a cracked mason jar in the foreground, something her father might have thought of: jagged angles and greening sunlight in the jar, the springing buds of a willow adangle down. In contrast the life study of her in oil was barely sketched out.

Barry retired to her corner, where there was a fake fur rug by the iron stove. She kicked off her moccasins, unbelted her jeans, took them down, folded them over the back of a chair. She pulled off the lightweight cotton sweater she'd been wearing, which left her in leopard-print underwear – a tank top, string bikini pants. She had the beginning of a tan, was already a little too red from incautious exposure along the tops of her thighs and across her face. She put a single gold earring in the left pierced lobe, walked barefoot across the floor to an empty space with a neutral background ten feet from the easel that had her outline on it. She took up a stance there, facing the vertical rack of lights that duplicated sunlight and bathed her evenly from head to toe, stood with arms folded below her breasts waiting for him to leave his landscape and resume with her. Neither of them spoke.

She waited five minutes, ten. Then he broke off suddenly and approached her, picked up tubes of color, squeezed them onto his palette.

'Why were you so upset at supper?' he asked, mixing colors, laying on strokes. 'You didn't eat.'

'Oh,' she sighed, 'it was just something that happened this afternoon.'

'At the supermarket?'

'No, later. On the way home. I saw something I wish I hadn't.'

'What was that?' Mark asked, glancing up from his brush-work. He painted with surety, energy, and a quickness that even her father couldn't duplicate.

'I was visiting Alexandra Chatellaine – do you remember her?'

He thought about it. 'The old woman at the hospital?'

'Yes. She has a little cottage at Kinbote estate. I left and drove straight home. Just after I came through the gates I saw her again in our woods. But I swear, Mark, it couldn't have been more than five minutes! And it's at least two miles. I don't know how she – I've been thinking about it a lot. Alexandra's a mystic, and she lived in Tibet. I had some tea at her place that made me feel funny and she was burning incense. The whole experience must have got to me in some strange way.'

'What did you see?'

'I saw a ghost in the woods that I thought was Alexandra. Now I know you don't believe in ghosts –'

Mark said practically, 'Show me one and I'll believe.'

'Enoch is very shy around you for some reason. Anyway, I thought it was Alexandra. I got out of the car and followed. When I touched her – it – nothing was there. I mean, what *was* there just drifted away like smoke, and I was left with some sticky cold stuff on my hand.'

Mark stopped painting and shook his head slowly, disbelieving.

'Weird, huh?' Barry said with a game smile.

'Maybe you ought to stay away from her.'

'*Right*. Except I already invited her to dinner Saturday. But I'll get out of that somehow.'

They were silent for a while. Then Mark said. 'On second thought, I think she ought to come over. I'd like to talk to her. She sounds interesting.'

Barry shifted her position unobtrusively; a muscle had begun to ache. With her father it didn't matter how often she changed – he never transcribed a pose – but she didn't want to throw Mark off his mettle. At this point he seemed to be having a little difficulty in sizing her up.

After another quarter hour of painting, he put his brushes down and cleaned his hands. He came over to Barry and just stared her up and down, frowning, preoccupied. Then he went on one knee and placed his still faintly slicked fingertips sensitively on her feet and ankles, where he read, like a blind man, the skin-deep bones, arches, and hollows, the youthful sinew and sumptuously fatted calves. He slid both hands up her long right leg to the knee, probed there the complicated cap, tested the bulky articulation.

Barry had begun to flush, from thigh to groin to belly, she was as rosy as a sunrise from his explorations before he stood and stepped back.

'Will you take everything off?'

'Yes,' she said faintly.

Her hands tingled as she pulled down the spotty triangles of bikini, flicked the bottom aside with a foot. Barry skimmed the top over her crackling head and dropped that too, then faced him, hands at her sides, feet well spaced. Mark went behind her, and Barry's blush deepened in anticipation of what he might do. Her skin crawled pleasurably. After too long a time she felt his touch again as he gently lifted, then separated her velvet cheeks at the base of the spine, spread them wide in order to trace the tremulous crescents of under-flesh to the slightly steely texture of mons veneris; the half-hidden petals of her tender sex unfolded humidly as she posed.

'Ahh,' Barry said, tensing. One of his hands was enormous but unmoving, thumb bulging in her gluteal grip, the other

154

edging upward past the rib cage to a well-inflated breast. Then Mark took his hands away, rose, and began to circle her slowly, again and again, pondering musculature, the prim high navel, the sheen of pelvic bones just beneath the opal skin, apparently not well aware of the peak to which he had raised her. After four times around, he came to rest facing her with both hands snug on the staunch outcurve of her hips. She was jolted – there was a nearly unbearable grit of passion behind the reddish cleft mask of her loins. She could barely swallow, the room seemed about to keel.

Barry looked dumbly at Mark in his paint-daubed denim shorts.She whimpered in dismay and tugged with her own hands at his beltline. He was puzzled.

'I want,' she murmured, eyes slitted and with a kindled touch of lunacy, 'to look at you too.' She was on fire to the tips of her ears. She unfastened the belt and tugged at the shorts, forcing them down over his hard-packed thighs, then in a fog reached for the French briefs. She got rid of those as well, leaving him almost as naked as she was, but with an important difference. He was not aroused.

Barry could have cried. She looked at the lengthy indolent penis – splendid, like carved faintly blushing ivory, a truly Corinthian cock that had not, would not work for them. In the brief span of her affair with Ned she had made fledgling love to him three times, never achieving an orgasm, out of ignorance, reticence, or just fear. She had loved, idolized Ned but had never cared for the appearance of his bulky brutish member, with an excess of liverish foreskin hanging down, a cowl over the sweet apple. It had been, in her eyes, ugly as a Gila monster. But Mark's was a real slave driver – just what she wanted and couldn't have.

Barry kneeled, a cheek against his thighs, stroking his cock as if it were a temperamental animal that had snubbed her. 'Oh, Mark! Everything else is so perfect. Why can't we make it work?'

She knew she shouldn't have said anything; it could only make his impotence worse. Time and patience were the answer. She bathed his naked legs in frustrated tears. His arms went around her. He lifted her, then sat down with her across his body, her weight in his lap.

'You want me, don't you?'

'I want to paint you,' he said. He always seemed afraid of her tears.

'You can, you can. I'll be all right. It's just that you get me so – I love you with all my heart, and I need – but it'll be okay. It'll happen! I know I shouldn't be like this, so anxious. Will you touch me here, and – here? Thank you. Thank you. And *there*! Just let it slip in. Out. So good. In, in. *Oh, my God!* Now take me to bed. Just like this. I don't want to put any clothes on. Don't worry, Dad won't see us. Sleep in my bed tonight. Will you, Marky? Hold me very tight. What would I ever do without you? My love. My love.'

TWENTY-SIX

THE PERPLEXITIES of this side of their relationship resulted in a certain amount of torment for Barry. Although sexual longing was like an unpleasant, nagging beast she had conjured and that shadowed her throughout the day, Mark's clear devotion to her, his passion for creating and recreating her in his sketchbooks and on the large canvas slowly taking shape in Tom's studio, acted as balm. They filled each other's days; no one else was needed.

He had grown daily more accomplished in his art, and more alluring physically. He took time to add to his store of strength, building stamina with weights and running and feats of agility that made her gasp: he could leap like a stag, walk on his hands, nonchalantly juggle a miscellany of sharp kitchen knives without suffering a scratch. He made her laugh with her heart in her mouth and butterflies in her stomach. His love of play not infrequently approached recklessness, as if, like a very small but precocious child, he had no firm sense of his limitations or mortality. He was getting much better at handling Dal's raffish Mercedes at high speeds, but he'd come close to wrecking it twice on the mile-long hilly stretch of disused road beside Caugus reservoir, where he practiced driving. On the second occasion Barry had been with him in the car and it was her life too, not to mention that the automobile cost a fortune. She had yelled at him, more afraid than angry, and Mark was contrite, but the experience didn't come close to slowing him down. Barry found herself having to sneak off for catnaps in order to have the strength to meet the demands that he exuberantly placed on her.

She sometimes felt as if she were caught up in a fandango that dimmed the senses and blurred her perspective, and she regretted that she did not have the power to resist the flow of time, cherish at greater length the most satisfying moments they spent together.

After daybreak thunderstorms, Friday turned into a day of noble-looking cumulus and racing cloud shadows across the dark inlay of pond where Mark and Barry coasted in a dented aluminum rowboat among islands of tangled sedge. Meanness rode with them in the bow, barking at a splayed snapping turtle that dived down into the tea-colored depths ahead of the boat. Mark had taken his shirt off for greater freedom as he rowed. He was tireless: they'd been around the large pond three times already. Barry had made a nest of flotation cushions in the stern where she lounged, drowsy, trying to read aloud, lulled by the delicious sounds of oars lightly stroking through the water. She read from Yeats. *Caught in that sensual music...*

From time to time Mark shipped the oars to pick up his sketchbook and draw something that excited his bump of artist's intuition.

'Who was Dionysus?' he asked idly, tuning in to a snatch of poetry.

Barry yawned and put the book face down in her lap. They had come to one corner of the triangular pond, a place roughly two-thirds of a mile distant from the gristmill, where there were rock ledges and tranquil willows alight with a simmer of sun like Japanese lanterns. Low hills rose from the pond. On the other side of these pine-covered hills Tuatha de Dannan ended and Kinbote began.

'Dionysus? Oh – the Greek god of wine and, let me think, drama. Something else. Fertility.'

'The Greeks had a god for everything. The Irish only have one.' He had been with her to Easter mass and she had tried to explain her religion, but Catholicism was still a mare's nest in his mind.

'The Greeks had honey and wine; the Irish got beer and potatoes, freckles, and sin.'

158

'If you only have one god and he doesn't like you, I guess you're out of luck. What does *sin* mean?'

'That which is hateful in the eyes of God and contrary to His laws, according to my catechism teacher.'

Meanness was barking again and rocking the boat, as if he meant to go overboard; Barry sat up shielding her eyes with the paperback Yeats, looking up into the hills. She felt a cold rush of dismay.

'Oh, no.'

Mark looked up at her, puzzled. 'What's wrong?'

'It's Alexandra. I think she sees us. Why don't we row back home before –'

But the unguided boat had bumped against the embankment. Mark turned on the seat, also looking at the hill where Alexandra Chatellaine strode energetically with her black cane, threading her way downhill between thick trees on a needle-cushioned path. She raised the cane and waved it in a relaxed, carefree way. She was wearing a wide-brimmed straw hat with what looked like a beekeeper's net attached to it.

'Why?' Mark asked.

'You know why. I haven't recovered yet from Tuesday.'

'Oh, the ghost. You said that you decided it was your imagination.'

'I said *probably* it was my imagination. It wouldn't surprise me if I was drugged. I don't think I like her, Mark. Let's go.'

'No.'

She saw he was going to be stubborn, so that was that. Meanness had leapt up to a rock ledge and he stood there quivering. Scents he was good at, he could bark with the best, but aggression wasn't his long suit. Mark stood, picking up the bow line, and stepped ashore with it. Barry rankled silently. It had been a fine mellow afternoon in their hectic life; now, prematurely, it was over. She had the sickly superstitious feeling that there would never be another like it.

Alexandra came down beneath the glowing willows and

flung aside the veil that kept the sun from her milky skin. Mark held out a hand to the doyen and she took it gratefully, inched down over the rocks to the ledge at the level of the boat, looking closely all the while at his face. Mark smiled toothsomely.

'You've changed a good bit since I last saw you! Filled out. And what a glorious head of hair. You mustn't ever cut it. You'll be like Samson..'

'Samson?'

'Hello, Alexandra,' Barry said icily from the boat.

'Hello, Barry.' She sounded somewhat winded. 'I believe I've walked farther than I intended today.' She held a hand to her heart and gazed at the pond, the shallow massing of cloud reflections, a repeated treeline. The water vista rippled and vanished in fathom darkness, reappeared tremulously at the dying-down of the wind. 'You've been rowing? What fun.'

'Come with us,' Mark invited.

'If you promise I'm not intruding.'

'You're not intruding.' He was more than polite; Mark seemed genuinely taken with Alexandra. She was an old flirt, and Barry felt a ridiculous spate of jealousy.

So Alexandra came aboard with Meanness, and they all set out in the twelve-foot boat, with Mark in the middle seat at the oars, facing Alexandra, who delved into his sketchbook. Barry studied the play of muscles in Mark's wedge-shaped back, occasionally reaching out to flick away a mosquito, to let her fingers trail lovingly down the bumpy groove of backbone. Dragonflies coursed around them. The wind rose. Alexandra's sun veil fluttered. Her face was indistinct except for what might have been a smile, but her eyes pierced through.

'I love to draw and paint,' Mark told her. 'I want to be as great as Tom is.'

Alexandra closed the sketchbook. 'Now that I've seen you again, I have no doubt you'll realize your every ambition.'

The wind suddenly picked up the hat from her head, whisking off the veil, leaving her with a wan, surprised expression as the hat went sailing a dozen feet to the surface of the pond and floated there. Then, the muslin taking on a heavy load of water, Alexandra's hat looked as if it might sink.

Mark hastily brought in the oars and stood up, which caused the boat to rock violently. Before Barry realized what he was going to do, he did it, jumping in after the hat.

'Mark!'

He sank like a stone. They were in the deepest part of the pond, and although she leaned out almost far enough to throw the boat over, Barry couldn't catch a glimpse of him. There was nothing but bubbles and froth.

'Can he swim?' Alexandra asked, alarmed.

'I don't know!' Barry wailed. She sat down and pulled off her shoes, ready to go in after him. She'd had lifesaving at camp and knew what to do, unless he got mired on the bottom. Then it would be dicey.

She was unbuckling the belt of her jeans when Mark reappeared eight feet away, floundering, looking shocked but laughing too as soon as his head broke water. Meanness began his distinctive deep belling, a sound that provoked goose bumps in fugitives and the bereaved.

'Mark, are you crazy?'

'Alexandra's hat,' he burbled, looking around for it.

'You don't know how to swim!'

'What do I do?' he said, beating at the water with both hands, holding his chin high. But he didn't sink again, and he didn't seem panicked. 'Hey, it's cold!'

'Of course it's cold – you're right over a spring! Can you make it back to the boat?' He couldn't. Barry picked up an oar and held it out to him. Mark seized it with both hands and relaxed, and she was able to pull him back. When Mark was beside the boat, Barry helped him get a leg over, and he rolled in without capsizing them.

'I'm sorry,' he said breathlessly to Alexandra, whose hat had gone under.

'Don't worry about that old thing.'

'Mark, it's more than twenty feet deep here!' Barry said.

The sun had disappeared and his teeth were chattering. He looked at her and just shook his dripping head.

'I didn't think. Sh-show me how to swim.'

'When it gets a heck of a lot warmer. Let's go, before you turn into a chunk of ice.'

Mark insisted on rowing, which was the best thing for him to do; the exercise kept him warm, and his skin soon dried in the intermittent sun. But his shorts were soaked. They had left Dal's car by the gristmill. Mark tied up the boat at the dock below the mill. Barry dropped him at the house for a hot shower and a change of clothes. She took Alexandra home.

'He is so well spoken. Manly. And so full of life.'

'Yes,' Barry said, driving faster than she normally would go, anxious to be rid of Alexandra.

'I must say, I think you've worked a miracle.'

'Thank you.' She tried to hold in her bitterness, but couldn't. 'I thought we were friends. Why did you do that to me?'

Alexandra was silent for a time.

'Perhaps it was not well advised,' she conceded, looking at the grim jut of Barry's jaw.

'*How* did you do it? What was it I saw?'

'I am, among other things, a *gyud* lama, well versed in magic ritual. Producing the double is not difficult. It was not a literal double, of course – I dressed her up. As an attention getter, you might say. Call it showmanship.'

'Why?' Barry repeated.

'To further your education. Reality is, in every instance, in every moment of your life, what you wish it to be.'

'Mental hospitals must be full of people who believe that.'

'The mentally deranged, poor souls, have suffered loss or impairment of *angkur*.'

'Self-empowerment, you called it.'

Alexandra beamed. 'You *were* listening. If there is no organic brain damage, they can all be put right again, but physicians specially trained in this healing art are required, and few of them exist in the world today.'

'Why did you – your *double* just float away when I touched it?'

'That is the agreeable nature of a double – to serve, to do one's bidding unfailingly. *Tulpas*, however, are more complex. Not all of them are so accommodating. They take on a life of their own and can be reluctant to let go of it. I told you about my little monk.'

'Yes.'

'After he became lifelike, and to move around, and others became aware of him, he changed. He grew taller and thinner. His face assumed a diabolical character. He had a more commanding, sinister appearance. He began to leave my control, to rule my life. I rather felt, when he looked at me, that he intended doing away with me in order to achieve total independence.'

Barry suppressed a shudder. 'You were hallucinating.'

'Strictly speaking, hallucinations may not exist outside of the mind. Remember, others with no knowledge of his origins gave credence to my mind creature, passed the time of day with him, in all respects found him a most engaging fellow. So, to save my own life, I determined to dissolve the obstreperous phantom.'

'How did you do it?'

'My mind was stronger, better trained than his. Of course, being *of* my mind, he had psychic awareness of my decision, and I had to be quite devious in my strategies.'

'That's spooky.'

'I can tell you, it was a suspenseful and fatiguing few months before he vanished.'

'Vanished?'

'Poof. Solid one moment, the next gone as if he'd never been. I was forced to take to my bed for a number of days until I recovered from our duel of wits.'

'Reminds me of imaginary playmates,' Barry said thoughtfully.

Alexandra beamed. 'Childhood is rife with such creations. Fortunately the little *tulpas* are not imagined with sufficient strength to become apparent to others. And they do not

163

persevere as human children mature, become preoccupied with the demands of society and their coevals. It is interesting to speculate about what *might* happen if these phantom children grew to adulthood. Those *tulpas* I have heard of are totally without inhibition and have an unending appetite for power. They would, however, have to reproduce by mental parturition. It is one of the failings of *tulpas*. They are asexual creatures, as neuter as mules.'

'Here we are.' Barry stopped in front of the cottage on Kinbote estate. Alexandra got out with her cane, paused with a hand on the door of the Mercedes.

'I hope you'll forgive me for saying, but I sense a great deal of pain in your relationship with Mark.'

'You're wrong. It couldn't be better.'

'Good. My intuition, I presume, has begun to fail with age. He *is* what you've always wanted. Dreamed of.'

'Yes,' Barry said, meeting impassively the strong green eyes.

Alexandra smiled and nodded. 'I can't thank you enough. Until tomorrow night. I shall look forward to meeting your family.'

Barry drove away feeling, again, ambivalent toward Alexandra. The old woman was alternately infuriating and spell-binding. It was just about impossible to be cold or cutting with her. Alexandra merely smiled indomitably, gracious crinkles around her eyes, a song in her heart, and left Barry feeling like a pile of shit.

She was a witch, a philosopher, a mesmerist probably – that aspect of Alexandra Barry didn't take to at all, even though she had always accepted ghosts and associated phenomena. They were a part of her heritage and upbringing: her mother's no-nonsense attitudes about the world of faerie, her father's powerful, creative mind, his love of nature and the hidden, motivating forces of the world.

What bothered her, and would continue to be a problem, was Alexandra's ceaseless prying, her avid interest in Mark – frequently Barry was left dry in the mouth for answers, a defense of her feelings. She sighed. Face it. They were neighbors and, unavoidably, she was going to be seeing more of Alexandra.

At least Mark didn't seem to mind having her around.

TWENTY-SEVEN

THE MERCEDES was almost out of gas and was looking grungy. Barry drove the car to the Shell station where they did business and had it spruced up. When she returned home there was an unfamiliar sedan parked in the drive; she thought it probably belonged to Niels Finnstadter, who looked after their orchards, or the farmer who leased acreage from them.

'Dal's home,' Mrs Aldrich said when Barry walked into the kitchen.

'He is! When did he get here?'

'Half hour ago – right after you left. I hope I can stretch the green beans.'

Dal came into the kitchen through the laundry room, walking gimpily, wearing unpressed clothing and a Greek fisherman's cap. He had a straggly beard along the jawline. His eyes looked as if they were about to bleed. His lips were white, and the end of his nose raw from the Med sun. His hands trembled. She ran to him, but he stopped her with the forbidding intensity of his stare before she could embrace him.

'Hey, how'd you get here?' she asked joyously.

'Olympic from Athens. Barry, I need to talk to you. Right now.'

'Sure! What's the matter? You look – is Dad –'

Dal jerked his head toward the studio. 'He's inside.'

'He's okay, isn't he?'

'See what you think. My God, kid – why didn't you call me sooner?'

Scared, the skin of her face shrinking tight, Barry ran by

him to the studio.

'Dad!'

He was standing by the window wall, some sketches in one hanging hand, when she burst in. The immensity of light in the studio blanched and dwarfed him. Barry ran to her father and Dal followed.

Tom moved only after she touched him pleadingly, but it was a scant erratic sort of action, the residue of momentum in a discarded windup toy. There was a muscular twitch in one desiccated cheek, giving him a jumpy unmeant smile. He held up the batch of sketches.

'This was my idea,' he said in a voice without shading or emphasis; yet it built up a mountain of apprehension in her breast.

'I don't understand either of you! What's going on?'

Dal steered her away, in the direction of the easels on which Mark had left various pieces of work unfinished. He pointed to the full figure of Barry in oil.

'Is Mark painting that?'

'Yes. Isn't he good? Dal, you have no idea how hard he's been –'

'You posed nude for him?'

'What does it look like? Is there anything wrong with life studies?'

Dal laughed derisively and said, 'What else are you doing with him?'

'Don't you dare ask me a question like that!' Then, hands on hips, she answered it. 'What do I do with Mark? Anything I want, Dal. I'm not a child. And I don't meddle in *your* life.'

'This isn't meddling, Barry. Something very serious is happening here. What about the landscape?'

'It's marvelous! I'd like to see *you* do something that good.' She didn't care by then what kind of wounds she left in Dal.

Tom, behind them, said, 'The landscape isn't Mark's.'

Barry whirled, astonished. 'Dad! I've watched him working on it.'

'That's not the point,' Dal said with a hissing intake of

167

breath. 'Just listen to what Dad is saying.'

Barry backed away from both of them. Tom followed her with the sketches, holding them out, his eyes tired and dull.

'The painting, the idea of the painting, is mine. I conceived it almost two years ago. He stole it from me.'

Barry glared in disbelief, then took the sketches from her father.

Most of them had been rendered in watercolor, and they were, as he had said, ideas, austere jottings, the shorthand that preserved a glimpse, insight, or emotion that might someday evolve into a major painting. Barry had looked at these dashings of her father's all of her life; she knew his methods well. She looked up now at the landscape that Mark had made. Yes, there were common elements, a certain elegance of line, although one could not have guessed from the sketches how the finished painting might have looked. That was always a result of experience, intuition, exploration, the illuminating flash of genius that sometimes occurred and sometimes didn't.

'But – what if he did see these? If *I* saw them I couldn't make a painting from them – any more than I could make a cow from a cow's udder. Mark's done a fantastic –'

'Barry,' Tom said, 'the painting on that easel is exactly what flashed through my mind when I first saw that cracked jar in a field; I saw it whole for an instant and then I put it out of my mind – deliberately, after drawing just a few lines the way I always do, as a reference. Then I tossed the idea into that cupboard in the back of my mind and purposely didn't look at it again for a long time. Mark couldn't have seen those later sketches because they'd been locked in a cabinet drawer. For months. But there's the painting, the exact painting I would have done!'

This rush of explanation seemed to leave him ill and faint. He sat down, mouth ajar, and leaned back in a low collapsible deck chair, slanting out of the light and into the shadow of a cabinet, turning as black as if he were charred: a consumed, dead thing.

'It's uncanny, all right,' Barry said with a worried look at her father. 'But just what is everybody accusing him of? Where *is* Mark?'

'I told him it would be a good idea if he fed the chickens,' Dal said.

'Well, I want him here! This isn't fair. Mark and I know how hard he worked to do that landscape! A couple of hundred hours to get it right! And he didn't *steal* a damn thing – I watched him work it up from scratch. He happens to be a tremendously gifted–'

'But where is the talent coming from, Barry?' her brother demanded.

'How should I know? If I did I'd go get myself some.'

'He couldn't paint a lick when I left here two and a half months ago.'

'He learns very fast.'

'Barry, it's just impossible! I started formal training when I was fourteen years old! Dad worked for *twenty years* to be able to do a painting as accomplished as that landscape.'

'Mozart –'

'Musical prodigies and freaks are irrelevant – it's another discipline entirely. There aren't any teenage geniuses in the art biz. That landscape isn't just technically good, it's phenomenal! It's Thomas Brennan at the top of his form, painted with all of his talent –'

'A talent I don't have anymore,' Tom said, his voice sliding high from emotion. 'He's taken it all away from me.'

'This is ridiculous! You two killed a bottle before I got home. Admit it, now.'

'No, Barry,' Dal said. 'We're sober and we're scared. Because we're artists, and neither of us understands how a painting like that can exist, out of nowhere.'

Barry looked at the father and brother whom she loved and felt a surge of contempt. And she also felt a real paddywhack coming on, the falling-down, foaming-at-the-mouth kind that had so terrified them all when she was younger. It would serve them right. But it would also have been a negation of the maturity she had proclaimed to Dal, and it wouldn't help make right a ludicrous, evil situation.

She knew what to do. What to say. Barry banned all emotion. She smiled.

'Well, I can explain.'

'Can you?' Dal asked wearily.

'These paintings didn't come out of nowhere. Mark *is* an artist, and he's always been an artist. He's always had enormous talent. His parents were artists. They saw his potential, so they made him work very hard. He – he never went to school. He wasn't allowed to have friends. He hated the discipline but he was afraid to fail. His father – would beat him.'

Tom's head came up slowly.

'How do you know this, Barry?'

'Mark remembers more about himself than he wants to tell anybody. That's his privilege, isn't it?'

'His parents are artists?' Dal said. 'Draven? I never heard of –'

'*Were* artists. They were killed in an accident, in Europe. An avalanche in the Swiss Alps. A whole village was buried. Terrible. And Draven isn't his family name – it was his grandmother's maiden name. Mark adored his grandmother. But she's dead now too. His past is really painful. He trusts me not to talk about it. I just can't say any more.'

Tom looked at the splendid landscape, his sense of outrage dimmed.

Dal said reluctantly, 'Barry – it doesn't explain enough. How could he have changed so much in just a few –'

'I don't want to hear any more! I've told you the truth!'

Then the emotions she had so resolutely placed under control burst through her facade of calm and reason.

'You two are going to ruin everything!' she said, sobbing bitterly. And she stalked out of the studio.

She found Mark in the barn hunkered down in a long reach of sunlight, sketching a bantam cock. He put down his materials and the cock went crazy-stepping away at Barry's stony approach.

She wiped one eye with the heel of her hand and threw herself down in a pile of fragrant straw near Mark.

'They don't want me here,' he said.

'I don't care! They have no right to act this way. I know my
dad hasn't been feeling so hot, but this afternoon he was
carrying on like he'd lost his marbles.' She rolled toward
him. 'Mark, I told them a story about you getting some of
your memory back.'

'Why?'

'I had to. They forced me. And it was the right thing to do.
They feel just a little better about you now, believe me.'

'What did you say?' he asked with a slight perplexed smile.

Barry told him about his abusive parents, his instinctive
desire to adopt his grandmother's maiden name as his own.

'I know it's all bullshit, but Mark, please, *you need a story
now*. I'm still thinking up parts, but here's what I've got so
far. You came to this country last year, you were hitchhiking
across the U.S., you fell in with two guys in a van who gave
you some kind of drug that had a terrible effect on your
system. They stole your clothes, money, passport –
everything. The drug wiped out your memory, and you still
can't recall very much about your life. Just some of the rough
times you've had.'

'Why do I need to say this?'

'For my dad's sake. So Dal will stop being so suspicious.'

Barry sat cross-legged and began picking filaments of hay
out of her hair, eyeing him lugubriously. There were times
when he could be very still and inscrutable, and after a while it
never failed to bother her.

'Do you feel better?' Mark asked quietly.

'It doesn't matter to me! I've told you over and over, I
don't need to know who you were, I only care about who you
are. I love you, Mark. And I love Tuatha de Dannan and my
family, and I want us all to be happy here. I want you to be a
part of it.'

Mark nodded. 'That's what I want.' But he sighed and
picked at chalk beneath his nails. 'I'll tell them what you
want me to. But it won't help. Dal just doesn't like me. He
never has. It was better with him away. I'm sorry he came
back.'

'Oh, he's crazy jealous. That's his problem. Don't worry. For now I just want to smooth things over. Maybe if we find you another place to paint, they'll calm down. The gristmill has good light.'

Mark didn't say anything.

Barry rose and dusted herself off and put her arms around him. 'Guess we'd better go face the music. Don't worry.'

'I'm not.' Mark knew she wanted to be kissed; he pressed his lips against hers. Arm in arm they walked slowly out of the barn and to the house.

Dinner was a tense affair – very nearly unpleasant. Dal was eating when they got there, as if he planned to make short work of his meal. There was a glass of whiskey at his place. Tom sat in his chair at the head of the table looking famished, but food didn't interest him. Neither did conversation.

Barry, on the upbeat, said to her brother, 'You didn't tell me. How was Greece?'

'Hot.'

'And a wall fell on you.'

'Uh-huh.'

'Didn't improve your looks.'

Dal's fork scraped his plate unnervingly. 'Is that supposed to be funny?'

'Hey, Dal, give us a break?'

Dal gulped some of his whiskey, which made him sweat. He glanced at Mark, who was eating and looking troubled. Their eyes met.

Mark said evenly, 'I want to be your friend, Dal.'

'You can be.'

'How?'

Dal dropped his napkin on the table beside his plate, pushed his chair back.

'Since Dad isn't in a proper frame of mind to make decisions for the family –'

'No, Dal,' Barry said warningly, 'don't keep this up.' Out of the corner of her eye she saw Mrs Aldrich just beyond the doorway to the kitchen, raptly attentive.

172

'I'll have to assume the responsibility,' Dal concluded, ignoring his sister. 'Let's just get this over with. Mark, I don't think it's in the best interests of this family that you stay on here.'

'Dal, you shit!'

'Shut up, Barry. Or go upstairs to your room while we discuss –'

'Who do you think you're talking –'

'Barry,' Mark said, 'don't fight with your brother.'

'Look,' Dal said, sensing cooperation, 'I don't want to be unreasonable. You had a tough time for a while, we were accommodating, and I'm not trying to throw you out on your ear. Take a week or so to make plans. We'll help. I can lend you money –'

'If Mark goes I'm going with him!'

Mark turned to Tom Brennan, who had sat listening with his head bowed.

'What do you say, Tom?'

Tom didn't look at him. 'I don't want you in my studio anymore.'

Mark accepted the edict with no change of expression. 'I love to paint,' he said, but his petition met with indifference. 'All I want is to be as great as you are.'

Then everybody was silent, including Barry, whose eyes brimmed with furious tears. Mark got up slowly from the table. The sunset light that filled the room was as thick as marmalade. The ceiling in the dining room was low and coffered. Its lowness accentuated Mark's size. By contrast Dal seemed slight, carelessly made in his chair across the trestle table.

'I want to think about what you said,' Mark told Dal. 'I'll go for a walk now.'

Barry started to rise; he put out his hand. 'No. Don't come, Barry.' Then Mark went quickly out through the kitchen with a slight shrug and a glance at Mrs Aldrich. She gave him a tight-lipped smile. Barry heard him whistling up Meanness in the backyard.

Mrs Aldrich came in with helpings of strawberries and ice

cream.

'All I can say is, that is one of the sweetest boys I've ever known in my life.'

Dal lighted a cigarette and shot smoke through his nose. Tom took his pipe from a pocket on one sleeve of his cardigan sweater. Barry got up without excusing herself and walked into the kitchen, stood looking out the screen door as Mark, accompanied by the hound, moved briskly downhill in the direction of the pond, flickering through peaceful lighted glades, losing definition among trees already gone dark except where the tips of leaves, stirring mildly in the twilight, exploded like powderflash. The pink dogwood outside the kitchen windows, the last thing the sun glorified as it set, was of a hue and richness that caused her eyes to ache.

'Barry?' Dal called from the dining room.

She shook off the sound of his voice like a horse twitching away a fly.

TWENTY-EIGHT

'MEAN, WHERE would I go?'

By the black pond, where a collapsing bank had thrown a willow half into the water, he had walked up the supple overarching trunk, barely wider than his foot to begin with, tapering to a wand that dipped almost subsurface at the cautious offering of his weight. It was an act of precision, of exquisite balance that he maintained almost effortlessly, the whole of the withering tree asway at his will, with each slow breath. Bats flew in charmed parabolas from greater heights, fish jumped silkenly from the musty depths, cicadas illuminated the inner ear. The bloodhound had the scent of muskrat in the marshland but found the mud a chore and slunk round again to the sound of Mark's voice, a rising eye as rosy as the moon. Meanness flapped his head and chewed ecstatically at a fleabitten ear.

'I have to stay,' Mark reasoned, looking at the house on the knoll, where a figure appeared now and then at an upstairs window, indistinct but swarming with life, like a fleck of embryo in the warm yolk of an egg. It was Barry, of course.

'I have to paint,' Mark said, momentarily forlorn. 'But Dal's a shit.' He looked up abruptly, risking his balance, filling his eyes with the passage of stars. His body, bent, wavering slightly, seemed fatally crippled then, as if he were suspended from an invisible gallows. The spacious act of breathing revived him. He gathered himself and came in a twinkling, a lanky run down the tree trunk to land with a plop beside the aging hound.

'You're my dog, my dog, my good dog,' he crooned, giving

Meanness an affectionate drubbing behind the ears. 'You want me to stay, don't you? So does Barry. It's my home. So if I stay, Mean –'

He held the dog's face close to his, pinned by the ears, and looked him in the eye. He made, in his throat, a low warlike growl that caused Meanness to twitch and try to back away from him.

Mark laughed and released the hound, laughed at the freedom he felt, luxuriating in the security he had provided himself by arriving at a fair solution to the dilemma.

'If I stay, then *they'll* have to go.'

TWENTY-NINE

BARRY WOULD have canceled their Saturday night dinner
plans, but Tom woke up the next morning saying he felt
better than he had in weeks. He ate some breakfast and
showed no inclination to lie abed until noon. He told Barry
that he was looking forward to having some company for a
change.

He was even conciliatory toward Mark, who obviously
didn't hold a grudge and indeed seemed to have forgotten all
of the unpleasantness at the table the night before. The two
of them worked, before the sun rose too high, in the garden.
Barry went over the menu for dinner with Mrs Aldrich and
her cousin, a big husky woman in her seventies with an
obscure biblical name from the lengthy roll call of Genesis;
everybody just called her Aunt Sparky. She was a swift
worker, but jerky from an arthritic hip.

Dal disappeared early into his studio with a portfolio of
watercolors and line drawings he'd done in the Mediterranean and which he wasn't ready to share with anyone,
including Tom. Just as well he chose to lie low. Barry felt
sore as a boil whenever she caught a glimpse of her brother.
But she realized the wisdom of temporarily avoiding a nasty
set-to. Mark had been given, rather autocratically, a grace
period, and all the nonsense (Barry's interpretation) might
well dissipate once Dal settled in and concentrated on his
own work. There was peace and quiet again, time to enjoy
life – they had another pretty day of dappled clouds and
sweet breezes, although rain was forecast by nightfall.

A search through her wardrobe convinced Barry that she
had nothing suitable to wear, and her hair was too long and

frowzy at the tips. She drove down to the big shopping centers in White Plains, had a wash, cut, and set at Bloomie's, bought a hostess skirt and a new pair of gold shoes at Charles Jourdan to go with it.

Midafternoon she arrived home. Mark was sprawled in a big hammock strung between oak trees with Meanness in the shade beneath. She leaned over and kissed Mark and glanced at the book that lay open on his chest. A biography of Mary Shelley.

'Had my hair done,' she said, showing off her stylish tresses.

'Um-hm.'

'What did you and Dad talk about while I was gone?'

'The garden.'

'Didn't he say he was sorry or anything?'

'Should he?'

'Well – it's all Dal's fault, really. But I don't want to get started again.' She gave him a fresh kiss – an ear this time.

'Tickles,' Mark said amiably. He was glad to see her. He loved the attention. He held her hand.

'I could eat you up,' Barry said, and she clicked her front teeth rapidly at him. She felt more than a little steamy. Under the hair dryer she had dreamed of Mark, buying shoes she had seen him in every passing pair of strong shoulders and trim hips. His shirt was open; his thick hair curled against her lips. She sighed.

'Do you want to make love?' he asked, recognizing all the signs.

Barry straightened and looked tenderly at him. It was what she called it and it was the rite they performed. Mark participating to the best of his abilities, but still too much was lacking. Not his heart, she was sure of that, nor his soul. Otherwise she couldn't have been with him at all – it would have been, ultimately, humiliating and demeaning, despite her passion. She did get a lot out of their lovemaking, Barry had to admit. She only wished there could be more. While remaining hopeful that any day –

'Later. I'd better see that Mrs Aldrich and Sparky have

everything they need. Let's see, did I call the bartender? Yes. Flowers, flowers—'

'They came.'

'Good.'

'How many will there be for dinner?'

'Oh, a dozen, not counting us. Not a big crowd.'

Mark looked relieved. He was basically shy and didn't care at all for crowds of strangers; he didn't even like sitting in a row with anyone else at the movies.

'Maybe you'd better try on that blazer we bought,' Barry said. 'You may have gotten bigger with all the weights.'

'Okay.'

'Oh, and why don't you drive over and pick up Alexandra for me? I won't have time. I'll tell you how to find her.'

By seven o'clock black clouds had moved in. The light was dusky and the air storm-heavy. The trees on the property had begun to show the pale undersides of their leaves in anticipation of a big rain. Barry was occupied with last-minute details – setting out place cards, lighting tapers on the round tables for six that had replaced the trestle table in the dining room, removing a chipped goblet no one else had noticed, chilling white wine, and letting the youngest of the red Bordeauxes breathe. She coaxed her father into changing jackets, borrowing one of Dal's because his own hung on him, emphasizing his recent loss of weight. Tom did have some color from his exertions in the garden, and he was bright-eyed in anticipation of good conservation with old friends.

The first guests to arrive, by limousine from Manhattan, were Les Mergendoller and the Broadway actress he'd been squiring around, and Dal's date, a Eurasian girl named Tepei, who wore a clinging jade-green dress. Tepei had warm oaken eyes, skin like a saucer of cream with two drops of coffee added, nutmeg hair so thick and luxurious she must have had to currycomb it. Barry had earlier spent two and a half hours dressing and felt, by comparison, as if she were wearing the kind of stuff that came in packing crates.

Les was a big shambling man with fat features and twinkly

179

little spectacles. His actress was named Stacey; she was one of those dieting women who seemed to be all cheekbones and brightly frosted, famished mouths. She was currently unemployed and had just returned from three weeks in Barbados, where she had baked herself the color of a Virginia honey-glazed ham. Her eyes opened wide in wonderment when she took in all of Mark, and she spent the rest of the evening auditioning for him. Barry felt that she could afford to be good-natured about the intended trespass.

Claude and Millicent Copperwell arrived with the first raindrops; Mark ducked out for Alexandra and returned in a smoking downpour.

Alexandra had with her a package wrapped in what looked like paper bags she'd saved from the supermarket. She presented her gift to Tom and Barry, which Barry unwrapped and then almost dropped in surprise and apprehension.

'Careful, Barry,' Tom said, getting his hands on the heavy leather casket. Together they placed it on a table in the family room. Barry was certain it was the same casket she had seen earlier in the week under the arm of Alexandra's double.

'It's gorgeous,' Stacey said breathily. 'It must be very old.'

'Perhaps a thousand years old,' Alexandra affirmed. 'It was the property of a very rich monk and a substantial figure in the cabinet, the government of Tibet, whose house on the Lingkor Road contained many such treasures. Unfortunately only a few of them survived the last rape of the Chinese.'

'Priceless,' Les said, licking his lips. Dal and Tepei were transfixed.

'Can you read these inscriptions?' Dal asked her. Tepei was multilingual.

'No. I have no idea what language it is.'

'Sanskrit,' Alexandra informed them.

'We can't accept this,' Tom protested.

'But you must! I have many things, and nothing would give me greater pleasure than to know how often this casket will be seen and appreciated by your friends, people of taste and discernment.'

'Will you open it?'

Barry was a little shaky, but the lock, though old, accepted the key easily and worked at once. The lid of the casket clicked open. Inside there was nubby orange silk, two long objects wrapped in a parchmentlike paper, which also was heavily inscribed in Sanskrit.

'What are they?'

Alexandra obligingly unwrapped the ceremonial bronze daggers for her. But she was careful not to separate them entirely from the paper.

'Ohhhh!' Stacey sighed.

'They are called *phurbu*–ritual weapons of sorcery.'

'Look at that workmanship!' Les said, frankly lusting. 'I've never seen anything to match them–maybe some odds and ends at Topkapi or the Cairo Museum.'

'There is a most interesting story about these particular daggers.'

Alexandra looked around at their faces slowly, already knowing she had their full attention. Her eyes lingered on Mark, who smiled encouragingly.

'They belonged to a Grand Lama famous for his magic who used them often in his rites. In this way they acquired considerable power, they became possessed – just as humans, animate creatures may be possessed. When the lama passed on, the weapons remained in the monastery, but without his influence to guide them they became, shall we say, pesky. They began to float around in the air by themselves, interrupting prayers, creating havoc. A monk who encountered one of the floating *phurbu* was attacked and died of his wounds. The entire assembly was in terror. Prayers were conceived to invoke the spirit of the Grand Lama and they gathered, huddled together, for three days and nights around the banner of benediction in the courtyard, having abandoned the interior of the monastery to the frightful *phurbu*.

'At last there arose from the monastery a terrific racket, a howling as of demons provoked. They shook and prayed louder. In the morning, at first light, the bravest of them crept inside to see what had happened. He found the *phurbu* wrapped tightly in the paper you see there, on which the spirit of the Grand Lama had written charms that rendered the daggers forever harmless. But who knows what might happen, even today, if they should become separated from the parchment?'

The steady drone of rain had lulled them all, along with the sound of Alexandra's voice. At a crackling bolt of lightning nearby they all jumped, and laughed edgily.

Alexandra, not looking up, her lips moving slightly as if she were reciting a brief, arcane ritual, wrapped the *phurbu* again in the old, decaying paper. The bartender offered drinks. Barry looked again at the daggers. Only a little bronze showed as Alexandra closed the lid of the casket on them.

'Hundreds of years have gone by,' she said with a shrug and a fatalistic look at the guests. 'It isn't likely that the *phurbu* have any wanderlust or wrong intentions. But perhaps you can't be too careful. Yes, just a little white wine, thank you.'

'Alexandra,' Tom said, 'this is too kind of you. The story would have been gift enough.'

'Wouldn't it be terrific if it was true?' Barry said cynically in an aside to Mark, and he squeezed her elbow, looking amused.

'Hey, I like her. She's fun.'

Barry had placed Mark as far from Dal as she could, seating him next to Alexandra, so there would be someone he knew at the table. She had made the mistake of also seating Les and Stacey, of Broadway fame, at the same table. Oh, well. Barry sat with her father, the Tad Kameos (he had been an early ardent collector and booster of the artist's reputation, and still continued to buy everything by Tom he could get his hands on), and a sculptor named Harry Ott Frankel, a friend of her father's whom she detested. Frankel was about sixty, a squirt of a man who dyed his hair crow

182

black, greased it away from his forehead, and wore dark glasses day and night, perhaps because he was careless with his arc welder. He looked, from a distance, as if he had stepped out of one of those gritty fifties flicks about high school delinquents. *Rock Around the Blackboard Jungle*. He liked tough talk, too, and never spared the sensibilities of the company he was keeping. He said 'fucken' a lot. Women were 'cunts'. And so on. He created, for huge prices, behemoth structures commissioned by the architects of ritzy office building plazas.

Frankel's wife was named Estelle. She was his age, but unlike Harry Ott she certainly showed it. Carelessly kept hair, the strands equally divided between white and black, a nose that looked as if it had been shaped with a hammer, a hairy wart or two, a shapeless body in the only dress Barry had ever seen her wear, a not-quite-in-season cotton print with big blue dahlias all over it. She was never bidden to open her mouth. When Frankel wasn't ignoring her, he was critical, in his irritating, side-of-the-mouth manner. They had been together twenty-five years. Barry had heard that once upon a time Estelle had drawn a bead down a hallway of their home with a Fox .410 and had just about blown the seat of her husband's pants away. She hoped the rumor was true, while deploring Estelle's lack of aim.

Chalyce Kameo, who sat at Barry's left hand, took a break from art biz gossip and said, 'Is Mrs Prye going to tell fortunes for us tonight?'

'I'm afraid not. Mrs Prye, uh, had sort of a breakdown.'

'Oh, dear. Can she be fixed?'

'I don't think so.'

Chalyce leaned a little closer. Her blued hair was intricately whorled and looked as hard as glazed ceramic.

'Tom just doesn't look well at all.'

'He's a lot better than he was.'

'Is he working?'

'He will be soon.'

'Your young man is delightful. Is he the one who—'

'He's the one.'

183

'You'd just never know what a trauma he's been through. He said something about being a painter.'

'He's a whiz, but not ready yet.'

'Oh. Well, you know how interested Tad and I would be in seeing the work of one of Tom's protégés.'

'I'll tell Mark. He'll really be excited.'

Barry glanced at Mark. She felt heady from wine and the pleasure of a candleglow evening that had been, so far, without a hitch – excellent food prepared by Mrs Aldrich and good company except for Harry Ott Frankel, whose only virtue as far as Barry was concerned was his tendency to mumble; half the time you couldn't understand what he was saying. Her father seemed to be holding up pretty well, although he became more of a listener than a talker as dinner progressed. Dal, absorbed in the cultured and beautiful Tepei, was behaving himself. Outside the dining room the rain fell on the terrace without letup, a pleasant silvery backdrop. She envisioned Mark famous, celebrated for his talent and his portraits of his favourite subject, who happened to be Mrs Mark Draven. Barry was having a lovely time.

The party ended early, around eleven o'clock. Mark brought the Volvo around in the rain to the front door and Barry, holding an umbrella, took Alexandra out to the car.

'I feel so badly, putting you to all this trouble.'

'Mark doesn't mind driving you home.'

Mark got out, came around to help Alexandra into the front seat. Alexandra seemed to suffer a chill as she was about to step inside. She trembled and dropped her purse. It spilled open at her feet; some things from the purse rolled underneath the Volvo.

'Oh, how stupid!'

'Let me help you,' Barry said; she was mildly exasperated. They were all getting soaked. 'Mark, there's a flashlight in the glove compartment.'

She let Alexandra hold the umbrella and stooped to retrieve the purse, a comb, a pair of reading glasses. Mark leaned inside the Volvo, left hand braced against the door frame, and opened the glove box. He handed the flashlight back to Barry, who turned the beam on the driveway beneath the car. Mark stood beside the open door, hand still on the door frame.

'Is that everything?' Barry asked Alexandra, making another sweep with the light.

'My gold atomizer's missing.' Alexandra tried to check her purse and hold the umbrella at the same time.

'I think I –' Barry started to say. She reached under the Volvo.

'Need help, Barry?' Mark asked.

The moment his attention was diverted Alexandra moved decisively, shutting, with all of her strength, the door on Mark's left hand.

Mark let out a scream. Barry leapt up, casting the flashlight beam on him. She saw at once what had happened. Alexandra was paralyzed. Barry forced her out of the way and opened the car door. Mark snatched his bloody hand away, pressed it beneath his other arm, and sank to his knees. Dal came running out of the house, followed by Tepei and Tom and those guests who had remained for a nightcap.

Barry was on her knees too, holding Mark, who was crying in agony.

'Oh, my God,' Barry said. 'Mark, let me see.'

He slowly revealed enough of his left hand to the flashlight's beam so that they could all see the little finger had been severed.

'It's my fault,' Alexandra said. 'I don't know how it happened–I'm so sorry–'

Dal took the flashlight from Barry and looked inside the car. Tom and Barry got Mark to his feet. Alexandra just stood there, mouth open, looking petrified. Dal found the cut-off finger and wrapped it gingerly in his pocket handkerchief.

They helped Mark inside to Tom's study and sat him down. He was gray and gasping.

Tepei assumed control of the situation. 'Barry, can you

find some clean gauze pads?' Tepei said. 'And bring hot water.'

'Tepei, what do I do with this?' Dal asked, showing her the wrapped finger in the bloody handkerchief.

'I think a surgeon can restore it. Put it on ice right away.'

'You do it. I'll call the hospital so they'll be ready for him when we bring him in.'

Tom was left alone with Mark, who sat, drenched and moaning and shivering, in Tom's favorite chair. Mark's eyes were open but he wasn't focusing on anything. Tom's nerves were bad. He poured whiskey for himself and whiskey for Mark.

'Mark, drink this. It'll help the pain.'

Mark looked up slowly, teeth chattering. He looked so hurt and devastated that Tom felt a rare moment of empathy for him.

He was so unprepared for the rage that flooded into the boy's eyes that he couldn't react at all when Mark, finding strength from his pain, bolted up from the chair and struck him brutally in the face on his way to the door.

In the kitchen Barry watched numbly as Dal and Tepei packed Mark's finger in a small lidless Tupperware bowl packed with ice. The finger, Saran-Wrapped, was blood dark and ragged at one end. She looked quickly away, thinking, *left hand, left hand*. Mark was ambidextrous, but he usually painted with his right.

Alexandra appeared in the kitchen doorway, pale and bedraggled. She looked at Barry, groped for a chair, and sat down.

'He's gone,' she said.

'*What?*'

'Mark. I saw him running out of the house.' She gestured vaguely. 'That way. Into the woods.'

Tom was sitting on the floor of his den when Barry and Dal got there. He looked dazed. There was a little blood at one corner of his mouth where a tooth had cut when Mark hit him.

'I don't know what happened,' he said. 'He just got up and

ran out. Hit me as he was going by.'

'But where did he go?' Barry cried. 'He'll bleed to death!'

Tepei, who had some nursing experience, pointed out that there was little chance of exsanguination, but shock might set in and leave Mark helpless in the rain. They had to find him.

'Shouldn't we call the police?' Tepei said.

'Saturday night,' Dal replied. 'They're spread thin. Might take them half an hour to get one man out here.'

Millicent Copperwell volunteered to drive Alexandra home. Mrs Aldrich's husband had shown up to drive her home and offered to help look for Mark. Tom insisted on going out too. The searchers divided into two groups. Barry went with her father and Ethan Aldrich; Claude Copperwell teamed up with Dal and Tepei.

Barry had let Meanness out about ten thirty to do his business; now he was nowhere around, though she called and called. The rain had begun to slacken, but it was dark and dangerous in the woods. The groups went separate ways. For a while each group heard the other calling for Mark, but there wasn't a trace of him.

Dal, Tepei, and Claude Copperwell reached the gristmill first and went inside. Dal flashed the light around. Since being banned from Tom's studio, Mark had moved his incomplete paintings and materials to a corner of the mill.

Tepei's fingers dug into Dal's arm. 'Look over there. What's that?'

Dal angled his flashlight toward an easel, the portrait of Barry taking shape. Mark had been working on it recently; there was a gleam of fresh paint like drying blood. Barry had changed in the portrait. Her pose was lewd, cynical, a flaunting of her nakedness. Her eyes had a demonic opaqueness; there was a brutish look around the mouth.

'Is that Barry?' Claude asked.

'Why does he make her look like that?' Tepei said.

Dal shook his head, feeling short of breath, oppressed by the distortion of everything he knew his sister to be. He no longer felt even a little sorry for the injured boy they were

187

hunting.

'I don't know. I don't know anything about Mark Draven. I just want him out of here, and for good.'

THIRTY

ALEXANDRA, WEARING her saffron yellow robe, opened a small aluminum ladder and stepped up on it to cover the cages of her parakeets for the night. She had turned off the lamps in her cottage; only the incense brazier nearby provided illumination. It was enough. She did not need light to sit on the floor and meditate, and her mind's eye was all-encompassing: it burned with anticipation.

Perhaps an hour after she composed herself and became so still one would have thought she had ceased to breathe, she heard a subtle increase in the loudness of the rain outside as a door opened soundlessly, then closed. There was a footstep. She didn't move, and the sounds of entry were not repeated.

After a time she turned her head slightly, toward the kitchen, as if in response to an unspoken query.

'Yes, I know you're here. I've been expecting you. Show yourself.'

Mark Draven appeared, his eyes, his wet face taking on highlights from the gleam of the brazier. The rest of him was murky, shadowed, mud encrusted. His left arm was across his chest, the hand out of sight beneath his sodden blazer. His eyes were inflamed. He stared at the lama.

'Why did you hurt me?'

'There was no other way to prove what you are, where you came from.'

'What do you mean? What do you know about me?'

'I know that you live and breathe, you have human appetites. You are a nearly perfect work of art. Barry's work.' He shifted his weight, as if to dodge a blow; the floor

189

creaked. Alexandra continued calmly. 'She created you in a moment of supreme tension from the chaos that surrounds us all. We all struggle daily to control this chaos with our minds, the force of our wills. But Barry's abilities are of a higher order than most.'

He came closer in two strides, knelt down. He trembled.

'I'm flesh and blood! You hurt me – my hand –'

'Let us see your hand.'

It was a simple suggestion, but he bared his teeth. He wanted to look away then but Alexandra's green eyes held his attention, as if she had him at the point of a spear. He twisted in pain, aching to deny the truth of what she had said. But the truth was taking possession of him. He was in torment; he was in ecstasy. Suddenly he pulled his left hand from beneath the coat and held it high. The hand was intact, undamaged.

Alexandra didn't even look at it. She nodded slightly, and he screamed. It was a haunting scream that was only vaguely human. It became, in the end, a howl of pure pleasure. Alexandra could not subdue a tremor of fear, and she felt her strength, inevitably, lessening.

'You have fulfilled all of Barry's expectations except two: you have no soul and no conscience. Therefore you must be denied the life you cling to with such passion. Before you destroy that family.'

He made a fist of his restored left hand. It trembled with power above her head.

'Can you stop me?' Draven said. 'Can you dissolve me, like you did your phantom monk?'

'I'm no longer young. I haven't the stamina. But they are all under my protection now. Barry, her father, Dal.'

'Your magic,' he said scornfully.

'It will do.'

'Go to the house. Bring the casket back.'

'I will not,' she said, aware of the fist but refusing to look anywhere other than into his eyes.

'Then don't interfere with me. Go away.'

'I must try to help them.'

'I won't give up my life! And no one can take it away. Who has to know what you say or what you think?'

He reeked of confidence, of animal cunning. Alexandra smiled slightly, but she felt another tremor. She continued to oppose him with all of her serenity and her power. But the realization was there, stark as bone: it was not, in this instance, enough. She had overmatched herself.

Draven reached down, he reached out. His right hand brushed her cheek, leaving a trace of mud there. Alexandra steeled herself and tried to force him back with the power of her mind. He hesitated, teeth clenched, breathing harshly. She felt a giving, a moment's uncertainty on his part. But she was fading, hovering at the edge of a misty blackness, unable to assert full control.

One of his large hands went to her shoulder, the other to the back of her head. Her mind seethed and then flared like a dying star. He saw the light flicker from her eyes and yelled in triumph, at the same time giving her head a sharp jerk. There was a snap – her body seemed to leap an inch or two off the floor. Blood trickled from her nose, her head continued to turn loosely almost a full half-circle.

He sat there holding her for a few seconds more, puzzled that it had happened so simply. His enemy routed. He swallowed once and released her. Alexandra's shell fell back in silence, head glancing off a silk pillow, falling aslant. And silence, and silence. The body useless now, unable to renew itself as his had done. Draven picked himself up with a surge that carried him on a run from the cottage, back into the falling rain, the dark of night.

THIRTY-ONE

By ONE in the morning they had explored all possibilities. Dal
had finished calling every hospital in the area. Barry sat in
the kitchen of Tuatha de Dannan with glazed eyes, drinking
strong tea, at times almost nodding off from the shock of the
accident, Mark's inexplicable disappearance. The rain was
down to a drizzle. Tepei sat close to her, murmuring, trying
to coax her into going up to bed. Barry moved to the family
room and announced her intention of staying there, close to
the telephone. Dal yawned and pulled Tepei away, and they
went upstairs together.

The light of the single lamp in the room hurt Barry's eyes;
she turned it off. Rainwater dripped from a clogged gutter
above the front windows. Then the clouds thinned and the
moon shone forth, adding shadows to the room. The gold
hardware on the casket Alexandra had brought to them
gleamed in the nocturnal light.

It made Barry uneasy to look at the casket, to dwell on the
brace of enchanted daggers within. Omens and superstition.
The woman was nothing but a witch, Barry thought. All this
grief was *her* fault. Barry got up and shrouded the casket
with a newspaper, then returned to her rocking chair.

The clock in the upstairs hall struck two. *Mark, Mark,
where are you?* She dozed and dreamed he was walking on
his hands along the roof peak of the house. Then she started
awake, perspiring, her throat wet and cold. She had heard
something strange and listened tensely for the sound to be
repeated. But her ears were ringing faintly from tension, her
orientation was awry.

Scratch, scratch.

192

For a few moments she thought the sound was close by, in the room. Mice in the walls. But they'd had the exterminators there at the beginning of spring.

Scratch.

Like something nibbling or digging. Teeth, claws ...

Barry exhaled nervously and got up. It could only be Meanness, at the kitchen door; she decided that her perspective on the sound was distorted by her own fatigue, the silent house. The dog had been out for hours, she'd forgotten all about him. There were places outside where he could have found partial shelter from the downpour, but still, by now he must be one wet, miserable dog.

She started for the kitchen and noted in passing that the newspaper she'd covered the casket with was now on the floor. A strong draft would have done it. Barry had the urge to take up the casket and drop it in the well on the high side of the barnyard, but she knew her father would have a fit. And if Les Mergendoller were any judge, Alexandra's gift to them was exceptionally valuable.

Barry turned on the kitchen lights and opened the back door there. Meanness was not sitting on the stoop as she had expected. Maybe he'd been trying for some time to get in and had gone away to sulk.

Scratch, scratch, scratch!

Loud enough this time to make her jump and look around. A branch of a tree rubbing against the roof or a side of the house? But there wasn't a tree near enough. No, it was something *in* the walls, or even within a closed space like a pantry or closet, working tenaciously to get out.

Barry made a face, thinking of mice again. She drew a glass of water at the sink and drank it slowly. She couldn't help listening for the sound, her nerves tingling. But she didn't hear it again.

On impulse she went to her father's studio but found no sign that Mark had been there. Moonlight came through the high windows. She turned slowly and looked at the corner where Mrs Prye's machine was covered by a dropcloth. Shuddering, she walked slowly toward it.

'Please, Mrs Prye. Help me. I have to find Mark. Tell me where he is.'

She waited, her fists clenched. There was, momentarily, a faint glow beneath the dropcloth. But it vanished, and nothing else happened. Mrs Prye didn't speak.

'*Talk to me!* Why is this happening? Where has he gone? You know! You must know. You know everything about me!'

Scratch, scratch.

The sound was distant, but chilling. Barry whirled. Through the windows she saw the moon, the distant universe. And, closer, Meanness was clearly visible a hundred yards or so from the house, ambling uphill from the direction of the pond.

Forgetting the capricious Mrs Prye, she ran back to the kitchen and opened the door there, whistled sharply. Meanness soon appeared and squeezed past her into the kitchen. He cruised by his empty food dish and looked around at Barry in disappointment. She gave him a couple of Gaines-Burgers.

'Where have you *been*?' Meanness was almost completely dry. Just the toes of his big feet and the edges of his ears were muddy from his perambulations around the farm. His brindled coat glittered dustily in places. Barry stooped to pat him and examined the husks that clung to her hand. It was chaff, from the floor of the gristmill near the grinding wheel. But the mill was closed up tight – there was no way he could have gotten inside.

Unless someone had let him in.

'Mark!' she said, and went running from the kitchen into the yard.

THIRTY-TWO

DAL AND Tepei got up at eight thirty Sunday morning. After Dal showered and shaved, he went down the hall to Barry's room, which was halved in sunlight and empty. Her bed hadn't been disturbed. He left Tepei dressing leisurely, trying on this and that, with a humming and a quietness around her eyes, and took the back stairs to the kitchen.

Tom, in a ratty plaid robe, was making coffee. The back door was open to green things – turf and garden and faintly damp air from all the rain. Tom still looked half starved but also rested and collected. His cough was nearly absent. Dal noted the improvement with satisfaction. Meanness slumbered noisily on his braided rug, as if he'd spent a long night in carousal.

'Where's Barry?' Dal asked his father.

'Haven't seen her.'

Dal rubbed his pink shaved cheeks and poured coffee for himself. 'She's probably out looking for Mark.'

'Damn fool thing for him to do,' Tom reflected. 'Why run away like that?'

Tepei came down wearing an aquamarine silk blouse and striped St. Laurent pants, her long satin-finish hair brushed smartly over one side of her face. She sat at the kitchen table with her hands folded, eyes on Dal.

'Shouldn't we call Alexandra?' Tepei suggested. 'Barry could have gone to her house. There may be some news.'

Tepei had jotted down Alexandra's number the night before. She placed the call, but no one answered.

'Now what?' Dal said, scrambling eggs with diced onion and chunks of cheddar cheese.

'Well – the police,' Tepei said.

Dal thought about it and shook his head. 'What can they do? They'll come out, ask some questions, file a report, check the hospitals again.'

Tom took a long pull of coffee, leaning, like a light-deprived plant, where shuttered sun bent in at the windows.

'What about Edwards?'

'If Mark had gone to him,' Dal said, 'he would have called us right away. If he showed up *anywhere* we would have heard. But I can't believe he's lying unconscious in the woods, either. What happened to him was pretty damned awful, but it's not likely to be fatal.'

They ate their breakfasts. Tepei had to be in San Francisco by seven o'clock that night, so Dal drove her to Kennedy in his Mercedes to catch her flight. Coming back, traffic was heavy on the parkways; he arrived home a little before two.

No Barry. Tom hadn't seen her. He didn't appear concerned. He was back in his studio. Everything that was Mark's had gone. Tom had set up a panel he'd been working on before he was weakened by illness. He had mixed little cups of color from the big jars on his worktable. Tom's pipe was going, and he gave off waves of contentment and satisfaction as he trimmed some sable brushes with a razor blade.

There were no messages from Barry or messages concerning Mark on the service. Dal piled up the Sunday papers, carried them to his room with a large bottle of Grolsch beer. He turned on the television. The Yankees had a laugher going in the fourth at Toronto. He couldn't interest himself in the game or in a *Times* magazine article about the Mark Rothko retrospective at MOMA. Barry's absence nagged, then actively worried Dal. It wasn't her style just to go off and not tell anybody where she was.

He tuned out the baseball game and stretched, shoeless, across the bed, closing his eyes. He was still suffering from jet lag and hadn't slept all that well, despite the soothing presence of Tepei next to him, her bittersweet fastidious love-making. The knee that had been hurt in the Corfu quake was throbbing – he knew he'd better see an orthopedics man about it. And where the hell was Barry?

Scratch, scratch.

It began unobtrusively, but became annoying after a while. Dal could neither identify nor home in on the sound. Fingernails, claws, something digging away in or at the house.

Dal got up and drained the rest of the now-tepid beer. He didn't care for it that way, preferring his beer so well chilled it was ready to turn to ice. Right now it was midafternoon, and what he really craved was a dollop of Jameson's with a frosty-cold suds chaser.

He went down the back steps, and there was Barry in the kitchen, making sandwiches. She looked around in surprise.

'Hi, Dal!'

'Hi. What're you doing?' There was a brown bag on the butcher block counter next to her, and it was already bulging with goodies. One sandwich was done, the crusts neatly trimmed away, and she was spreading mayonnaise on another.

'Just fixing something to eat. I haven't eaten all day, I'm really hungry.'

Her blue jeans were dusted with chaff, there were husks in her tangled hair. She had dark brown smudges of ordeal, of sleeplessness, beneath her hazy eyes. Dal looked her over carefully in passing, opened the refrigerator door, and pulled out another beer, which he popped into the freezer.

'Where's Tepei?'

'On her way to Frisco. Magazine assignment. Missed you this morning, kid.'

'I went out early.'

'Worried about Mark?'

'Oh, God! I don't know what to think! What could have *happened* to him? I've looked everywhere.'

'Not like him not to get in touch with you.'

Barry sighed and slipped her sandwiches into Baggies, then packed them in the brown bag. There was a quart-size thermos bottle on a shelf beside the sink. She took it down and fumbled it badly as she was unscrewing the cap. Sometimes she was so inept he had to grin. But today her nerves, her air of suppressed frenzy, dug like a big barbed hook into the pit of his stomach.

'Get the milk for me, Dal?'

'Looks like you're having a picnic. Can I go?'

'Well, I'm – I just thought I'd go rowing, you know, by myself. I'm really depressed. I need to be alone. Maybe Meanness will go with me – he's outside somewhere.'

'Still pissed at me?'

'Yes. But I don't want to fight.'

'Me either.' Dal took a long look inside the refrigerator for the Tupperware bowl and the cut-off finger that had been packed in ice the night before. They were missing. He took a deep breath and closed the door. 'Here's the milk.'

'Thanks.' She spilled some of it as she was filling the thermos.

'Did you hear that?' Dal asked her.

Barry turned her head sharply. 'No. What do you mean? Oh – that scratching noise. I *did* hear it, late last night. It gave me the creeps.'

'Where's Mark, Barry?'

She jumped about a foot. 'I don't *know*!'

'Trouble is, even when you were a little kid and tried to lie to me, I always knew. You get crinkly lips. And I've never seen you so on edge. And one more thing – you couldn't put away that much food in a week.'

Barry picked up the thermos and gripped it under one arm. She grabbed the bag of food with her other hand. Then she backed toward the door, wary of him. There was a look in her eye, reflection of an unhealthy spirit, that gave Dal pause. He could barely breathe.

'I don't get crinkly lips and I'm not lying and I don't know what's the matter with you since you got home. You'd poison a rat if it bit you!'

'What kind of trouble are you in? What the hell is Mark Draven doing to you?'

'Nothing!' Barry shook her head vehemently, which caused her face to redden. 'Nothing's wrong. I'm fine!'

'No, you're not – you're depressed. You just said so.'

'Okay. So I'm depressed. I have a right to be.'

'And you're scared too. What's going on with you, Barry?'

'Dal, can't you just leave me alone? Stop being my big brud-der. *Stop* trying to be *anything* to me – I haven't asked for it and I don't *need* it!'

Barry elbowed her way past the screen door and walked quickly away from the house. Dal was about to follow, but he wasn't wearing shoes and his knee was aching – there was no way he could hope to match her pace. Instead, forgetting about the beer he had placed in the freezer, he went up the stairs at a limping run, ignoring the pain.

In his room he had to search both closets and a chest full of possessions collected in his recent youth before he came up with the binoculars. He took them to Barry's room, where he had from her windows a better view down toward the pond, unobstructed by the high long barn. Barry was in the trees by then, Meanness slouching along behind her, but he easily picked his sister up with the powerful glasses. She did, indeed, appear to be headed for the dock and the rowboat. Needles of sun shot through the trembling image he maintained; her head in close-up seemed disembodied, like a balloon drifting away from a holiday parade, her hair windswept and pale red, firing off glints of magnetism.

About forty yards from the water she paused, looking around, taking her time, as if she were afraid she had been followed. Then she took a different path, to the gristmill.

Dal put the binoculars down, took off his own glasses, and rubbed his strained eyes. After half a minute, when his vision cleared, he tried to find Barry again. She wasn't in sight, but Meanness turned up, flushing woodcock from low brush on the near side of the diamond-faceted millrace. And the boat remained tied up at the deserted dock, another two hundred feet away beyond a cattail marsh.

Dal returned to his room, pulled some hunting clothes from a cedar closet – boots, camouflage jacket, and loose-

199

fitting trousers – and changed. He put the binoculars into the case and hung the case from his shoulder.

As he walked down the stairs to the foyer he was conscious of the insidious scratching sounds again.

Something – he couldn't have said what – drew him to the family room.

As if his presence had been detected by whomever – or whatever – was making them, the sounds stopped suddenly. His heart jumped to a faster beat.

Dal's eyes lingered on the leather casket Alexandra had brought the night before. He had much on his mind, but, paradoxically, he was drawn to the casket as if nothing else mattered for now.

There was something unexpectedly cold in the air of the room. It was as if, within a few steps of the foyer, he'd become immersed in a pool of ether. He wanted to back out, but couldn't. And his hands no longer seemed to be under his control. He was, suddenly, almost ill with fright; but his hands wanted to open the casket.

It was locked. He couldn't budge the top. Relief jetted through him. The key was nowhere in sight. Barry must have done something with the key, but for his life Dal couldn't recall what.

Scratch, scratch.

The leather of the casket was cured hard as paving stones. He remembered the silken lining, the crisp parchment wrappings around the daggers. He thought he heard, in addition to the persistent scratching, a crackle of paper – as if the daggers were moving around inside the casket, trying to dig their ways out of it.

The hairs on the nape of his neck stirred icily.

Dal, unlike other members of the family, never had had a fondness for lore and legends, the mysticism of his forebears, although Barry's queer talents had always been matter-of-fact for him. Those things he could live with. But this was something without the realm of faerie stories and shadow shows, an uncharmed evil that, he felt, threatened death in their house. He was pale as a wafer; his heart throbbed as if it

200

were racing toward a seizure. He turned and got out of the room, evading the thickening atmosphere of disaster, and went after his sister.

He went down to the gristmill the hard way, deliberately off trail, approaching from the hill side, where there were no windows. Then, limping fiercely from the strain on his weak knee, he edged around the millrace. There was a fluent runoff from all the rain with the surfaces of the big boulders, usually high and dry and dappled with lichen, now inches under the clear spuming water. The mill wheel loomed woodenly and almost to the top frames of the second-story windows, which had so much dirt and cobweb on them they rejected the quivering light of the sun.

Dal found, lower down, a smaller window to look into. His view was of interlocking dark angles past which, as if in the center of a kaleidoscope, Barry and Mark could be seen, both of them bright and small, sitting face to face by the grinding stones eating the lunch she had packed and talking tranquilly.

He fumbled the binoculars from their case, shifting his weight to ease the hurt in his bad knee, and focused through the window. Something cold and blunt insinuated itself between his legs, causing his balls to shrink tight. It was Meanness, but he'd almost let out a yelp of terror.

'Go on,' Dal said sternly to the dog. 'Get home!'

The hound looked at him, a side gash of teeth where his lips didn't come together; it was a benign sort of sneer, then Meanness sat down and went after a flea with a big paw that for the most part just fanned the air with comic futility. Dal gave up trying to get rid of him and raised the binoculars again.

Barry came into his line of sight first, talking with her mouth full, pausing to brush away an airy gleam of blue-bottle fly. Then Dal picked up Mark.

His hands began to shake so intensely he could barely keep the boy in focus. Mark was smiling. By now, needing surgery on his mutilated hand, he should have been half berserk from pain, too nauseated to put anything in his stomach.

Mark reached for the thermos and poured himself a cup of milk. He held the thermos in his right hand, the cup in his left. For four seconds Dal had a good close look at the left hand of Mark Draven. No swelling, no blood. All five fingers were intact. It did not look, in any way, as if a car door had been slammed on his hand.

Bitter liquid shot up into Dal's throat; he choked on it, lowered the binoculars for a few moments, then raised them quickly again and tried to steady his hands.

Barry's back was turned as she tidied up from their meal. Mark got up from the broad flat stone on which he was sitting. He stretched and yawned, dusted off the seat of his pants. Chaff flew like insects in the light. He returned to his easel and the painting he was working on, which Dal couldn't see.

Then Mark turned and looked deliberately at the window where Dal was watching, as if he were perfectly aware of Dal's presence and had been for some time.

Dal, shocked, spun away from the window, nearly dropping his binoculars; as most of his weight shifted to his bad knee, he groaned. He began a hobbling panicked escape – he could not have managed to move more quickly if he feared that all the fiends of hell were contained inside the mill and would momentarily come flying after him. He had seen nothing in Mark's haughty handsome face – he had seen, or sensed, as he eavesdropped too much that was uncanny, beyond explanation, ultimately horrifying.

Meanness trotted along as Dal hauled himself, sweating, up the long slope to the house. In the kitchen he pulled a bottle of Irish out of the pantry and had a generous four ounces, chased it with tap water, got his breath, and considered what he should tell his father. But nothing he rehearsed sounded right because he didn't know enough – not yet.

Dal limped through the house and went out the front door to his Mercedes. He had left the keys in the ignition. He drove madly to Kinbote estate. The gates were open. There were two girls on magnificent horses on the greensward in front of the manor house. Dal took the right-hand fork of the drive to Alexandra's cottage.

The front door was locked. She didn't answer his knock or his inquiry. He waited, knocking intermittently. Five minutes passed. Dal walked around the cottage, peering in at narrow leaded windows with occasional clear panes of glass. Not much of the interior was visible. What he did see seemed submerged in gloom, like a house in the ocean.

The girls on horseback had cantered nearer. He called to them. They told him they hadn't seen Alexandra all day.

A diamond-shaped pane in one of the living room windows had been cracked in half and patched, long ago, from the inside with transparent tape. The windows were draped. The broken pane punched out with little effort on his part. He reached through the opening and twitched the thick drape aside.

Sunlight over his shoulder pierced the room with the intensity of a laser. Birds chirped in high cages. There was an odor of cat food and incense. In the shaft of light Alexandra looked up at him from the floor with a steely composure, one hard emerald eye narrower than the other. The light was dazzling. Her pupils did not react. Still, it took Dal a few moments to accept that she was neither meditating nor in a mystical trance of some kind. She was dead.

THIRTY-THREE

DAL GAINED entrance to the cottage without difficulty, by reaching in and turning the handle of the casement window. Then he parted the drapes and stepped over the low sill. He was looking at the body and almost planted his foot on one of Alexandra's cats, which shot up in front of him with a horrendous screech. The birds went crazy in their cages; little feathers floated down through streaks of sun. He heard the clear voices of the two girls as they circled their horses on the lawn.

He touched Alexandra. She was rigorous and cold. There was a line of dried blood from one nostril to her chin. She was lying on her back near a small aluminum ladder with nonskid rubber cleats. His first assumption was that she had fallen from the ladder trying to reach the bird cages overhead. It was apparent that her neck was broken.

Then he saw the faint outline, in mud, of a man's shoe near one of Alexandra's outstretched hands. He looked more closely at the floor. There were more traces of dried mud, along with gristmill chaff.

Dal stood up, his head pounding violently. Her death suddenly seemed less easy to explain.

While they had been hunting for Draven, he had been here.

One of Alexandra's cats scratched in the litter box next to the murmurous refrigerator. Dal looked around carefully for more footprints, followed them all the way to the kitchen door. Then he took a wet paper towel and began carefully to obliterate all traces of mud, working backwards to the dead woman. There he knelt, picked up all the bits of chaff and germ he could find. Dal wrapped them in a handkerchief, which he stuffed into his back pocket.

He left the house by the front door, the sun in his eyes like knives. He walked around the cottage and gestured urgently to the girls on horseback.

They rode up to him, and he expained that Alexandra was dead. The girls went galloping to the manor house.

Dal sat down on the stoop to wait. He'd left the front door ajar, and the cats wandered outside.

Within a few minutes Bob and Ellen Kinbote drove down from the manor house. He'd known them casually for years. They were in their early fifties, indescribably rich, without pretensions. Bob was partially bald and disliked hairpieces. Ellen had spent years working to fund health-care facilities in Third World countries and at the age of forty-seven had decided to become a doctor. She was now interning at a hospital in the city.

They went in at once and looked at the body. Dal stayed behind; he was so tense he felt as if his lungs were turning to stone. Bob made a couple of phone calls inside. Ellen came out dry-eyed but greatly saddened.

'Poor thing. Poor thing. She was such a delight to all of us.'

'What do you think happened?' Dal asked.

'She must have fallen off that little ladder. At her age –' Dal nodded.

'How did you happen to find her?'

Dal had prepared a story. She'd been over for dinner the night before, they'd made a date for today: he was greatly interested in looking at Alexandra's art collection. When she didn't answer his knock and he heard the cats crying inside he'd become concerned, found a loose windowpane, looked inside to see her lying on the floor. Ellen Kinbote accepted all of this without a flicker of suspicion.

'If there's anything I can do,' Dal said. 'I know Barry was really fond of her.'

'We'll just have a simple service in a day or two. I'll call.'

Dal went home, so sick with dread he could scarcely

concentrate on the road. It was a quarter after five and getting cloudy when he walked into the house.

'Barry! Barry!'

Tom Brennan came out of the kitchen, where he'd been making a sandwich from the leftover veal roast.

'Dal? What's up?'

'Is she here?'

'No, I don't think so. I haven't seen Barry. I've been in the studio all afternoon.'

'Would you pour me a drink?' Dal pleaded. 'I'll be right down.'

He dragged himself upstairs to his room, his face inflamed, and opened the gun cabinet there. He took out a Mossberg twenty-gauge slide-action shotgun and filled the tube with three-inch magnum shells. He carried the shotgun to the kitchen and gulped the whiskey his father handed to him.

'What's the gun for?'

'Barry's with Mark. They're in the gristmill. I may need to use it to get her away from the son of a bitch.'

'Dal, have you gone crazy?'

Dal laughed in an ugly way.

'I have to be crazy, don't I? There's no other explanation. *Because these things can't be happening.'*

He stopped suddenly, head cocked, listening.

Scratch. Scratch.

'There it goes again. Hear it?'

'I've been hearing it all afternoon.'

'Coming from inside that casket Alexandra left us,' Dal said in a high voice. 'God knows why she brought it here. I'm scared to look at it again.' He sat down suddenly, the shotgun across his knees, and began to cry.

'Dad, I think – when Draven ran out of here last night, he went down to the gristmill. But he – didn't stay there long. Before we started to search for him he made his way over to Alexandra's place. She – she's dead – her neck was broken! And I'm sure – Draven killed her.'

'For the love of God!' Tom said, almost as upset by Dal's

206

nervous tears as the accusation Dal had made.

'No, no listen to me! I don't know who – or what – Draven is. But Alexandra must have known. What I can't answer – the awful thing is – Barry probably knows too. And she doesn't *care*.'

'What do you mean about Mark? Try to calm down and make some sense –'

Dal had to nod a couple of times, painfully, to get the words flowing again.

'I was down at the gristmill this afternoon. I was able to get a good look at his left hand – the one that was smashed by the car door last night. *But there wasn't anything wrong with it.* His hand was as good as new. Now how could that be?'

Tom looked on silently, doubtingly; Dal, aroused, cried out passionately, 'We saw the finger that was cut off! I put it in the refrigerator. But it's not there now. So there's no evidence the accident happened!'

Dal pulled the wadded handkerchief from his back pocket and spread it on the table; bits of chaff clung to the cotton cloth.

'This came from Alexandra's house. Mark must have had chaff on his clothes and shoes from the gristmill. Some of it fell on the floor when he killed Alexandra. But I – I rubbed out his footprints and picked up all the chaff. Because – how could we explain to the police what he is, when I don't even know myself?'

Dal paused, feeling as if he were coming apart, nerves unraveling, the bones of his chest separating; the heart of him was going to drop on the floor like an egg falling from a bird's nest. He looked at the whiskey bottle, but willed himself to stay out of that refuge.

Tom, groping to make sense of his son's confused explanations, said, 'His hand – are you sure you saw –'

'I'm not mistaken! I know what I saw! *He grew a new finger overnight!* God, oh, God, Mary Mother of Mercy. Mark got so good at painting, and you got so sick. If I hadn't come home, in another week you might have been dead too.'

Dal gazed at his father, loving him, his tongue horror-struck to the roof of his mouth. He wiped tears from his cheeks.

Scratch, scratch, scratch.

'What are we going to do, Dad?'

Tom shook his head, still unable to fully comprehend Dal's fright. The screen door opened and Barry came in like a breath of fresh air, cheeks reddened and humid, as if she'd sprinted partway up the hill.

She barely gave them a glance as she headed for the back stairs.

'Hi, everybody!'

'Barry!' Tom called. 'Where're you going?'

'Take a bath, I'm itchy.'

'Barry!'

She came back to the kitchen, sobered by her brother's thunder, and looked from his face to the gleaming shotgun.

'What are you doing with that?'

'Barry, where's Mark?'

She gave her head a fractious twitch and scrubbed a mosquito bump near one ear.

'Gristmill. You know that. You were spying on us this afternoon.' She looked at both of them grimly for a few moments, then smiled slightly. 'Mark'll be up in a little while.'

'He's not coming in this house,' Dal said.

'Is that so? Dal, he has just as much right to be here as you do.'

'Why did he run away last night? Why has he been hiding in the gristmill?'

'Hiding? That's bullshit! He was forbidden to set foot in Dad's studio, or have you two forgotten? So now he's working – trying to work – in the mill. Dal, you're being impossible, I don't want to talk to you. I need a bath.'

'He's hiding because neither of you know what to say about his new finger, do you?'

Her chin came up. Her indrawn breath hissed almost inaudibly between clenched teeth.

'What new finger? He's just like he always was. Perfect. Nothing happened.'

'Barry, we saw –'

'Nothing happened! Nobody can prove any different, can they? Can they!'

'Oh, kid. What kind of trouble have you got yourself into?'

'I'm fine! I've never been happier. Why don't you leave –'

'Barry, Alexandra's dead. Draven broke her neck last night.'

The girl faltered then, as if she'd lost her place in the fast shuffle, the desperate game of emotional Ping-Pong she'd been playing with them. Dal had a glimpse of just how frantic his sister was, the lengths to which she might go to keep Mark Draven with her. Instead of being angry he felt a new surge of fear, followed by a brief unstable period of calm.

'But you know that already,' Dal said. 'Mark told you all about it – over lunch.'

Barry shrugged, not admitting anything. 'He told me – he said – she had an accident. It wasn't anybody's fault! Mark wouldn't hurt –'

'Alexandra must have shut the car door deliberately on his hand. Because she knew something about him, had to prove something.'

Barry just stared at him, mean and on edge. 'I wonder what stupid, irrational thing you're going to say next. But I don't intend to be here to listen.'

'Stick around anyway, kid.' Dal stood up and laid the Mossberg shotgun on the table. He looked at Tom. 'Dad, I'm afraid nobody in this house is going to know the truth about Mark Draven until it's too late. Unless Mrs Prye is willing to help us.'

Barry suddenly was headed, like a whippet, for the screen door. But Dal had anticipated that move. He latched on to her and spun her around, tightening his hold on her upper arm as she squirmed and thrashed and tried to kick his sore knee.

'Let go!'

'It's for your own good, Barry. You've fooled yourself long enough!'

209

'*Mark!*' Barry shrieked. '*Mark, help me!*'

Dal muzzled her. Barry bit his hand, grinding her teeth into the meat at the base of his thumb. He knocked her loose with a jarring open-handed blow to the forehead with the heel of his other hand and threw her across the kitchen, where she rebounded from the pantry door and collapsed, sobbing. Dal hobbled over to his sister and pinned her to the floor.

'Dad, let's take her to Mrs Prye!'

Tom took in his struggling daughter, her head at an angle off the floor like a pinned snake's, bad blood in her cheeks, and Dal's desperation. He hesitated for only a few moments, then helped Dal wrestle Barry to her feet. She groaned and cursed, but the two of them were too much for her – they walked and half dragged her past the back stairs and through the laundry room to Tom's studio. By then Dal's grip was tight enough to cause Barry to cry out in pain.

'Dal, don't be so rough!'

'Just plug in Mrs Prye!' Dal pleaded.

They came to the fortune-telling machine in a corner of the studio opposite the high window wall. It was nearly full dark outside. Barry was silent again but breathing harshly; she kicked and bucked, face dead white except for high spots of Mick anger. Tom went down on his hands and knees with the snaking cord to reach the nearest electrical outlet.

As soon as the machine was plugged in it began to light up, but wanly. Barry snorted. Dal gave her a push and with his right foot kicked the machine. It made a high-pitched sound and the dome brightened, glowing from waves of light: scintillating amber, bronzy blues, and electric greens. In the midst of this swarming display Mrs Prye's mannikin head lifted holographically, like some strange fish in the sea. Her eyes fastened on them unwinkingly. Barry let out another sound that might have been derision, or displeasure, and resumed her tense deadly fight with a weakening Dal.

'She won't talk to you! *I won't let her!* Let me go!'

'Dal, what do we do now?' Tom said.

'What day was it?' Dal demanded of his father. 'The day

John Doe showed up in the park?'

'Friday – uh, December fourth.'

'Nooo!' Barry wailed.

'Punch in the date,' Dal said. 'If Draven has a birthday, that day is as good as any. Just get Mrs Prye talking, that's all.'

Tom's fingers hovered over the keyboard. Barry tried to muscle him out of the way but failed. With the information fed to the machine tiny lights resembling stars began to flicker electronically within the eerie dome that contained the mannikin-medium's head. Her lips writhed unnaturally as a mechanical, vaguely womanish voice intoned:

'You were born under the sign of the zodiac known as Sagittarius, the Archer, which is ruled by the planet Jupiter. You are an adventurer with the soul of an artist, and you have a flair for the dramatic –'

'This is not the information we need,' Dal said to the machine. 'What we need to know is not on your tape, Mrs Prye. Speak to us now in your real voice. Come out, Mrs Prye.'

The recorded voice stopped. The head froze in midword, which gargled away on a querulous electronic note as currents of twinkly light flooded the interior of the dome. Barry moaned hollowly and went a little slack in Dal's hands. She had bitten her lower lip; blood flowed.

'Stay – away from me!'

The head of the mannikin began to disintegrate, crumbling into sparkles and flashes. A new face, more sharply defined, was forming gleefully. Artificial curls piled high, a heart-shaped beauty mark by the preposterously overpainted, coquettish mouth. Mrs Prye had aged into a thousand undisguisable wrinkles; her lashes were so thickened and extended by mascara she could barely keep her eyes open. But her spirits at once again being admitted to their company were unbounded.

Good day, your worships! Good day, mistress. What's this? A fit? Havadone, my precious dove! Thou shalt blame

211

no one but thy capricious self for the turn the matter has taken.

Barry, the will to fight now drained out of her, was slack in Dal's hands. He could very nearly feel her skin crawl, and she was turning alarmingly cold. Her mouth hung open; her voice came out queerly, not sounding too much like Barry and with the same speech pattern as the mannikin.

'Don't tell them, goody – for the love of – heaven, tell them *not!*'

The doll took over. *I ne'er scruple a lie to serve my mistress. But this be severe duty, depend on't. There is dire work in the offing.*

'Then tell us about Draven,' Dal insisted, staring into Barry's glassy eyes.

Hold, sir! The voice of Mrs Prye now came, imperiously, from the depths of Barry's throat, although neither her lips nor tongue moved – as if she were some strange ventriloquist possessed by her own dummy. Saliva coursed down over the girl's chin. She gave an odd twitch or two, but was entirely manageable. *A moment. I shall bear witness to that which has astonished all your senses. But I would be remiss not to plead for your indulgence on behalf of my mistress. She is in thrall to that which she has created. Nay, not blameless, but a victim as well of her heartmost desires.*

'Who *is* Draven?' Tom said.

A brute, lacking all conscience and scruple. By nature parasitical, as those creatures that feed on the flesh and blood of their hosts.

'Where did he come from?' Dal asked her, but he now suspected the fantastic truth.

Draven owes not to angels, nor the devil. He was created by the power of my mistress's aspiration, wrought in a single mighty impulse from the chaos of matter that separates your world and mine. Barry wished her old love back again, but in more perfect form: clean of limb, graceful in his bearing. Once her mind-creature had need of her; but he has taken his full purchase on life, and would discharge her.

Barry gave a great shudder and a despairing cry, eyes

212

rolling back in her head. Dal waited anxiously, glancing at the medium in the machine. Mrs Prye was still there, looking sternly out at them. Then the mannikin took over again.

Pray, be quick, My moments are few.

'Then he isn't human,' Tom said, trembling.

He need obey no natural law.

'Did Alexandra Chatellaine know about him?' Dal asked.

Ay. 'Twas by her design the finger was lost from his hand. But Barry conceived another, poor booby. And the old dame for her suspicions has paid with her life.

'If Barry made Draven,' Dal said, 'can she unmake him?'

'Tis within the realm of possibility. But he is now nearly as powerful as she, and my mistress knows not the strength of this outlandish art.

'Then how can *we* get rid of him?'

A flicker like lightning went through her face, nearly decomposing it. Mrs Prye grimaced.

Sirs, there is naught you may do. Think not of dirty action – it will hasten your own end. He is a plague-y sort, and divines easily your intimate thoughts.

'Barrrrrrrryyyyy.'

Tom said in a hoarse low voice, 'Dal, listen – he's outside.'

'Christ!'

Yet stay – it may well be the old dame has provided for your safety with her magic.

'Mrs Prye!'

The image of the elderly medium had flattened and begun to waver, forming a whirlpool of iridescent light inside the dome.

Oh my. 'Tis too much for me to tarry so long. Fly, fly from the mind-creature.

'Barrrrrrrryyyy.'

Dal shook his comatose sister. Mrs Prye's voice had settled deep in her chest. It emerged as a kind of growl.

Pray, sirs, that the magic is strong enough to stay the deed. I would not lose my hussy, my dear little girl –

'God! Dal!'

Dal looked over his shoulder at the fortune-telling

machine. In the dome where the mannikin and the medium had been now loomed the head of Draven, a face of lean grinning evil.

Dal dropped Barry and lunged for the plug in the socket. It resisted his first pull and when he yanked with all of his strength everything came out of the wall in a blinding burst of sparks. A circuit breaker was tripped and all of the lights went out. They found themselves in near-darkness, the rising moon obscured by miles of cloud.

'Barrrrrryyy!' Draven called, sounding very near the studio.

She sat up at once, hands to her head, hair tousled, and began to tremble.

'Let's get upstairs,' Dal said. 'Quick!'

He tried to get Barry moving. Barry, on her knees, was deadweight. The huge windows at the north end of the studio were soft gray with cloudlight and featureless, like dreams waiting to begin.

'She won't budge. Help me!' Barry, dragged, seat of her pants squeaking, made sounds in her throat like a kitten they were trying to pop into a sack to be drowned.

They were halfway to the door of the studio when Tom stiffened and pointed.

'Dal! He's out there!'

Dal stopped, panting, and looked out into the dusky yard under the flowering cherry where Draven stood with what looked like a club in his hands. The windows were mirror glass – he could not see in. But he had to know where they were from the sounds of their voices.

Draven raised the narrow club in his hands, and Dal's blood turned cold. There was a dull glint of metal, and Dal realized it was the shotgun Draven held, which he had carelessly left on the kitchen table.

There was a gust of orange flame, a hammering report, and a good-sized section of the window wall disintegrated. Bits of glass flew at them, gigantic cracks sped glossily through the remaining panes, the wall trembled and began to fall down in huge death-dealing shards.

Dal found the necessary strength to yank Barry from the floor and propel her through the doorway, with Tom right behind them. Dal had a quick glimpse over one shoulder of Draven striding toward the house. He experienced a rip of terror, his already bad knee going weak as water under him. He pushed his father toward the back stairs.

'Dad, upstairs, I'll try to –'

Barry was like an eel: she got away from him and headed for the kitchen. Tom surprised Dal by being on her in three steps, he hung on desperately with both arms until Dal got there. The kitchen door was open; he heard the greased easy stroke of a shell being chambered in the shotgun for firing. Frantic scratching sounds came from the family room.

Dal had only an instant to change his mind. No use going upstairs, they'd just be trapped there. The front door was the only answer. He pushed and prodded his father and sister, herding them toward the dining room and the foyer.

They were only a few feet from the door when Barry got a hand free, turned, and dug her fingernails into Dal's face. He staggered back, blood gushing from above one eyebrow. Barry ran soundlessly to the dining room, and Dal couldn't stop her.

An arm reached out to Barry. She collapsed into the protection of Draven's encircling arm and he brought her slowly back to them, the other hand holding the shotgun, muzzle-eye looking straight at Dal.

For several seconds there was a hush, marked off by the pendulum swing of the clock in the upstairs hall, the *scratch, scratch* from the family room.

She leaned against Draven, her eyes like the opening of the shotgun boring down level and strange to them. Dal, half blinded, frustrated with rage and fear, conceived something almost nostalgically heroic about the two of them, valiant defenders of the homestead. Barry *belonged* there with him, and they – her brother, her father – were interlopers. There was nothing of the ogre about Draven; he was not the fiend they had glimpsed in the fortune-telling machine. He looked like a serious, responsible young man in command of a nasty situation, the sort Dal would always want on his team when choosing up sides. He thought, with horror growing all over him like some sort of loathsome extra skin: No matter how he does it, no matter what happens to us, everyone will believe his version. And before a day goes by he and Barry will believe it too.

THIRTY-FOUR

THE INVERSION of reality almost cost Dal his life. He arose
snarling from where he'd been crouched against the wall,
foolishly braving the aimed gun. But a last-second blink of
intuition stopped him. *He isn't all that sure. He doesn't
know, yet, how to pull this off.* There was time for a plea,
which he directed to Barry.

'For the love of us – for your mother's sake – for God and
sweet Jesus, break away from him, Barry, while you still
can.'

Scratch, scratch, scratch!

A small frown momentarily marred Draven's calm
expression; his eyes flicked to the doorway of the family
room.

'You've done no real evil yet,' Tom said, and the strength
of his voice was a marvel to Dal. 'You can redeem yourself. If
we still matter to you.'

Draven tightened his arm around Barry, and she pressed
closer to him, gazing up at his face with a fervor and
devotion that had Dal shouting: *'He won't need you either!
You'll be next, Barry!'*

Draven tilted the muzzle of the gun, one of several spots of
brightness in the darkening foyer, but the most entrancing,
to point at Dal's chest.

'Barry,' Draven said quietly, 'you should go and take the
casket from the family room.'

'What do you want me to do with it?'

'Bury it beside the stone wall along the drive. Pull stones
down on top of it – a pile of stones.'

'All right, Mark.'

She walked to the family room door but hesitated there, put off by the sounds of frenzied scratching. She seemed a little afraid. Dal turned cautiously to watch her.

'Go on,' Draven urged.

Barry went all the way in as if pushed, and Dal lost sight of his sister momentarily; then she emerged carrying the casket in both hands, hurrying with it toward the front door. She seemed to trip, and cry out, but the light was poor – it was hard to distinguish what had happened. The casket fell to the floor and Barry turned with a look of anguish, blood welling in the palm of her right hand.

Tom and Dal went for Draven almost simultaneously.

Tom got his hands on the barrel of the shotgun and nearly succeeded in wresting it away from Draven as Dal barged into him from the side, using his head and shoulders like a bull, then hitting Draven a sharp follow-up blow in the ribs with his elbow, driving the three of them – awkwardly joined, grappling – against the staircase.

Draven was so quick and strong they had no chance to subdue him. He took the gun back with a twist of his wrist and, holding it by the pistol grip of the stock, whacked Tom in the side of the head with the barrel. Tom dropped without a sound at Draven's feet. Dal began pounding Draven in the style that had won him fights with bigger boys in the past: in close, head down, short fast knuckly jabs to the stomach and kidneys.

For a few moments he had Draven sagging, weakened, unable to counter the ferocity of Dal's attack. He was no fighter, didn't know how to use his hands, but his strength and stamina won again. He let go of the shotgun and simply picked Dal up, then heaved him over the banister behind them. Dal landed awkwardly on the steps and came tumbling down again. A baluster had been broken off earlier. Draven reached for Dal and dragged him through the space, pinning his arms tightly to his sides. He began twisting Dal's head with both hands, trying to break his neck.

'Barry!' Dal cried, having had a glimpse of her huddled

against one wall, looking on with the furtive, fascinated eyes of a bystander in an alley brawl; and he glimpsed something else, a gleam of ceremonial daggers spilled from the casket that Barry had dropped. He was strangling; his vision danced with bloodspots and his perspective was distorted by the tortured angle of his head. But before he blacked out he saw his sister approach.

'Mark –'

'Get away,' Draven said to Barry.

'No, you're killing him –'

Her hands pulled at Draven. Blood was running from Dal's mouth, and he felt, despite his agonized resistance, his neck bones about to sunder. He gazed helplessly into his sister's eyes.

'I don't want you to hurt him anymore!' Barry said urgently. 'Why do you have to hurt him?'

Abruptly Draven's big hands lifted from Dal's head, the terrible torque was removed. Draven turned and slapped Barry – hard enough to drive her back on her heels. She screamed in pain. Dal couldn't make a move to free himself and within seconds Draven resumed trying to twist his head off.

Barry groped along the floor and came up with a dagger in one hand. She stood there uncertainly, trembling, the dagger raised high.

'Mark!'

He turned quickly and scowled at the dagger. Barry was all but shaking to pieces.

'I d-don't want it t-to be like this! Why can't we –'

'Barry,' Draven said, alarmed. 'Put that down!'

'I can't!'

She took a faltering, out-of-control step toward him. But the hand that held the dagger was steady. She struck at Draven with the speed of a cobra, piercing the palm of the hand he had raised protectively with such power that his hand, with six inches of blade through it, was thrown back against his heart, nailed securely to the chest wall. He fell down hard, back to the stairs, rose to one knee with his eyes

219

filming over, and pitched forward in front of Barry.

Barry kneeled down beside him, shocked and moaning. She rolled Draven onto his back, wrapped her hands around the hilt of the dagger, and pulled at it, grunting with effort. She had the strength of the possessed, but the dagger wouldn't yield. Dal freed himself from the balustrades and sat up holding his head, barely able to move it at all without terrific pain in his neck. He was afraid he would pass out.

'Barry,' he said hoarsely. He couldn't see out of one eye and his larynx felt half ruined. There was blood in his throat and on his tongue, some of it dribbled down his chin. 'Barry, don't do that. Get away from him.'

Now her hands were slippery with Draven's blood and she couldn't hold tightly to the dagger. She began sobbing in frustration, cursing Alexandra.

'Barry, stop.' Dal forced himself to his feet, came haltingly down the steps, his knee bad but holding him, his head at a wry angle. His mind kept wanting to make a dream of this. He sank down beside Barry, who didn't spare him a glance, nor rest in her efforts to free Draven of the lethal dagger.

'Look – what she did to him. That dirty old thing. I hate her! I knew I should never have let her in the house. She always wanted to hurt us. She couldn't stand seeing us happy together. You were all the same. Jealous of Mark.'

'No, kid. No. Look at me. Look at Dad. Draven almost killed us. He took you over, and he was taking us over.'

Her hands flew into the air like white birds escaping a sacrificial altar. They dripped blood.

'I can't do it! It won't come out!'

'Because – it's finished. You'll see.'

Barry got up, wiping her hands on the front of her shirt, shaken by sobs and devastating hiccoughs, her body jumping, throbbing freakishly in a dozen places.

'I need your help,' Dal said. 'I can't do anything without you, and we've got to get him out of here. He has to – disappear, like he never was. Barry, do you understand?'

But she had gained some control over her body and walked away, indifferent to his pleas. She stopped at the second dagger, which had spilled from the casket, and stood looking down at it. Her mouth was open. The sobs became dry sucking windy sounds that unnerved him. Cold sweat was in his eyes. Dal crawled up the wall to a standing position.

He heard the somewhat melancholy voice of Mrs Prye from Barry, though again her lips didn't move.

Ay. There's an end to all the trumpery. But do not trifle long, my beauty, my insensible cub.

Barry stooped swiftly and snatched up the bronze dagger, held it vertically very near her face, her exposed throat.

'Barry, no!' But he realized, as she turned and walked to the family room, the dagger lowered but still threatening, that Barry was beyond his hearing. Dal made a lunge to intercept her and fell down, twisting his neck again, and blacked out.

Barry turned in the doorway, face smooth now, body still palpitating but with less force, her eyes sorrowing to blandness. She gazed at her brother for a few moments, then stepped into the room and closed the doors behind her.

THIRTY-FIVE

DAL AWOKE with his father shaking him. He let out a cry of pain, eyes filling with tears. The clock above their heads chimed the hour, but he had no idea what time it was.

'Dad – are you okay?'

'Worst headache I've ever had in my life. What happened? Did you kill him?'

'No. My God! Where's Barry?'

'I don't know.'

'She went – give me a hand up.'

His father helped him stand. They leaned against each other, aching, crippled. Dal smelled smoke.

'What's that?'

'Fireplace. Family room.'

Dal turned slowly and saw, in the space beneath the closed doors, the glazed light of a tremendous fire on the hearth inside.

'Barry,' Dal groaned. 'Oh, no, God, please spare her!'

He went hobbling to the doors and threw them open, then stood swaying just inside the family room, a hand groping along the wall for support. The heat had him perspiring instantly. The light from the flames hurt his eyes.

Barry was seated cross-legged on the floor in front of the raised hearth, almost close enough to the fire to singe her naked body. She had the dagger in her right hand. As she gazed at the flames she severed great locks of her hair and threw the locks onto the hissing pyre she had made. She had already trimmed the left side of her head to a ragged pinkish turf of less than an inch.

Dal saw there was no stopping Barry; and, with a flood of

relief, understood that there was no real need to interfere. He sensed that the dagger could not, would not be used by her hand to harm her. A necessary ritual of expiation was coming to completion: a purge of demons, the uninvited.

By the time the clock chimed again – twelve times, Dai realized with a distant shock – it was over for her, the dagger still in her limp hand and lying by her side. He had brought a change of clothes to Barry; she had burned the other things, which had been soaked with Draven's blood. He helped her to dress. She moaned a little but was cooperative. The fire had shrunk to half its former size. Dal forced her to drink brandy. She choked on the first sip, then was greedy for more. Her eyes cleared as if a driving rain were washing mud from stones.

Dal had taken two powerful painkillers, and while Barry completed her ritual by the fire he had been busy, with the occasional aid of Tom, who had a goose egg over his right ear and complained of double vision.

'Where is he?' Barry wanted to know, as soon as she could talk. She huddled against her brother.

'Outside.'

For several minutes Meanness had been howling: a death siren, a dirge. Barry listened apprehensively.

'What are you – going to do with him?'

'In the pond.'

'Ah!'

'Barry – look, kid, there's no other way. We're all guilty of murder here. No one will ever believe what he was, what happened tonight. He just appeared one day, and he's going to disappear now. Who's going to ask a lot of questions? Barry, I need your help. I can't do it alone and Dad's hurt.'

'No, don't ask me!'

'I've wrapped him in canvas, with stones. Too heavy even for both of us to lift into the wagon. I'll tie him to the bumper, drag him down to the dock. There's no moon, no chance we'll be seen. Let's get going.'

He had a good grip on her elbow, but she came along

223

docilely. Tom was at the kitchen table, head in his hands. 'Go to bed, Dad,' Dal said. He and Barry went out into the yard. Meanness was nowhere to be seen, but his howling continued.

She almost turned and ran at the sight of the canvas bundle, stoutly lashed with Dacron cord. Dal put her into the front seat of the Volvo, went around to the back to tie the shrouded corpse to the bumper. He drove down to the pond at five miles an hour, dragging the bundle.

Then came the most difficult part – getting the two hundred pounds of deadweight out onto the none-too-solid dock and rolling it into the boat. With the corpse taking up much of the space lengthwise there was no way to row; instead they squatted Indian fashion, Dal in the bow and Barry in the stern, and paddled across the dark water. Dal guided them through the many little islands, frog tones fading at their approach, resuming behind them in the marshy thickets. The oars dipping, gliding, Dal's neck killing him despite the analgesic, which was so strong it had left him woozy. Once he leaned so far the wrong way he almost toppled out of the boat.

'Dal? Where?'

He couldn't take any more either; he pulled in his oar. 'Here.' But Dal wasn't sure where he was. He thought they must be in one of the deeper places, but it was very dark and he couldn't orient himself by the lights of the house; too many trees in the way. Then the prow of the boat scraped across a barely submerged concrete spillway that had marked the end of the pond originally, before a dredging operation in the twenties enlarged it. This place would do.

With the boat grounded he stepped out on the spillway. It was easier that way to get the body out of the boat. Barry pushed with all her strength and sat back crying as the awkward bundle splashed in, drenching Dal. It sank immediately.

He pushed the boat gratingly off the spillway and jumped back in, sat breathless with his arm around his sister.

'Dal, I'm sorry – I'm sorry!'

224

'It's over now.'

'I tried to say a prayer. But it stuck in my throat.'

'A prayer wouldn't have meant anything to him. Offer one for us instead.'

'Maybe a convent's the only place for me. I can't do any harm in a cloister.'

'The best place for you is with Dad and me,' Dal assured his sister.

They drifted awhile, feeling extraordinarily light without their burden, until Dal had the strength to man the oars and begin the slow work of rowing them home again.

MID-SUMMER'S EVE

Every movement, in feeling
or in thought, prepares in the dark
by its own increasing clarity
and confidence its own executioner.

– WILLIAM BUTLER YEATS,
'Per Amica Silentia Lunae'

THIRTY-SIX

TIME AND the season healed them all.

The stab wound in the palm of Barry's right hand, caused by one of the daggers piercing the leather casket as she was carrying it to the front door, was superficial. It left a small scar across the heartline. Dal had torn neck muscles and a herniated throat, and he was required to wear a brace for four weeks. His knee responded to heat treatment. Tom's headache lasted a day, his goose egg was gone in a week, and his vision was soon sharp enough for him to resume work in his studio. The replacement windows had to be specially ordered, which took a month and a half. Pieces of translucent dropcloth served to keep the weather out and allow light in.

On the second day after Draven sank into the pond Dal, with the aid of a neighbor's boy, loaded the fortune-telling machine into the back of a borrowed pickup. They drove it to a ravine a couple of miles away and dumped it into a collection of rusted old refrigerators and portions of automobiles.

Before the party Mrs Aldrich had asked for, and received, a week off: her oldest daughter was having another baby, her fourth, up in Mechanicville. She returned to find the house in good order and was shocked by Barry's punk haircut, which showed her shapely head to good advantage but gave undue emphasis to her ears, never her best feature. Barry felt a little like Dumbo, the flying elephant, and took to avoiding mirrors and wearing Dal's Greek fisherman's cap when she had, infrequently, to appear in town.

Strawberries ripened, nestlings emerged, gawky and

almost immediately twice too large to be stuffed back into the fragile shells from which they had broken free. Trees settled into a mature, denser green. There were bumblebees and clover blossoms and wild climbing roses. The days grew languorous with a dry and fragrant heat and bronzy, domeshaped thunderstorms. The broad light of day lay on the surface of the pond until nearly nine o'clock in the evening.

Mrs Aldrich was disappointed to find Draven packed up and gone so abruptly. For several days she asked thorny questions about his departure. The story they had decided on was simple enough: a phone call from Europe, an authentic inquiry, flashes of memory on Draven's part that resulted, almost overnight, in a joyous reunion with his family. Of course he would write. Of course he would call, once the excitement of homecoming wore off. And someday he would return to see them. They appeased her curiosity while embroidering as little as possible and hoped that her appetite for news of Draven gradually would diminish.

Barry did well enough with Mrs Aldrich, although her smile was seldom there and the cropped head and melancholy stare were like that of a survivor of the Nazi horrors. Mrs Aldrich readily understood. Barry was only eighteen, but she'd had, thus far, bitterly bad luck in affairs of the heart.

Dal was trying to work again, but for the most part he kept a close eye on Barry, gave up most of his social life, and became her constant companion. The Mercedes coupe reminded her of Draven, so he went out and bought a yellow Lamborghini. They took long flashing rides together. He tried to tempt his sister with Europe, Morocco, São Paulo. She only shook her head. Not ready yet. After a while. Thanks, Dal.

She ate well enough, but the flesh mysteriously left her bones. She picked up books and put them down again, could not concentrate, even on her own conversation, which she seemed to be steering around obstacles, continents of difficulty in the psyche: a deep sense of dejection, of guilt, of morbidity that was becoming more apparent in the pained tone of her eyes, the set of her mouth.

One night they stopped in a tavern high up on the Connecticut border, having set out for Lime Rock and an auto race they decided not to attend. They danced pleasantly to hillbilly torch songs on the jukebox, doing the Texas two step, which had become the rage in the effete preppy East. Dal ordered schooners of malt liquor for both of them. Barry got tight, then pretty well loaded, and began to shine forth in a way her brother recalled tenderly. Still, in the blued light and wraparound mirrors of the low tavern there was something off-key and faintly horrid about her gaiety: the flush in her cheeks was that of silk roses on a grave site.

She began paying more and more attention to the pond, although at first from such a distance he was unaware. In the rain, by sun and starlight, she gazed at the liquid, dreamy, shifting surface. Then she began to walk down there, venturing as far as the gristmill.

'Barry, don't,' he said, catching up to her one afternoon beneath some swaying pines along the race.

'It's the bad in me,' she said earnestly. 'Can't sleep it off, walk it off. It just *is*. Why so much bad? It was never him. He wasn't the real horror. Aren't you afraid of me, Dal?'

'I love you, kid. And you'll get over this.'

'He's down there, and he's painting me in his head.'

'Oh, Christ.'

'I want him to stop. What can we do?' She looked at her brother, without hope.

Dal talked to Tom Brennan about selling Tuatha de Dannan, moving away. Tom wouldn't hear of it.

'But this place is spoiled for her – worse. It's an *influence* – I can't describe what I mean. The house, the land around it, is saturated with the Celtic curses, the haunted twilights, the wretched immortals, all the sorcery we swallowed whole as children. Now I've put it away, but Barry can't – she's charmed.'

Tom had his work back, his appetite, his dog by his side. He was less concerned than Dal thought he should be.

'Maybe a psychiatrist –'

231

'There's no form of psychiatry that can deal with her.'

Barry, without being party to their conversation, somehow caught the drift of Dal's intent and began to shun him, which made him nervous and peevish.

She found privacy for herself in an upstairs room of the gristmill – a closed place with a powdery bare floor, just a trickle of air coming in around the loose-fitting windows set at different angles to frame every moment of the daylong sun. She entered into this seclusion in a week of warm clear days before the solstice. Nothing to sit on but the warped floorboards. For company wasps in a cornered nest. A reflection of rippling water on the ceiling. Nailheads rusty in the wallboards, like the leavings of poison red berries. Her mind watered by the reflection, her face a plane of the ordinary, smoothed out to the mildness of water, without surface tension; but the eyes, sometimes, hotbeds. Sitting, lying down, walking around, a weight tilted against her, inescapable. The sun a giant wasp machine buzz and then a boil on the surface of the mind reddening out to a shocking eruption that would not come, although she made the effort sometimes, squeezing, squeezing. More often just sitting blankly, going out a time or two the first days but then not going out, peeing down a knothole when necessary, the smell of splashed urine bleached out by the sun in time. On a Thursday for curiosity Barry disturbed the wasps' nest, broke off a piece of it, and the wasps, though swarming, wouldn't touch her. Proof of something – she didn't know what. Mostly waiting, though, humdrum – waiting, as her favorite Irish poet had put it, for vision to come to her weariness.

THIRTY-SEVEN

DAL CAME home from having his neck brace removed late in the afternoon on June twentieth; he had been pronounced fit and was in the mood to call a girl or two.

There was a stranger in the yard, stranger to Dal. Apparently he had just arrived and hadn't rung the bell. He waited for Dal to get out of the yellow Lamborghini.

'I'm Dr Edwards.'

'Oh, yes,' Dal said, on his guard right away. He introduced himself but made no move toward the house. 'What can I do for you?'

'Mark's expecting me.'

Dal tilted his head carefully, afraid of feeling a twinge. 'Is he? How do you know?'

'He called me.'

'Today?' Dal said, foolishly.

Edwards looked queerly at him. 'Yes.'

'You spoke to Mark Draven on the phone today?'

'No, I didn't speak to him. I only keep office hours until eleven on Saturdays. He left the message with my service at two thirty this afternoon.'

'I don't know how that could be. Mark hasn't been here for a month.'

'Oh? Where is he?'

Dal came out with the story they had crafted for Mrs Aldrich, but in the telling, under altered circumstances, it sounded somewhat absurd, highly suspect. Edwards listened, with his arms folded, like a man who is sure he is being lied to.

'When was the last time you heard from Mark? He may be

back. Is it possible he called me from New York or the airport?'

'I don't know. I wouldn't think so. I'm sure he'd let us know his plans.'

'There *was* a message. It was very plain. He wanted to see me right away, as soon as I could get here.' Edwards looked around at the house. 'May I come in? Barry might know something more about this.'

Dal couldn't think of any respectable way to refuse.

'Fine. Come in. I'll call Barry.'

She wasn't around; Dal was, for once, thankful. Mrs Aldrich took Saturday afternoons off. Tom was working in his studio. Dal explained, when he rejoined Edwards in the family room, that Tom wouldn't relish being disturbed.

The doctor still had his arms folded. 'There's no sign of Mark?'

'No. I'm sorry. No. I don't understand, but – obviously he just isn't here. If he's coming later, well then –'

'By all means have him give me another call,' Edwards said, not concealing his disappointment.

'Could I fix you a drink, doctor?'

'No, thanks. Sorry to have bothered you.'

'That's all right.'

They closed with banalities concerning the weather, while the weather in Dal's brain worsened by the moment; then the doctor got back in his car and drove away. When he was out of sight, Dal hurried back to the family room for a huge whiskey to calm his screaming nerves.

After that he went hunting for Barry. The sun was nearly down but the light lasted, a hot radiance in the woods, creating illusions from commonplace things: in shafts and wells and alluring beams of touchy sunlight, visions arose from the rootbeds of earth like half-realized heavenly bodies.

Barry was a shadow slanting out of shadows, accidentally crossing his path. She took off, startled, and he went after her, hauling her aground only after a strenuous all-out footrace.

234

'Did you call Dr Edwards?' he said furiously.

She had turned too wild in a week , creeping in the back door for occasional meals, sleeping outside, anywhere, not bathing too often. Something had to be done, and right now. He sat on her, pinning both wrists, made her face him. Barry gasped for air. There was something rank and feral and carelessly incestuous in the way she worked her body against his.

'Mark made me do it!'

'What do you mean?' he asked, sickened by her fatal, fascinated expression.

'He isn't dead. Alexandra's magic didn't hold. He's coming back, Dal!'

'Don't give me that shit. He's twenty feet down in muck, where he belongs.'

'None of us can keep him there!'

'Is that what you want? You *want* him back?' He picked her up in disgust and gave her a shaking, until her teeth sparked together. But he failed to get rid of the surly deadpan, the cast of unreason in his sister's eyes.

'Then I'll give him back to you!' Dal shouted. 'I'll give you back what's left, after a month in the water! When you see him, maybe you'll believe once and for all he's finished.'

He dragged Barry from the woods toward the dock and boathouse, a hard hand clamped on one wrist. But she had stopped resisting him so much, and her eyes were on the sinking twilight of the pond.

In the boathouse Dal took down from the rafters a thing of lightweight rusting chains and ganghooks, used for clearing out choked areas of lily pad. He dumped the dragline into the stern of the boat and told Barry to sit forward, facing him, while he rowed. The oars sliced through a calm chartreuse skin forming in the shallows around the dock and carried them into deeper water, lavender and rose-streaked but all black and impenetrable in their wake. Barry gripped the gunwales with both hands, looking around, looking avidly all around at the dimming shoreline, the sky going slowly to seed, and then down into the depths where they rowed, seeing her reflection glide, grow faint, vanish in negative dissolution. Dal grappled with the water, breathing hard, his neck stiff, propelling them past thin looming snags and islands fixed but shaky, incapable of supporting their weight. A large water bird coasted apace, then with an outcry and lazy explosion of wings shot on beyond tiptop shafts of moody evergreen to feed in the the brilliant granary of stars.

'Dal, go back!'

'No!'

There was enough light remaining for him to row to the approximate spot, by the sunken spillway, where the body in canvas, embracing stones, had gone down.

The boat rode over the top of the spillway and came to a halt; Dal scrambled forward and stepped out. The water over the spillway was ankle deep. Mosquitos were humming in; they had a fiery bite. He slapped and cursed and dragged the boat more securely onto concrete.

'Get me the dragline,' he said to Barry.

She crept over the middle seat and pulled the chain with its several hooks off the bottom of the boat, shuddering as she turned to her brother.

'Help me,' he said.

'But I don't want to do this.'

'You'll only go crazy if you don't. Get out of the boat.'

Dal held out his hand to her. Barry stepped out of the moccasins she was wearing and came over the side, slipped, and almost fell sideways into the water. Dal put his other arm around her, and they teetered together for a few frantic moments.

'Easy. Easy.'

He took the dragline from Barry, walked carefully a few feet toward the shore, looking down. Then he stopped and lowered the hooks, began feeding the dragline into the black water. Barry knelt and washed her steaming face; she watched her brother.

With the hooks deep he began walking again, going faint in her eyes against the line of hills a hundred yards away.

Almost out of sight, he stopped, the chain taut in his hands.

'Dal?'

'I don't know – wait.'

She felt too much alone by the boat; she ventured nearer him, wincing at the whine and stab of mosquitos, moaning a little in her throat. Dal was pulling hard, straining, hands climbing inch by inch the straight wet chain, which piled up behind him on the spillway.

'What is it?'

'Coming up. Don't know – if I can –'

Over Barry's shoulder, breaking through the trees, the old moon shone forth; a milky pallor clung to them, to the surface of the water.

With a shocking splurge the thing in the hooks came for his knees, black and dismally deformed, a dripping fright wig of vegetation contributing to the corpselike effect. Dal almost jumped backwards into deep water before he saw what it really was – the gnarled bole on a thick crooked tree branch. He stopped to get his breath, his heart hammering wildly. Then he hauled the six-foot branch up and out of the way, freed his tangled hooks laboriously, and cast them once again. Barry stood by with her thin arms clasped across her breasts, not even responding to the mosquitos anymore as Dal fished and cursed. Tears slid down her cheeks.

'He's in my head – that's where your hooks should be. He came to rest in my head, Dal, not down in there. And that's why I'll never be free of him.'

'Do you want to be?'

'I don't know – I don't know how.'

Again the chain tautened, and Dal bent his back to it. As he handled the rough wet links Barry smelled blood. Dal was groaning, heaving, his footing precarious in the shallow water atop the wall.

'Barry!' he cried. 'I can't do it – myself. Help me!'

She stood at his side, reaching down. They pulled together. Behind them both the rowboat rocked, as if from an unseen current, and scraped almost inaudibly across the concrete, pulling slowly away.

It was dead, slow weight, and Barry knew, this time, the hooks had found what they were looking for.

Raising him was the problem. It would have been a chore for three strong, fresh men. But Dal by now was in a fanatical frame of mind – he would pull and pull until a blood vessel burst or his hands became too skinned and slippery to grip the chain.

'Son of a bitch, son of a – bitch, you're – coming up!'

Once free of the silt that was thickly deposited against the base of the spillway, their hooked burden rose more easily, but still invisibly, through the cold water to the moonlit surface. Dal's limbs were trembling, but he was exultant.

'We've got it, we've got it!'

It might have been a chest of gold, rather than a water-logged body turning to a soaplike fatty blob, that he was after. At the first glimpes of greenish canvas still securely tied with the Dacron rope Barry's stomach turned on her and she almost let go of the chain, but Dal snarled at her, and she gave one last convulsive tug as he reached down and grabbed a rope with both hands. He pulled the lumpy shroud atop the spillway, then sat down; he was already soaked with perspiration, and the water lapping around his waist felt good.

'You see? You see? *That's* where he is. Alexandra's magic – is still good. And you don't have to be afraid – anymore.'

'Something's wrong,' she moaned, her skin flashing with prickles, her mouth drying out.

'For the love of – God, Barry, what do I have to do? Okay –'

Dal reached into his trouser pocket for a clasp knife, dug it out, leaned forward, prying open the sharp three-inch blade. He began to hack and slash at the tough ropes. They parted. He closed the knife and, on his knees, tore open the canvas.

Barry covered her mouth with her hands, but not in time to keep from puking in terror all over herself.

Dal looked up, eyes rolling with shock toward the distant moon. His hands sank a litle deeper between stones into the silt that was slowly washing out of the canvas. There was not a rag, a bone, a tooth to be found.

Barry turned with her throat burning up, gagging on the vileness in her mouth, and saw that the boat had drifted almost twenty yards from the spillway; rather, it seemed to be backing slowly out of sight, stranding them nearly a hundred yards from the nearest shore.

'Dal – the boat –'

He rose slowly, and she sensed he was going to dive in. *'Don't leave me!'*

An instant later he arced, splashed, disappeared. But after a few moments his head bobbed up, then an arm, gesturing.

'Jump in, Barry! Swim!'

'No! Where is he, Dal – where's Draven – *what's he going to do to us?*'

'I'll get the boat!'

'Oh, my God, hurry!'

'He doesn't exist anymore, that's all – he just doesn't exist!'

'You're wrong! Please! Bring the boat!'

Despite the moon she could barely make it out anymore. Dal took a deep breath and struck out in the direction the boat was moving. He was fast, an expert swimmer. But for Barry the stars had locked in their flight, the night had darkened beyond hope of illumination; Dal would, in his nightmare crawl toward the dwindling boat, swim mindlessly on to the edge of the universe.

She swayed but didn't faint. She closed her eyes. That made it better somehow, sightlessly experiencing nothing but the brush of a mosquito against her skin, the odorous water around her feet.

'Barry!'

He sounded all right – calm. She looked out across the pond but couldn't see him.

'Dal? Where's the boat?'

'I've got it – I'm coming.'

She heard the oars then, saw the flashes of water out there.

'You doing okay?' he asked, in a normal tone of voice that carried very well.

'Yes. Yes. Just hurry.'

Then she took a wrong step somehow, awkwardly nudging the piled chain and hooks. Suddenly, inconceivably, it was all falling off the spillway. And her other foot was caught, wrapped tight. Barry screamed in panic as she was yanked into the water. She scrambled against the sunken side of the spillway, trying to hold on to it, though it was slick with algae. Her face was submerged, she couldn't scream again for Dal. It was all she could do to keep from being dragged to the bottom by the weight around her ankle.

She knew the hooks and chain combined weren't that heavy. Something had hold of them.

She heard the metal boat scrape against the spillway. She had found a piece of rusted iron reinforcing rod to cling to. But the pull from below was stronger now, the chain cutting into her ankle.

Barry felt Dal's hands groping for her. She lifted her own hand, and he grabbed her arm. At the same time the drag on her foot eased, and Dal was able to pull her up.

'What happened?'

She couldn't speak. She pulled herself half into the boat, and he saw the tangled mass of chain and hooks dangling from her foot. He reached out and unwrapped them, let them drop.

'Dal! Dal!' she said, and began to retch.

'What a mess you got into.'

'No – accident. Afraid. Row. Row!'

'Calm down, kid, you –'

'He wants to kill us!' She reached up and seized him by his wet shirt, eyes blinded by fear. 'He's right here! In the water! No! Don't look. Just row.'

Dal stared at her for an instant longer, and then he looked at the laceration on her ankle where the chain had bitten. Not believing, but fueled by her extreme anxiety, he grabbed the oars and began to pull away from the spillway.

'I don't know, kid, I don't know what we're going to do now. You've got me sick worrying about you all the time.'

Her hair was stuck to her face, her lips were blue.

'Oh, Dal, it's so horrible what I got us into! I want to kill

240

myself.'

'Easy with that kind of talk, we – Shit!'

Barry went rigid in the seat facing him, seeing the oar jump from his right hand and drop into the water.

'What happened!'

'Don't do that – hit a log or something, but – I can reach it –'

He was leaning over the gunwale, hand extended for the oar floating only a foot or so beyond his grasp, when the water between erupted and Draven arose, as if catapulted from the bottom, clutching in his right hand the ancient ceremonial dagger they had last seen driven through his heart.

Draven came up out of the water to a fearsome height, his feet almost to the level of Dal's astonished eyes; for three or four seconds he hung there, leveling out as if by the impulse of the moon behind him, and then he was in the boat with them, driving the dagger into Dal's shoulder as Dal screamed in horror.

The boat rocked, and before Barry could react she was thrown into the water.

Her head hit something, possibly the other oar; it knocked her dizzy and water gushed into her throat. She swam instinctively beneath the surface for a dozen feet or so before lunging upward to gulp sweet air and hear, renewed, her brother's agonized screams. She turned her head quickly and saw the huge dark figure of Draven, the flashing dagger in his hand, Dal down in the boat, only his feet feebly kicking as he was stabbed again and again by the weapon which Alexandra had contrived to protect them from the mad and indestructible *tulpa*.

But Draven had caught sight of her; the dagger was poised beside his head. Dal made no further sounds. Barry turned and thrashed away.

'I'll find you,' Draven said, his voice echoing across the pond.

She heard him. Terror turned to despair as she swam, and then to a small but glowing coal of anger in her heart.

241

THIRTY-EIGHT

BARRY'S FIRST thought when she crawled ashore was to look for her father and then get help. But who could help them? And she was afraid to go back to the house. Draven would anticipate that. She had to hide somewhere, try to think what to do.

The tree house, long disused, had been her secret place deep in the woods. Dal had helped her build it, years ago. Now it was a potential refuge. She had shown Draven everything but the tree house, had forgotten it herself. The tree house had a trapdoor entered by squeezing between two branches of an elm tree, a feat that, despite her thinness now, she found difficult.

Inside it was snug and dry. There was a small latched window, too dirty to admit much of the light from the moon, which faced the pond. But she felt safer, less vulnerable, without the moon shining in.

She hadn't left much behind when she'd outgrown the tree house. A box with some toys and an old bedroll. She untied the bedroll, shook it in case there were spiders, then took off her soaked clothing and crept into the bedroll, teeth chattering, to dry. Despite her terror, or because of it, she fell asleep and awoke to an owl's screech just outside.

Barry started up, listening for other sounds, perhaps the crunch of footsteps beneath the tree.

Barrrryyyy.

She shuddered violently, not certain she'd actually heard him call her name. He just might have been trying to get inside her head again, from wherever he was. Her heartbeat slowed, but she felt too edgy and confined to stay much longer in the tree house.

What had happened to Dal? Was he dead?

The hopelessness of her predicament struck her full force. There was no one she could go to, even good friends like the Copperwells, who would believe her story. They'd be sympathetic, of course. And concerned. And call a doctor to give her a shot to calm her down. While she was lying helpless in a hospital bed, Draven would come ...

She couldn't take that chance. There was no one else who could do anything about Draven. She was utterly alone, with no idea of what to do next.

The jeans and shirt she'd had on were sodden – they wouldn't be wearable for hours. She had left her moccasins in the boat; her feet were already cut and bruised from stumbling in the woods, and a ripped nail on her left foot had bled. In rummaging through the toy box she found another pair of moccasins, the soles worn very thin. They were snug and stiff, but she could still wear them. There was, however, nothing else to wear.

Barry opened the trapdoor an inch at a time, pausing often to listen. She was wild with an anxiety she knew she must hold in check, or it would surely do her in. Movement was what she needed now – some sort of purposeful action that might stimulate her to think. Scared as she was, Barry was aware of the dangerous power of her mind.

But Draven was even more powerful.

She had killed him once – but *killed* was not the word. With an action of violence she had severed a vital connection between them, and so he had ceased to live, for a little while. Had he been lying in the water these weeks, secure, incorruptible, waiting for her return? Or had she created him all over again, out of desire? Yes, a perverse desire this time – to be punished for everything about herself she imagined to be wicked.

Barry climbed down the tree, trembling in the mild night air. Her heartbeat was so loud in her ears she couldn't hear anything else. With her feet on the ground and room to run she was calmer, but still indecisive.

243

I made him, I unmade him, I made him again.

Why, or how, she didn't know. She had no thought of getting close to him again, even with Alexandra's dagger. She lacked the strength and probably the courage.

Barry walked, not knowing or caring where she was, or if she was going in circles.

There had to be some way to keep him from springing back, recurring like a nightmare. But Dal was already dead – there was so little time for either her or her father.

She came to a deep ravine littered with the metal carcasses of defunct machines, threadbare old tires. In the midst of brambles and junk something glinted like the eye of a fallen giant. She stared, finding it familiar, then went clambering over the machinery, heart thumping.

'Mrs Prye! Mrs Prye!'

The glass dome was cracked but not broken. The eyes of the mannikin, jolted open by the fall of the fortune-telling machine into a grave of gutted autos, looked dustily out at her.

'Mrs Prye, help me. What can I do?'

Barry heard nothing. Worse, she felt nothing. She tried again to raise the medium. Tears came to her eyes. In desperation she put her mouth to a crack in the glass and blew her breath inside.

There was a flicker, a glow within.

'There you are!'

Has returned, has he? The medium's voice was weary, distant. *Alack. What a sad state we find ourselves in.*

'But what do I *do?*'

No more may I advise thee, mistress.

'You must know!' Barry sobbed in frustration. 'Tell me how I can put an end to him.'

Knowing may not be enough.

'Tell me!'

Very well. In the beginning, mistress, is his end.

Barry stared at the mannikin, the weakening nimbus of light within the dome.

'What does that mean?'

Must think on't, Mrs Prye advised.

'No, don't go!'

In her anxiety Barry leaned too heavily against the fortune-telling machine, which tilted, then slipped and fell away from her down the side of the ravine. The dome was smashed to a hundred pieces against an engine block.

Barry held her aching head.

In the beginning is his end.

'But it doesn't mean anything!'

And then it did. In a way it did. But she couldn't conceive of a way to make it work.

She had lost track of time. It seemed possible that a couple of hours had passed, but not the full night, and she was shocked to hear birds, see the faintest yielding of the dark – although there was no true light yet – in the eastern sky.

Barry worked her way back toward the pond. She heard Meanness whining somewhere close by. She stood very still, listening, trying to locate him, seeing the pond through the trees. She was afraid to call to the dog, afraid of Draven. And then she heard another sound, frail and human.

She moved closer to the pond, pausing frequently, alert to every sound, weighing what she heard. It was hope, not courage, that kept her going toward the exposed shore. The bloodhound seemed near, and his voice changed, as if he had heard her moving through the woods or caught her scent.

When she saw the beached rowboat and the shape of the dog sitting beside it she had to force herself not to run.

Meanness barked, not loudly, a gruff sound in his throat.

A hand came up slowly over the gunwale of the boat, fell back into darkness. She heard Dal moan.

Barry forgot caution and broke for the shore.

He was very bad. That was obvious at a glance, a touch. There was blood everywhere – on his face, his clothes. But he was alive. His eyes opened when she whispered to him.

'It's Barry.'

'Watch – out.'

She kissed him tenderly, crying. 'I know. Don't worry. I have to get you to the hospital. Dal, do you think you can walk? Just up the hill to the house.'

'Try.'

'Come on.'

Meanness was licking her bare legs. Barry got her arm
around her brother and helped him out of the boat. Most o
Dal's wounds had crusted over, but fresh blood appeared o
his lips, which scared her more than his appearance. H
muttered incoherently. He had no legs to speak of, but wit
her help he found the will to move.

By the time they reached the house the sky was paling, th
air was very still. There were lights on in Tom Brennan'
studio. But she had already guessed that Draven would b
there. Fully occupied, she hoped.

She put Dal into the back of the Volvo station wagon. Th
keys, as always, were in the ignition.

'I'm coming right back.' But he didn't move or reply. Th
effort of getting there had weakened him even more – sh
was afraid he was going to die.

She didn't want to go into the house, to be even closer t
Draven. But she had to find out what had happened to he
father.

Tom Brennan was in his room. He lay sunken in the bec
His eyes opened briefly when she shook him, but that was a
the response she could get.

First Dal, now her father. Barry knew that if she didn
lure Draven out of the house, her father would die too.

She took a minute to put on some clothes and a good pai
of shoes.

Then, before her fear could fatally weaken her, sh
plunged down the back stairs and ran to the studio. She too
a deep breath and threw open the door.

Draven turned from in front of the easel where he stoo
painting. A self-portrait was taking shape – he must hav
been at it for hours. The face was that of a man she no longe
knew – handsome, but cruel. Merciless.

'You found me,' Barry said. And ran.

She was behind the wheel of the Volvo when Drave
appeared at the front door. When she knew he would follo

her Barry drove away, in a hail of gravel, and saw, in the mirror, that he was headed for Dal's Lamborghini.

The light in the sky had turned from gray to faint gold. The gates of Tuatha de Dannan opened ahead of her.

No matter how fast she drove, Barry knew, he would be quicker in the Lamborghini. But that was all right. She wanted him there when it happened. He had to be there.

At this early hour the road to Anatolia was deserted. The woods by the road were in darkness – only the sky held light.

He was a hundred yards behind her before she'd driven a mile. Closing fast.

Fifty-five, sixty. Barry pushed the Volvo to the limits of her driving ability on the quick sharp curves.

At the same time she was concentrating on what had been: the beginning.

The window on her side was rolled partway down. The air had taken on a chill – the chill of winter.

Perhaps Draven already sensed what she was up to. He tried to overtake her on a level stretch, but she put the wagon in his way; tires screeched, they bumped, he fell back. She saw the anger in his face.

He would do anything to stop her; what did it matter to him? He would walk away.

Unless –

In the beginning is his end.

A few flakes of snow spotted the windshield.

Draven tried to come alongside again, to slip ahead and then force her off the road in passing. Barry's heart was pounding ferociously.

A sign whipped by: *Tremont State Park.*

Now the snow was thickening, slashing across the road; she had to slow down in order to see. She turned on the windshield wipers. Draven kept the Lamborghini almost on her back bumper, angrily sounding the horn.

The sky fell on them, in a great flaking deluge that rapidly covered the road, whitened the trees of the park. Summer had turned to winter; the cold wind clawed Barry's face through the open window. Her breath appeared in clouds.

247

The Volvo, without snow tires, slued dangerously despite decreasing in speed.

He rammed into her from behind; the jolt almost threw the Volvo into a skid. But there was a worse danger: her mind was tiring.

How much longer can I hold on to it?

Then the last hill, the road spiraling down to the covered bridge. Her lights were on now, but she couldn't see – the world had closed in on them.

One hundred yards to the bridge.

It appeared then, like a mote shimmering on the dense black pupil of the eye of the storm, taking more solid form almost instantly. It stood, naked and defenseless, staring into the headlights of the Volvo, hands flung up in a pathetic, frightened gesture.

Barry! Stop!

She almost obeyed the mind-cry from the car behind her; there was still a moment to twist the wheel sharply, risking death herself in order to save the poor befuddled creature in the road.

Instead she sank her teeth into her lower lip, pressed the accelerator, and drove straight into it.

The impact was enormous, more horrible than she could have imagined; and she heard it scream, a fierce inhuman caterwaul that trailed behind her as she drove at a clip through the bridge.

Just behind her the Lamborghini veered sharply, struck the side wall, and smashed through it, plummeting thirty feet to the water.

Barry brought the Volvo to a stop a hundred feet on the other wide, pulled weakly off the road, and leaned her forehead against the wheel, a migraine exploding like pinwheels, her stomach heaving emptily from nausea.

The sun came out. She looked up wearily.

The road was wet and black. The last of the snow, melting, slid off the windshield. Trees dripped beside the road.

She opened the door and got out, was staggered by the pain in her head. But she had to be sure.

The Lamborghini was down but right side up in three feet of swift water. She had to go down there.

The bank was slippery from an accumulation of melting snow. Barry stepped from rock to rock through green shrubs and dark hawthorne trees and stepped out into the water. It was cold, and her teeth chattered instantly. She waded on toward the middle and reached the Lamborghini. Still she was half-blinded by the pain in her head – she couldn't see well at all.

She cupped her hands against the glass and leaned forward to peer inside.

The car was driverless.

Dravenless, she thought, and giggled, but it turned into a sob.

Hands fell on her from behind.

'Nooo!'

'Barry! Jesus!'

Barry turned convulsively and saw her brother hip-deep in the water, looking pale and shocked.

There wasn't a mark on him. The ugly wounds, the dried blood had vanished, just as Draven had vanished the moment she destroyed his replica in the road. She leaned against the fender. Morning sun glittered through the trees above them. The confusion of seasons had been resolved, in the land, in her mind. Time flowed rightly again. There was no fear.

'What the hell is my car doing in the river?' Dal demanded.

Barry looked at the shattered hole in the bridge, and at her brother's face, now reddening, familiarly, to anger.

'I guess,' Barry said weakly, 'I have some explaining to do.'

THIRTY-NINE

AUGUST. TOM Brennan had finished his first major piece of work since the previous fall, and once he decided to let go of it Barry wrapped the painting in the old quilt, according to custom, put it in the back of the Volvo, and drove it to Copperwell's, where she had a glass of sherry and admired the new panel with her friends.

Blighty Mouse had a Queen Anne side chair in the shop that Barry was interested in; they chatted about price but Barry put off making a decision to another day.

It had been a rumbling muggy afternoon, and there was some sheet lightning in the west as she drove home from Anatolia. The day had taken on a pale green, prestorm cast, and the wind was rising.

Dal called from New York, where he had gone for a blacktie show at a friend's gallery, and they chatted for a few minutes. The line was static-y, sure sign of a big rain moving in.

After talking with Dal she tinkered awhile with the piano, trying to compose. Meanness drowsed, but the weather made him restless. He went to the front door, came back, barked at her. She knew what he was telling her. They had company.

The air was dense with unshed rain; leaves flew by the windows. Barry went to look out.

Someone was standing in the drive about thirty yards from the house. He was a young guy, wore a short-sleeved bush jacket, jeans, and desert boots. Blond, but she couldn't tell much else about him. The wind had his hair flowing back from the temples.

As she was watching him the day turned incandescent; there was a fork of lightning nearby that attracted her eye. When she looked at the young man again he was getting up from his knees, holding his head.

Barry ran outside.

'What happened? Were you hit?'

He stared at her, speechless, deafened perhaps. He looked glazed. He shook his head.

'You're okay?'

'I think so. That was close.' He smiled edgily.

'Where'd you come from?'

He turned his head. 'Oh – back down the road. I – I think I lost my way.' He glanced up as a couple of big raindrops splashed on his forehead. 'Looking bad.'

He was certainly nothing sensational, but his features were regular and he had a pleasant mild way about him.

Barry smiled at him. 'Better come inside. Before we get soaked.'

'Thanks.' They walked toward the front door, where Meanness had his nose pressed against the screen.

'I'm Barry.'

He still seemed a little dazed from the close call with the lightning. His tongue was a bit thick.

'Fred. Fred Wade.'

She liked the name. It suited him. There'd been a boy her freshman year in high school named Wade Blasingname – vice-president of his class, co-captain of the track team. A solid, dependable sort of guy. She'd deeply admired him. Fred Wade was the same type.

Barry held the screen door open, giving Meanness a little push out of the way.

'Come on in, Fred.'

'Thanks, Barry. Nice house.'

She was beginning to love the way his head was shaped. She liked his pale thick eyebrows and the trace of freckles she hadn't noticed before. Fred was aware of her interest and continuing scrutiny. He liked her too, she could tell. There was an instant rapport. Pleasant, not spectacular. He smiled

251

in acknowledgment, a little shyly.

'Have a seat in the family room,' she said. 'How about a Coke?'

'Great. Thanks.' Fred went in, looking around, and Barry hustled off to the kitchen, humming to herself.

The rain began its cozy preliminary drumming on the roof.

When it came to men, Barry had made all the mistakes she intended to make.

This time, she was sure, it was going to be just perfect.

THE SHINING
by Stephen King

Danny was only five years old but in the words of old Mr Halloran he was a 'shiner', aglow with psychic voltage. When his father became caretaker of the Overlook Hotel his visions grew frighteningly out of control.

For as winter closed in and a blizzard cut them off completely, the hotel seemed to develop a life of its own. It was meant to be empty, but who was the lady in Room 217, and who were the masked guests going up and down in the elevator? And why did the hedges shaped like animals seem so alive?

Somwhere, somehow, there was an evil force in the hotel — and that too had begun to shine.

NEW ENGLISH LIBRARY

'SALEM'S LOT
by Stephen King

Almost overnight, the population of 'Salem's Lot has gone from 1319 to nothing. *At least to nothing human!*

Thousands of miles from the small New England town of 'Salem's Lot, two terrified people still share the secrets of those clapboard houses and tree-lined streets.

One is an eleven-year-old boy who never speaks. Only his eyes betray the grotesque events he has witnessed.

The other is a man with recurring nightmares of a placid little township transformed into a tableau of unrelenting horror, a man who knows that soon he and the boy must return to 'Salem's Lot for a final confrontation with the unspeakable evil that lives on there . . .

NEW ENGLISH LIBRARY

NEL BESTSELLERS

Orbit	*Thomas Block*	£1.95
Forefathers	*Nancy Cato*	£2.50
The Citadel	*A.J. Cronin*	£1.95
Schism	*Bill Granger*	£1.75
Maura's Dream	*Joel Gross*	£2.25
Friday	*Robert Heinlein*	£2.50
The White Plague	*Frank Herbert*	£2.50
Shrine	*James Herbert*	£2.25
Christine	*Stephen King*	£2.50
Spellbinder	*Harold Robbins*	£2.50
The Case of Lucy B.	*Lawrence Sanders*	£2.50
Acceptable Losses	*Irwin Shaw*	£1.95

All these books are available at your local bookshop or newsagent, or can be ordered direct from the publisher. Just tick the titles you want and fill in the form below.

NEL P.O. BOX 11, FALMOUTH TR10 9EN, CORNWALL

Postage Charge:

U.K. Customers 45p for the first book plus 20p for the second book and 14p for each additional book ordered to a maximum charge of £1.63.

B.F.P.O. & EIRE Customers 45p for the first book plus 20p for the second book and 14p for the next 7 books; thereafter 8p per book.

Overseas Customers 75p for the first book and 21p per copy for each additional book.

Please send cheque or postal order (no currency).

Name ....

Address ....

....

Title ....

While every effort is made to keep prices steady, it is sometimes necessary to increase prices at short notice. New English Library reserve the right to show on covers and charge new retail prices which may differ from those advertised in the text or elsewhere. (A)